TROUBLE FINDS YOU

a novel

Joshua Marie Wilkinson

Fonograf Editions
Portland, OR

Cover and text design by Mike Corrao

First Edition, First Printing

FONO25

Published by Fonograf Editions
www.fonografeditions.com

Distributed by Small Press Distribution
SPDBooks.org

ISBN: 978-1-7378036-8-3
LCCN: 2022948245

TROUBLE FINDS YOU

Joshua Marie Wilkinson

FONOGRAF EDITIONS

for Lisa & Jude

When we ask for advice, we are usually looking for an accomplice.

— Saul Bellow

I discovered, though, that once having given a pig an enema there is no turning back...

— E.B. White

PART 1
MONTANA

HARRY

Two high school kids are sitting on the curb in the parking lot at Marty's Mart when Harry pulls in at the far pump after dark.

He takes out the nozzle, sets it into the tank, and squeezes, but his hand is shaking. He can't get the fuel lever to rest snugly in its clip. He shuts his eyes and leans against the truck's dusty fender as he holds it there, letting the gas flow in. His shoulder throbs.

One of the kids approaches, avoiding eye contact, and offers Harry five dollars to buy them a case of Busch. Tells him they're going to a party. Harry stares through him, tells him to fuck off. The kid shrugs and shakes his head as he walks back to his friend sitting beside the bundles of firewood.

Harry has the feeling that each of his movements is being clocked from above, like he's a rat in a maze. And driving a random route through the night had felt slightly less foolish than heading directly back to the cabin.

Dust is stuck to the dried sweat above his lip. He can feel the grit of it between his teeth. His shirt is soaked through with sweat. The back of his hand has been sliced by glass, but there's somebody else's blood on him as well. He doesn't even want to look at his ankle, but he knows he's going to have to wash it out. The pain from down there is electric. It feels runny. He imagines a nest of spiders wriggling under his sock.

He pulls his hat down on his forehead and pushes open the door of the convenience store. Lights blare. A pop station plays on a portable radio where the cashier is studying herself in a compact mirror. With her free hand she's doing something to one of her eyebrows. Harry makes his way past the frozen pizzas and ice cream to the heavy door of the washroom.

Inside, the mirror is scratched with profanities and extravagant symbols. In his reflection he finds someone else there: covered in dust, chin stained with tobacco spit, and sweat tangling the hair at his temples. He removes his hat and sets it beside the sink. His ears are still ringing from the rifle shot. That Harry in the mirror, he looks far away.

He washes the blood off his hands and notices two tiny cubes of glass in the breast pocket of his flannel shirt. He pictures Kristin in her dark hoodie at the edge of the fire pit, her face partly obscured by shadows. She'd pulled on his sleeve when the screaming started, but Harry had run the other way, back to his truck. He'd just left her there.

He pulls out his cell phone, but there's nothing from Kristin—only a missed call and a voicemail from his sister. He'll have no service out at the cabin, but his mind is too addled to know if he should try to call Kristin now, or call the police himself, so he returns the phone to his pocket.

He pulls up the damp leg of his jeans. He has to pinch the fabric of his sock and sort of tug it down—one side and then the other, gently—to see the marks. It's worse than he thought. Four clear holes full of blood, each the size of a ladybug.

Looking over his wound he allows himself to replay the scene. At first, all he sees is that woman in the headlights. Her arm splotched. Someone had lost a great deal of blood. Running from the field back to the truck, Harry had swallowed some of the chewing tobacco that had been wedged in his lower lip. His stomach is roiling now. There's a faint smell of dogshit.

Somebody is pounding on the bathroom door.

"Just a minute," Harry says, his voice breaking like a child's sob.

He brings a two-handed cupping of soapy water down from the sink, his arms trembling, and flings the warm splash onto his ankle area. He lets out a cry. Clenches his teeth.

He makes to leave but stops short. He can't bear the smell. He unlaces and pulls off his boot and then wedges its smeared-over sole under the sink's hot water. His hands are still shaky. It feels as if his eyes are going to fall out of his head, and he turns his face away, mashing his nose into his shoulder, to avoid inhaling the odor. More pounding follows. A man's voice telling him to hurry it up.

"Give me a second," Harry says. "I shit myself in here."

With a handful of foaming soap from the dispenser, he splashes water onto his shoe and then lathers it onto the stubborn excrement squished into the boot sole's rubber traction. It starts to come loose from the grooves, his fingers tickling it free in the hot water. The citrusy soap fragrance mixing with the scent of the warm dogshit all steam up into his face. He gags. Stifles it. Gets his boot back on over his wool sock.

A tall man in overalls, with a squirrel-gray beard, curls his lip when Harry comes out.

He hears the door lock click behind him as he walks back through the candy aisle. He's going to need Band-Aids and something stronger to douse his wound with, though he doesn't want to risk being recorded by the store cameras any more clearly than he already has. Harry counts at least four people who could ID him here, including the night clerk: a pale woman behind the counter, now lip-syncing to Mariah Carey's "Fantasy."

"Alcohol?"

The cashier gives him a bored look and points a long, turquoise fingernail at the coolers of beer.

"No," Harry says, "like for a cut."

"We don't carry nothin' like that. Sorry."

Outside, Harry leans on the trashcan and looks out at his truck. He'd swept the chunks of glass out of the passenger window, so that side just looks rolled down now. The truck is covered in dust and mud but for Montana this is hardly strange. A shinier truck than Harry's would have drawn more attention. If his Arizona plates weren't doing him any favors, at least Missoula was a college town, full of undergrads driving crappy sedans from Idaho and Washington.

The two high school kids are performing their forlorn boredom, drinking slushies out of child-sized cups on the curb between a cooler for bagged ice and firewood. One of them eyes Harry's damp pantleg before looking away.

This will all soon be evidence of some spectacular crime. A team of investigators will be tweezing everything into Ziploc bags. They'll spot the fresh puddle of glass on the road. A trained shepherd will sniff out the rifle in the weeds about nine seconds later, and some rubber-gloved, stubbly detective will whistle in a couple other uniformed cops without so much as a glance over his shoulder.

Harry's blood is on that rifle. So are prints from all ten of his sweaty fingers. There will be hair and saliva and perhaps even flecks of blood on the door of his vehicle.

"That truck look weird to you?" Harry says.

"I didn't touch it," one kid says, his hat on crooked. He looks up at Harry.

"We'll give you ten bucks, man," the other one says. Something's wrong with his ear. It's closed up like a dead flower.

Harry stalls a moment, pretending to consider the offer. He'd scooped the wad of chewing tobacco out of his mouth in the washroom, but its hot particles are in his belly, reacting with the acid in there. He can't tell if he'll be sick, but it passes.

An ambulance soars by on the interstate, headed east, in the direction of the party.

"That's the third one," the kid with the ear says.

"Third ambulance?" Harry says.

"No, cop car or whatever. Third or fourth."

Two more patrol Blazers scream after it, and the three of them watch the blue and red lights melt into the distance, the sounds of their sirens bending and fading.

"Must've been a fire or something," Harry says.

"Nah, no fire trucks," the other one says, squeaking the straw up and down through the lid of his plastic cup.

Harry practices walking slowly without any suggestion of a limp back to the pumps. The wound at his ankle feels unusual now, sort of fat and taut. Many moths and littler insects batter the lights above his truck. He takes a deep breath as he starts the engine, and he watches the red arm of the fuel gauge float itself up to full.

The cool night air is wetter as well. It pours in through the missing window with a feather of gasoline. Harry leans over to roll it up but catches himself.

Just before escaping the party, Harry had rolled down the driver's side window, stuck his head out, and started to ease back as if to push people out of the way until he got his pickup pointed the right direction.

Those who hadn't scrambled back into the house or disappeared into the high grass where the shooting started were running through the front yard. The white dog was barking at him as everybody scrambled into their vehicles, and for a moment Harry thought the animal might try to leap into the truck.

Two women appeared in his headlights, crossing in front of the truck, the sisters he'd seen earlier at the fire pit. The bigger one was sobbing, muttering something. The prettier one with short hair was stone mute with a brownish stain of blood on her dress, smeared down the length of her arm.

There was more yelling behind him from a scuffle of panicked bodies when he felt the unmistakable pressure of the truck's back end dipping down, pressed now with some load. He turned to shout at the white dog to get out, his mouth burning with beer and tobacco. But it was not the dog.

It was two men flattening themselves down into the bed of his pickup. He leaned out the window and screamed at them to get out.

“Go, motherfucker, go!” one said as he pressed himself down out of view.

Harry swallowed a gob of spit and tore out of the yard, following the beams of his headlights back to the county road. Dirt and rocks sprayed up behind him as he drove out the way he'd come in, Kristin's birthday flowers replaced by the shell of their plastic wrapping on the empty seat beside him.

Harry's heart was thudding like a trapped moth. He watched the high beams light up the road before him as the truck picked up speed and rattled along the empty lane. Something smelled of dogshit, and he glanced down to see that he'd stepped in a fresh one on his sprint back through the grass. He had no clue who was riding back there, but he was helping them escape the mayhem. Harry might have done the same thing had his own friends left him for dead. He'd drive down the road a ways. Pull over and figure out what to do. Maybe they'd know what the fuck had happened back there.

There was a hard tap on the glass of the truck's cab. Harry turned just enough to see that it was the nose of a rifle. Whatever momentary calm he'd felt vanished as his blood went to ice in his fingers. The rifle gave two more hard raps on the window, and Harry took a deep breath as he unlatched the black handle. He was driving sixty, then sixty-five, then nearly seventy. Without taking his eyes off the road, he slid open the window. And then the rifle slid its long barrel into the cab of his truck, like something with a brain of its own. One of the men said something Harry couldn't make out, and the rifle nosed his shoulder.

With one hand on the steering wheel, Harry reached his

left arm across his chest and wrapped it around the barrel, grabbed hold, and yanked. The force on the other end jerked it back and Harry lost his grip—his hand too sweaty to grasp the slick gunmetal. He stomped on the brake. The two men fell forward, ramming into the back of the truck's cab, and the rifle came free, its nose spearing into the empty cup holder at Harry's knee, and a cloud of dust was kicked up on the road and came over them like smoke.

Harry got his seatbelt off and turned around.

It was Tommy. Little blond guy in the yellow hunting vest from the field. He'd let Harry shoot his rifle and here it was in his cup holder.

"You tried to kill us," Tommy said. His teeth were small, his gums prominent.

"Just get the fuck out of my truck."

"Okay, okay," Tommy said as he got himself up.

"Tommy, you stupid asshole," the other one said. "Why'd you do that?"

"Keep your mouth shut," Tommy said. Then to Harry: "We're climbing out, okay? Just throw me the Ruger."

"So you can shoot me with it? Get the fuck out."

Harry opened the door and Tommy sprang forward, squeezing himself through the cab window again and grabbed the wooden stock up once more. Harry turned and got hold of the barrel before Tommy could pull it all the way through the back window.

Tommy pulled hard, but Harry managed to joust him in the ear, scraping his jaw with the hard rubber of the rifle's butt end. Tommy still wouldn't let it go. Sweat was dripping from Tommy's forehead and his yellow vest hung over his shoulder. The little guy was as strong as a cow. Keeping hold of the weapon, Harry pushed his head through the window and spit a wad of tobacco juice the size of a strawberry into Tommy's eye, and Tommy screeched and a shot was fired—shattering the glass of the passenger side window, which burst like so much water.

Harry pulled the gun back through the opening then, and he let it fall to the passenger footwell. It lay there, the business end jabbed into the lining between the dirty mat and the door. Crumbled glass was on the seat, on the cellophane bouquet wrapper, but most of it had splattered out onto the road. The ringing from the shot came into Harry's ears like a swarm of insects.

He shouted for them to get the fuck out of his truck as he held the horn down. Its far-away sound joined in some peculiar dissonance with the ringing of the fired shot, which lingered in his eardrum, and the horn's echo boomeranged strangely from the dark mountains around them.

Tommy and the bigger guy had stood themselves up in the truckbed. The dust from the gravel road was on them, and they had a scrim of dirt in the sweat around their eyes and mouths, visible in the moonlight. Both men's arms were held out, palms up, as if to say, *Do not take your foot off the brake.* They would've toppled, maybe bounced out like big sacks of corn. Harry screamed at the two of them once more, his voice coming from somebody else inside him, as if buried under a bed of soil. He kept his hand on the horn and it droned on into the darkness.

Tommy leapt out first and started to work at his eye with a finger.

"You better not hold onto that rifle. That doesn't belong to you."

"Step back," Harry said, "I'll throw it out."

The bigger man was moaning. Harry hadn't recognized him until now. He'd been with Tommy out in the field, shooting at empty bottles. The guy had a beer gut and a goatee, and he must have mashed his face when Harry had slammed on the brakes: a cut across his nose bled onto his chin. He had on a long white shirt and red basketball shorts. Even in the moonlight Harry could see that every part of him was mired with dust or blood.

The big guy was slow in hoisting himself out of the truckbed, like a baby maneuvering onto furniture. He gave out an awful groan as he wrangled himself over and fell hard onto the gravel.

Harry let go of the horn then. Its empty blat faded into the valley.

The two men stood there like ghosts, gaping. The bigger one kept his hands held up, palms out.

"My cousin's a State Trooper," Tommy said, his gummy smile back on his face. "You're fucked, man. I got your license plate."

"Get away from the truck," Harry said.

The bigger one looked right into Harry's eyes, pleading. "Don't fucking leave us out here, man. I didn't do shit. I swear to god."

With the flat of his hand, Harry gestured for them to step

back, and when they'd gotten far enough away, he reached across the gearshift, his shoulder squishing against the seat with a sinewy throb, and grabbed the weapon. The wound at his ankle—which Harry had forgotten till now—sent a ripple of wet pain through him. Both of the men moved back into the plants of the overgrown ditch, and the bigger guy sort of hopped one-footedly down into the weedy grade and then tripped, tumbling once more, and crying out.

As Tommy went over to help him up, Harry reached across and got the passenger door open, cutting his hand on a cube of glass as the last of the window crumpled out of its frame. He took up the rifle by its stock and flung it into the darkness opposite the two men.

"Tommy, you're so screwed," the bigger guy said, and Tommy told him shut his face as they scrabbled around the back of the truck to recover the weapon.

Harry put the truck in gear and tore off, laying another lake of dust over them both. The wind gushed through the truck's open window, and it sucked the bouquet's cellophane wrapping off the seat, letting it out into the darkness, like a thin membrane over nothing.

SHERIFF'S DEPUTY

As Harry pulls out of Marty's Mart with a full tank of gas, the highway is pure darkness, pocked by occasional lights, and reflective yellow signs at sharper bends along the Clark Fork River.

Harry takes it easy at the speed. The wind blows in through the truck's missing window. Bits of glass lay in the cracks of the seat. One shard takes the passing interstate lights like a diamond.

Tiny in the black distance of Harry's rearview mirror, another flashing police light appears. His head throbs like a heart. When he hears the chirp of the squad car, he pulls over and eases his foot off the accelerator, the gravel on the shoulder kicking up. The patrol car's lights are bigger and angrier, and soon enough it's slowed in behind him and rolls to a stop.

Harry watches the patrolman's shadow in the side mirror, which approaches before disappearing behind the back end. For a second he thinks the cop is going to climb into the bed of his vehicle and he cranes his neck around, when a young white trooper appears at the wide-open passenger window, evidently to avoid getting clipped by a passing car on the interstate side.

Red cheeks, a stubbly mustache. One of his eyebrows is split by a mole like the eraser on a pencil. The trooper peeks his head inside the cab.

"Howdy," Harry says, in a strange voice.

"You coming from that party out past Bonner?"

"No, sir. I was in town. Over at Child's."

"I'll bet you were," the cop says, his mouth hanging open for a moment. He rights himself and looks into the bed of the pickup. The patrolman leans back into the frame of the open window and cocks his head.

"You spot anybody along the roadway, thumbing for a lift?"

"Nope," Harry says, too quickly.

"Where is it you're headed?"

"Rock Creek. Is there a problem?"

"What'd you have to drink tonight?"

"Just a beer. Couple hours ago."

"One beer my foot." The cop shuts his eyes and lets out a sarcastic laugh. "Is that all it takes to get you fishtailing over my road out here?"

"I beg your pardon?"

"If I breathalyze you, you telling me you'll blow clean?"

"Yes, sir," Harry says.

"Arizona, huh? You up here for school?"

Harry hesitates, his fingers squeezing the steering wheel. "Yep."

The trooper nods, appearing pleased with his policework.

The officer draws his flashlight off of his belt and aims its beam over the truckbed, illuminating the spare tire, a flattened Pepsi can, and a red plastic cigarette lighter that must've fallen out of one of their pockets.

"Alrighty," he says, rapping his knuckles twice against the window sash. "You be safe."

Harry exhales and pulls out onto the dark interstate, not bothering even to wait for the officer to get back to the door of his cruiser.

His brain feels loose and clunky. At the slightest turn in the road it seems to thud against the inside of his skull like an egg floating in a glass of water. He gets the truck back up to sixty-five, and he watches the patrol car's blistering lights grow smaller in the rearview. The white glare from the cop's floodlight stains his retina as he tries to focus on the dark road ahead.

The grassy mountain air pours through the window once again, and Harry feels a familiar sob form in the back of his throat as he slows for the exit to the 102 out to Rock Creek, where the picked-over carcass of a small coyote lies near the offramp. He drives as slowly as he can over the big rocks and divots in the dirt road to keep himself from becoming panic sick or tobacco sick—whatever he is now.

The driveway's dark.

Harry leaves the truck lights trained on the cabin and waits there with both windows down, to listen. He cuts the engine.

Something sputters inside him, and his stomach flips over like a fish in a bucket. Harry belches hot air. Then he hears Greta's bark and he gets out, as if from a boat onto solid land. He steadies himself with his hand on the dusty metal of the hood, but the ground seems to lurch up toward him.

Harry's ankle is weeping. The fabric of his jeans clings to it like a wet curtain sticking to a window. He hears the familiar sound of the river pouring itself over the rocks beyond the pines. Greta barks and barks, and when Harry finally gets the cabin door open, his hands shaky on the knob, she leaps onto him and pushes him backward.

Her water bowl is nearly empty. He fills it in the sink and gives her two big scoops of kibble. She goes at her food noisily, and Harry drops down to his knees and falls back on his ass. He scoots over to her and rests his face against her warm flank as she licks her dish clean and starts lapping up the fresh water.

Harry figures he'd better call his sister now. As he listens to the phone ring in his ear, he can't decide what to tell her. Little factoids like inadvertently driving a getaway car, or lying to a State Trooper, or the wound on his leg now swollen and throbbing. He winds up spilling it all to her in precisely that order.

Adrienne is quiet on the other end.

"You there?"

"Jesus Christ, Harry. After you go to the ER, you should call dad's friend Calvin Hogan."

"I don't know…"

"He used to be a sheriff's deputy up in Whitefish."

"I thought he was a fly-fishing guide," Harry says.

"Tell Calvin what happened and have him go to the police with you. He probably knows half the cops in Montana personally. But, Harry?"

"What?

"Call me back before you do anything stupid."

Something low inside him burbles up in his gut, and he feels his insides yield to that unmistakable watery twist.

"Whatever. I gotta go."

Harry gets himself upright, hobbles through the open door to the yard, and throws it all up into the weeds.

CALVIN

Halfway through Idaho, on the last day of his drive north, Harry ordered a large coffee, fries, and a chocolate shake at a drive-thru.

The coffee was scalding but he got the plastic lid off, and stirred in a few strawfuls of ice cream to cool it down. He ate his French fries out of the bag.

Harry looked at his cell phone. Two bars of service. Probably enough to get through.

Pat picked up on the second ring, asking him to hang on, and Harry could hear the scratchy flint of his father's disposable lighter scraping until his cigarette crackled softly in his ear. Harry felt a sudden fondness for him, followed by pity for what he'd been through lately—radiation, all that chemo.

"Harry," he said, letting out a big exhale, "you don't sound so hot."

"Well…school's not really working out."

"What happened?"

Harry hesitated for a second, but went down in the first round. Told his dad he'd gotten into a fight. At a school function. The only way to appeal it was to see a counselor and Harry had refused. So, he got on the road and headed to Montana.

"What, like a shrink?" Pat said, interrupting with a laugh. "Better than jail, I guess."

Harry smiled at this. This is why he'd called his old man. Commiseration? Okay, not exactly. But it beat the hell out of his sister's water-boarding tactics.

Harry sipped his coffee, held the phone between his ear and shoulder to dump more chocolate shake into it.

"So, what now?" Pat said. "I'm a little short on scratch, Harry."

"Would it be alright if me and Greta stayed at the cabin for a while?"

Pat fell into a nasty coughing fit. Harry had to hold the phone away from his ear as his dad cleared phlegm out of his throat.

"Bad plan, Harry."

"Why? Is somebody staying there?"

"Cal looks after it for me, but you don't wanna go to Montana. It ain't—" and Pat broke off with a weary sputtering sound.

Harry remembered his dad's old high school buddy "Cal." Calvin Hogan: big teeth, wild eyes, 70s relief pitcher mustache. If you conjured up a guy who claimed to have had a *ménage à trois* with Playboy Bunnies or swore he once boxed a kangaroo, you'd picture Calvin Hogan.

Harry hadn't seen him since he was about ten and Adrienne was thirteen, but he'd call around dinnertime now and again. Pat would put him on speakerphone, and Calvin would regale them with tales about bears coming into town, or bobcats tearing through a neighbor's chicken coop in the middle of the night, leaving a mess of blood and feathers in the snow.

"That cabin won't clean the slate for you, kiddo. Whatever mess you got into—"

"Dad, I'm in Idaho Falls, standing outside a fucking Burger King. I'm four or five hours out of Rock Creek. I know I should've asked earlier, but I've been driving for two and a half days and I'm exhausted. Can I just stay there for a couple of nights, please?"

Patrick made a tutting sound of disapproval with his tongue against the back of his teeth. Then he let out a long smoky breath, and paused.

"No dice, Harry. You'll have to figure something else out."

Harry pulled into the parking lot of the Grizzly Grocery that evening. Greta was peeing in a litter-filled drainage ditch next to the phonebooth and Harry was trying to figure out what to do. There was a Yellow Pages dangling from a chain under the payphone.

It was worth a shot. Even if Calvin told Pat in a couple days, Harry would be settled in by that point and it's not like Pat could flush him out from Denver.

Harry let Greta sniff around in the weeds, her leash trailing behind her, when he ran back to the truck and grabbed a quarter because the battery of his cell phone was about dead. And there it was in the phonebook: *Hogan, Calvin. 716 Old Pond Road.* Harry picked up the receiver, dropped in the coin, and dialed.

"Yell-o?"

"Calvin? This is Harry."

"*Who?*"

"Pat Stables's son, Harrison… Didn't my dad tell you I

was gonna meet you out on Rock Creek at six?"

"Harrison? Holy cow. How *old* are you now? I didn't know your voice had got so low. I ain't talked to Patrick since Christmas."

"I cannot believe this," Harry said. "I'm gonna be staying out at the cabin, and he was supposed to call so you could let me in."

"*Pat* said that? Huh. What's your number? I'll call you back after I ring his ass, and we'll get this pickle worked out."

"No!" It spilled out of Harry like a cry. "It's just that—" He switched the phone to his other ear, then took a deep breath—"with the meds he's on, he's asleep by now. He's got that prostate thing, you know. It's too late to bug him about it tonight."

"Well, shit," Calvin said.

"Could you just do me a favor and meet me out there?"

"Nobody's been in that thing for a long time. Ain't much to the place."

"I'm sure it'll be fine."

Calvin snickered at that. "You might be surprised."

"I don't need much."

"Look, I got a rendezvous with this gal later on. The key's under the red bucket out back. You remember where that log pile's at?"

"Actually, it's been a while."

"You got a pen? Fifth one past the little angler shop on the right, about ten miles down the river road after you take the exit for the 102 to Rock Creek. When the asphalt turns to dirt, it's down another half mile there. No bigger than a bubble of soap."

"Thanks, Calvin."

"Yeah, well, you won't be thanking Pat when you see the shape that thing's in. He probably didn't tell you there's no cell service out there either, so call from the landline if that's still got a dial tone, and I'll tell you how to get the pilot light lit up so you can have a hot shower. Anyways, get going and call me back ASAP. If you get the machine, I'm already painting the town with Rhonda."

Harry left Greta in the truck with the groceries when he pulled into the cabin's gravel driveway that first night.

The sky was starting to get dusky, and everything smelled of dust and pine. He wanted to hike through the trees down to the river, but he'd have to wait till morning. He was afraid Greta would get loose and he'd spend the night searching for her in the woods with his Maglite.

Harry found the red bucket and the key beneath it, got the door open and flipped the lights on. Calvin was right. This was nowhere near the picturesque retreat he'd manufactured from the haze of his memory, formed when Pat had brought him and Adrienne out here as little kids.

First off, there was no TV or microwave. Nothing on the walls but peeled plaster and yellowish water blisters. Furniture-wise: a twin prison-issue metal bed, a "desk" that looked like a girl's make-up vanity from Little House on the Prairie, a folded card table, and two plastic chairs stacked obscenely, one inside the other. An oak chest of drawers that looked sturdier than the cabin itself, and a kitchenette with a hot plate next to a bathroom the size of an airplane lavatory that smelled like the septic tank it was plumbed to. Oh, and a crappy little radio Harry flipped on, which picked up Bing Crosby, some biblical wrath, and static. There was a gun rack over the bed, but no gun.

Harry unpacked the clothes from his duffel bag into the dresser. Put his pocket watch in the coin saucer on top, tucked his passport—with the picture of his mother slipped in along with a hundred-dollar bill for emergencies—into the drawer under his socks and went back out to the truck for the last of his supplies: a bag of bruised fruit, and a half dozen cans of Bud Light bobbing around in a cooler of melted ice.

Harry let Greta out of the truck, finally, and she leapt off the front seat and ran into the high grass, sniffing like crazy. He poured her kibble into a cereal bowl, called to her, but she didn't come. It was hard to blame her for bolting, cooped up for three days in the front seat thinking they were home every time Harry pulled into a rest stop or service station.

He stepped back outside, clapped a couple times, and hollered at her. His heart started to pound. He yelled out again, louder, and she appeared from the thick meadow grass, covered in tiny burrs and pollen. She darted through the doorway like a seal to devour her dinner.

Harry grabbed a beer, tucked the old rotary phone under his arm, dragged a plastic chair out of the kitchen, and sat down under the porch light luring bugs. He couldn't see the river yet, but he could hear it flowing up to the Clark Fork on the other side of the meadow, past a thick stand of pine trees and something that looked like a willow or aspen maybe. White bark, humongous branches covered in tiny green leaves quivering in the breeze. Bats were starting to wheel after floating insects. The moon was coming up.

He opened his beer and called Calvin back, figuring he'd just leave a message and say thanks.

"Another two minutes and I'd a been gone. You caught me brushing off the lapels of my tuxedo."

"Fancy," Harry said. "I found the key no problem. So, thanks. Think I'm all set. Don't worry about calling Pat, okay? I'll just talk to him in the morning and let him know I got in alright."

"You fish, Harry?"

"Not really, no."

"Well," Calvin said, "do you drink cold beer?"

"Sure?"

"We'll go fly-fishing this weekend. Season's good. I know the spots."

An owl gave off a throaty hoot right over Harry's head. His skin shivered.

"Okay…but one more thing—animals?"

"What about 'em?"

Harry told Calvin he hadn't seen anything on the drive up other than deer and a coyote's carcass getting worked over by crows near the off ramp.

"Well, there's black bear. And moose, though not many. If you keep your eyes peeled, you might see some bighorn sheep up on those cliffs, especially around dawn."

"Dawn," Harry said. "Right."

He pictured a cluster of sheep looking down onto the hood of his truck from the rocky ledges above the dirt road that snaked out to the cabin.

"Cougars?"

"They won't bug you." Then Calvin fell quiet before going on. "But don't go running over any foxes."

"Oh yeah?" Harry said, sipping the last of his beer.

"You'll have to ask Patrick. There's a story there. I don't want to foul it up."

"Sounds like a plan. And don't worry about calling my dad. I'll get ahold of him tomorrow."

"I heard you the first time, Harrison."

"Sorry." Harry gave a strained laugh. "Long drive, I guess."

"You aren't holding anything back from old Cal, are you?"

"No." Harry pictured Pat slamming down the phone after Calvin was sure to call him. He could see both men realizing they'd been duped. Harry stomped the empty beer can under his boot sole. "I just don't want to worry him. Truth is, he's not in good shape."

"Be that as it may, I owe him a jingle. Especially if he's not doing so hot. Hey, check that wardrobe, would you? Might still be a rifle out there."

"Hang on a sec," Harry said.

He stepped back inside the cabin and opened up the closet and leapt backward when he saw a pair of rubbery hip waders hanging from a hook.

"You there?"

"There's a mop," Harry said, lifting it up by the handle. Its tendrils frozen solid into a dusty brain of spaghetti.

"A *mop*? Well, the bears should leave you alone if you keep the lid bungeed to the can out back. Anything stinking, like fish parts or gizzards, you leave at the river or burn in the fire pit before bedtime. Unless you wanna have yourself a teddy bear picnic in there."

—

It's the morning after the party, when Calvin picks up the phone on the first ring.

Harry hasn't called him back for a week and a half.

"Dolores?"

"Hey, it's Harry."

The TV is on loud in the background, somebody guessing the price of something. Screams from an audience.

"Oh hiya, Harry. I'm in the middle of this thing. You mind if I call you later?"

"Actually, I'm in some trouble."

"Hang on," Calvin says, and the shouting gets louder before it goes dead. "Can't get ahold of you and Pat won't call me back neither. Thought I was gonna have to come peek in through the curtains and see what you'd got up to out there."

"Yeah, sorry I haven't called," Harry says. "I've just been tracking down a few things over at the library."

"Never mind the lame excuses. What kind of snag you get into, Harrison?"

"Promise you won't tell my dad?"

"Nope," Calvin says. "But I'll let you buy my breakfast at Flo-Ann's."

Calvin is already inside the diner, spread out at a booth with a newspaper.

He's much grayer and fuzzier than Harry remembered. Partially obscured by the drawings of sausage links and fried eggs on the window, but it's Calvin all right. Looks like he's yakking across the restaurant to the waitress at the counter, whose hair is piled on top of her head.

Putting weight on his bad foot, Harry feels it might burst like an overfilled water balloon. He stalls by leaning against the door of his truck, pretending to study his reflection in the side mirror. Dark bags under his eyes. A week's worth of stubble.

Somehow Harry's managed to look both oily and dehydrated. He bites down on the inside of his cheek to check the pain from his leg.

The hostess wiping down menus with her apron is not older than fifteen. High ponytail, streaked with fish tank blue. Lipstick so purple it's pretty much black. She just points to Calvin, like she knows exactly who Harry is, though he's never set foot in this place.

The *Missoulian* is spread out on the table beside Calvin's coffee, and Harry wonders if there's news from last night's party in there.

Calvin does not get up as Harry approaches. He grins maniacally, holding Harry's eyes with a crazed look, and makes a victorious *V* out of his arms up over his head.

"Well, well, well…" Calvin says, nice and loud. "You done playing pocket pool in Pat's rig out there or what?"

"Thanks for meeting me so early," Harry says, sliding into the booth, covering his wince with a cough.

Most of Calvin's clothing is some sort of camouflage and looks like he's lived in every article of it for years. He's smiling under his enormous mustache, toothy and googly-eyed.

"Little Harrison Stables, what on the bountiful earth did you get yourself mixed up in?"

"Can you keep your voice down?"

Calvin switches to a parody of a whisper, nearly as loud as his speaking voice. "Top secret stuff, huh? Looks like you need java." Calvin's breath smells like he's eaten a cigar dipped in manure.

Harry opens up the menu like a partition to steal a glance at Calvin's newspaper.

"How'd you slice your mitten there?"

"Why don't we order first and I'll tell you what's up."

"You afraid I'm gonna spill all your secrets to your lady friends?" Calvin says, pulling a long strand of hair out of his water glass. Harry waves the waitress over and Calvin watches her approach in a manner that can only be described as appraising.

"We're not quite ready yet, darlin', but we were hoping to know if there was any specials this morning. This young man is Patty Stables' kid, Harrison. And Harrison here drove all the way up from Tucson to buy old Cal a nice big breakfast."

"Sorry to hear about your dad," she says. "I haven't had the pleasure, but Cal talks about him nonstop. Special's chicken fried steak and eggs."

The waitress, "Linda" according to her nameplate, has

the voice of somebody much younger and friskier than she appears to be. She smells like cigarettes and hand sanitizer and wears an ocean of pastel makeup above her eyes and high on her cheekbones so that she looks like a doll that little girls had long ago had their way with.

She takes their orders and Harry starts in on his coffee. A wildfire at Glacier National Park is the story above the fold. The photo is a smear of orange and black, under which is something about a football player arrested at a bar in town. Looks like they used his team picture for the story.

"You can read about Smoky the Bear later. What the hell's going on, kid?"

"Did you ever hear from my dad?"

"Neither of you knows how to pick up the phone. Not until you need something, that is."

This relieves Harry somewhat, though it's not exactly his top concern at the moment. He decides to soften the ground by beginning with the minor offenses, but Calvin's not interested in Harry's life in Tucson in any way. Being expelled from a creative writing program sounds to Calvin like getting booted out of a Jazzercise class.

"The hell were you doing there in the first place?"

Calvin dips an imaginary quill into ink, pretends to scribble on his placemat, and then crosses his eyes and sticks out his tongue.

"Good question."

"Your hound dog loan you some fleas, Harrison?"

Harry must've been at his ankle under the table, not realizing it.

"I got bit up last night. Mosquitoes."

Then Calvin lowers his voice, "Never mind them. You gotta make sure you and your doggie watch out for rattlers up here though."

"Oh *yeah*?" Linda says, delivering their breakfast spread. "Calvin'll tell you all about the snakes we got here."

She sets an obscene platter of biscuits, gravy, and bacon before Harry. He has to look out the window and do some mouth breaths not to be sick. A big fuzzy mutt is padding around the bed of Calvin's truck in the parking lot. He gives out a doleful bark.

"That's Herkimer," Calvin says. "He's squirrelly to go nab an elk."

"And," Linda says, "here you go, Cal."

She places a towering stack of pancakes, topped with a single runny egg onto Calvin's paper placemat. Sausage links crowd the plate's edges. It's enough breakfast to kill a child. Calvin tears open three plastic cups of syrup and empties them one by one over the steaming food like somebody a little too eager to be lighting spiders on fire.

"We have rattlesnakes where I live in Tucson," Harry says, but Calvin doesn't hear. He's slurping coffee, breathing the hot smells, letting his eyes zigzag all over Linda again as she walks toward the kitchen.

"How do you keep Herkimer from going after snakes?"

Calvin sets down his fork. He glances out at his pickup and gives a floppy wave to a humongous man in bib overalls who's easing himself into a cream-colored Buick.

"Harrison, I think it's time you tell me what happened

last night. We can talk rattlers over our whiskeys later on."

Without breaking eye contact, Calvin leans over and snatches up a slice of Harry's bacon and bends the whole thing into the back of his mouth like a stick of Juicy Fruit.

"There might have been a shooting," Harry says, leaning forward and lowering his voice. "At a friend's party out past Bonner—"

"I figured you were out there."

"You heard about it?" Harry feels all the blood in his body rush to his face.

"All over the news, bud."

"Oh my god."

"Just joshin' ya, Harrison. That gal at the register painted up like the Bride of Frankenstein said something about a little gunplay at a fracas."

"A *fracas*? Jesus Christ, Calvin. Thanks for the fucking coronary."

"Simmer down," Calvin says. "You ring the coppers?"

Harry takes a sip of coffee to stall, not knowing what to tell Calvin. He remembers Paul from the party, one of Kristin's friends. Paul said he knew Calvin, that Paul and his dad fished with him now and again. The feeling of doom starts to work its way up from the pit of Harry's stomach, but he doesn't want to lay all his cards down yet. He's not sure he can trust Calvin. Harry imagines him calling Pat after breakfast. The two of them having a good, long chuckle about Harry's little quagmire.

Calvin leans across the table, waves his hand in front of Harry's nose. "Earth to Neptune."

"Sorry. I went to the precinct on the way over here," Harry says, "but I chickened out. Thing is, I ran out of there like everyone else when the screaming started, but I didn't realize there were two guys hiding in the back end of my truck."

This isn't precisely true, but Harry feels it more or less captures the spirit.

"Good going," Calvin says nodding sagely with a mouthful of pancake.

"Which part?"

"Not going to the cops. They'll trip you up and tangle that little yarn of yours into a confession. They train in horsepucky like that."

Harry pictures a beautiful female psychologist in nerdy glasses instructing these redneck cops on the subtle art of interrogation techniques to pry stuff out of dumbasses like him.

"Just between us girls then," Calvin says offhandedly, "who'd you have to shoot?"

"I didn't shoot anybody!" Harry's voice comes out high-pitched and loud.

Linda and the teen hostess both look their way like deer spooked in a meadow.

Cal flashes Harry his wily bucktooth smile. "Well I had to check, didn't I?"

Harry needs to calm down, but Calvin's not making this easy.

The itching at Harry's ankle flares up, and he scratches it below the table with purpose now. Liquid comes free from under his sock. A little relief, followed by hot pain.

"Calvin, if I don't go to the police, what the hell do I do?"

"What are you so worried about? If you didn't kill

nobody—like you say you didn't—then I think you should just go ahead and—"

"Go ahead and *what*?" Linda says in a flirtatious tone, glancing between the two men hunched over the table. She refills their coffee mugs. Harry purses his lips tight and glares at Calvin.

SUSPECTS

"I could tell from Siberia over there that you boys are up to no good," Linda says, cracking a sneaky smile.

"I mean, plotting and scheming first thing in the morning?"

"So, Harry. What you do is"—Harry shakes his head—"you catch a rattler and stick him in your icebox at home. You gotta freeze that sucker."

"Okay, I gotta hear this one," Linda says, sliding into the booth next to Harry, bumping her hip into his like they're kids in the backseat of the family wagon.

"What I wanna know is," Linda says, "how does that snake not die in your freezer?"

"Well, obviously it's much colder than a meat locker here by turkey time. And those things live through the winter."

"Okay, then, Mr. Snake Charmer," Linda says, "after you freeze this goddamn snake—pardon me, Harrison—then what are you supposed to do with it?"

Calvin's face lights up. "I'll tell you *then what*, lady."

His big mustache is webbed with syrup now. He makes his forefingers into a pair of crooked snake teeth. The three of them eye Calvin's curled finger fangs.

"But first," Calvin says, "I gotta drain the vein."

Linda rolls her eyes, pats Harry on the thigh, gets up, and walks back to the register. Calvin dabs his mouth area with a balled-up napkin, lets out a satisfied belch, and stands up too.

Suddenly Harry's alone in the booth. Fatigue crashes a cold wave through him. Linda's perfume lingers like wet fruit. Herkimer barks from the bed of Calvin's truck like an omen.

Harry wants to make all this—last night, Calvin Hogan, his throbbing ankle—disappear.

Word of "gunplay" had made it to the diner before Harry had. He wants to slip out the front door, drive back to the cabin, grab Greta and his scant possessions, and get on the road back to Tucson. Slide out of this mess back into the first one he'd run from. He can almost hear Pat saying that he'd known Harry's little calamity would follow him right out to the cabin.

Harry touches the wound under his pant leg, and its sticky dampness gives off heat.

Linda is looking at a TV over the counter now, leaning against the dessert case, its shelves rotating pies slowly inside.

Unless the shooters are still roaming the woods by the highway, Harry can't imagine it would've made the broadcast news yet. But when it does, people will be asked to phone the police with tips. There might even be a cash reward for details leading to an arrest—or *arrests*.

He recalls his mug shot, at 19, when Harry had gotten his one and only photograph taken by the police for driving under the influence. He'd buzzed all his hair off after his freshman year at CU-Boulder. He was nearly smiling in the picture, that's what stung. He'd looked shiny and smug. And his sister had floated him the cash for the ridiculous DUI classes they made him take so that he didn't have to mention any of it to his dad.

—

Harry watches Calvin, sauntering back through the diner, strike up a conversation with one of the line cooks.

Behind Calvin, two uniformed police officers come through the door, and they sit down in the counter seats nearest their booth. The hostess trails them with a pitcher of ice water and menus under her arm. Calvin gives them a big howdy-do nod, touching the bill of his cap, and slides back into the booth, wearing a look of intrigue.

"Now then, Harrison. Where was I?"

"Should we get a move on?" Harry says through his clenched teeth, giving a darting glance to their new neighbors.

Calvin raises up one hairy hand, as if to say, no sudden movements.

"You gotta *act natural*, because the next thing you're gonna do is de-fang the snake. And this is sensitive business. Once the rattler's good and froze up, you yank out his teeth with a pair of pliers, because you need this sucker and you need him angry—and you need him very much alive."

Harry drops his napkin over the remnants on his plate. With their backs to the booth, the cops are freakishly quiet, and Harry can't tell if they're eavesdropping on Calvin's anecdote or under the spell of a horrific crime scene they've surveyed this morning.

Somebody's blood smeared in the high grass out behind the house. A throng of cops pointing out indentations on the ground for evidence of the struggle. Maybe plainclothes detectives are interrogating people in the house, or loading them into their squad cars to question them down at the station. That whole back yard's probably cordoned off with yellow police tape, strung from the garage to the rear steps of the doublewide.

Calvin clocks Harry watching the two policemen and sucks his teeth to catch Harry's eye.

"You were gonna take me out to the river to go fly-fishing, right?" Harry says, like he's an actor in a bad commercial.

"Those trout aren't gonna grow feet and wander off, kid. So, anyways, you let the snake out in your garage, right? And then comes the hard part."

"I bet I know where this one's going," says the taller cop.

Suddenly Harry is falling through the sky, his ankle leaking a stream of blood into the air above him like a parachute failing to open. He coughs, glares at Calvin, and forces himself to smile like this is just another funny thing they're all doing together for a happy time.

The policeman—early 40s, gray at the temples, his nose broken at least once—has turned himself around, and is looking right at Harry.

"Maybe you do," Calvin says, not even glancing at the cop, "and maybe you do not."

The other officer chuckles, and keeps his back to the booth like he can't even be bothered. Broken Nose looks eager though, nodding with his eyebrows up, as if to say, Go right ahead, Weirdo. Finish your little anecdote.

Harry reaches down to his ankle, but his sock is oozing like a sopped dishrag now as he tries to breathe normally.

"Okeydokey," Calvin says, evidently delighted that his

audience is growing. "So, you wrap a shock collar onto your dog. One of those ones with the remote control. You let him wander into the garage. And he'll see that snake and he'll creep up on that son of a gun. And you got to watch real close now, because your pooch is gonna try and get a taste of rattler. So, when he goes in for a scratch-and-sniff on the serpent, thawed out in the warm garage, the snake's gonna rattle and rear up. Now, you're holding your breath here, because the moment that critter strikes, you shock your doggie with the current."

"I knew it," the taller cop says. His partner lets out an exaggerated sigh.

"Louis, you didn't know squat."

Calvin's eyes are all over Harry's face, unmolested by the cops' banter. Harry watches Calvin bite a sausage link in two, pause briefly to study the insides of the chewed-off end, then put the rest of it in his mouth before continuing.

"Gotta have that shocker up as high as it'll go. The moment that rattler uncoils and its empty mouth nips the nose of your mutt, why, you shock him *one more time.* Your dog'll shit the floor, of course. He'll be writhing in pain. Honest to God, it's a terrible thing. But I'll tell you something, bud—"

"What's that?" Harry says, leaning back in the booth, attempting to appear at ease.

"Your hound dog will not ever sniff up on a rattlesnake in the hills when you're out there hunting for chipmunks. That's that," Calvin says, nodding. "Consider your mutt *trained* off of snakes."

—

At the register up front, Calvin refuses to let Harry pay, but then he doles out the entire amount in crumpled up one-dollar bills and a pocketful of coins.

The hostess folds her arms, smacking her gum, and says, "Here we go again."

"Money's money," Calvin says.

"And Calvin's Calvin," she says and laughs till it turns to whinnying.

The two officers are sipping coffee and muttering under their breath without looking at each other in that spooky cop way, like they're watching a movie that nobody else can see.

Harry is pretending not to be too interested in the stray newspaper he's picked up on the bench by the gumball machines, but he is scanning it voraciously: Glacier fire, budget windfall from cigarette taxes, some lady's 101st birthday at the nursing home. The old woman is nearly bald, and looks neither aware of the sheet cake before her nor of the fact that her picture is being taken for the article. Then Harry sees yesterday's date in the corner and drops it back onto the pile.

In the parking lot, Harry pats Herkimer's fuzzy head, but the dog's big brown eyes are locked on Calvin and he paces the truck bed, whimpering. Calvin says he'll have to run back to his house on Old Pond Road to get some tackle and an extra pair of waders. Harry's cover about "heading to the river" has become their next move. He hasn't held a fishing pole since he was ten years old, but Harry's rolling with it. Evidently, Calvin Hogan is not somebody you jest about fly-fishing with.

"I need to do a few things at the library first," Harry says. "Meet you in an hour?"

"You can pull up dirty pictures on the net later, Harrison."

"I need to check my email."

Calvin shuts his eyes and brushes this away like a cloud of gnats. Herkimer's antsy, bounding around the back-end of the pickup, drooling. Calvin gets in and rolls his window down. The dog whines once, and Calvin tells him to hush. Harry looks at the dog, trying not to picture him as a puppy on the floor of some garage, writhing in agony next to a toothless snake.

"What happened to your window, Harrison?"

"Huh?" Harry slides into his truck and puts the key into the ignition.

Calvin stares at Harry and waits, his truck rumbling, a sparkle coming into his eyes. Harry has no idea how Calvin can see that the window isn't simply rolled down, that it had been removed by a bullet. But now Calvin's studying Harry's face, awaiting a real answer.

"I punched it out," Harry says. "Back home. I just—it's a dumb thing I did."

Calvin's brow comes down and ever so slightly he shakes his head. Harry can't tell if he can see through the lie, or if Calvin's just realized that he's about to go fishing with a moron.

"See you at the crossroads, Harrison. A couple miles past the cabin, right where it forks. Don't make me wait for your butt."

Calvin puts his truck in reverse and Herkimer gives out a happy woof as the vehicle jerks back before stopping again.

"Pick up a case over at the Grizzly Grocery on your way. And none of that yuppie stuff, neither."

Herkimer laps the air as they roll out of the lot. When Harry sees that they've turned the corner, he steals back into Flo-Ann's, slips past the hostess still sorting through Calvin's coins, and locks himself in the stall of the men's room. Under his sock, the wound is bruised and red. And it's much puffier now.

When Harry comes out, he plays dumb, and asks the hostess if she's heard about "some party."

"Yeah, my friend Regina was gonna go, but this other girl called her and told her not to. She said people went crazy. Somebody got shot and she got blood in her hair. Not Regina. Regina didn't end up getting a ride, thank *god*. The other girl got blood in her hair. I don't know her, but that's so gross. I mean, right?"

She pauses with her purple lips open, as her eyes scan Harry's face, like she's inspecting him for something. Many of her teeth are not where they should be.

"Are you okay?" she says. "You look kinda sick."

Not wanting to use his cell, Harry calls Kristin from a payphone across from the public library.

There's no answer, and he hangs up when he gets her voicemail. He doesn't want to sprinkle around any more evidence that he'd been at the party.

He's standing two blocks from the door to where Kristin works as the day manager at the Sapphire Mountain Bed & Breakfast. But he's keeping his distance for now. There could be detectives asking questions in there.

Less than twenty-four hours have elapsed since Harry was standing next to Kristin out by the bonfire, her hip nudging his. Now he doesn't know if she's even alive.

A minivan rolls by on the street and Harry leans against the glass of the payphone. She said, "You can bring your gun if you want."

It had seemed like such a weird thing to say. He even laughed about it when he got back to the cabin. Who brings a gun to a birthday party? He pictured the empty gun rack over the bed. That mop in the closet.

She'd tugged on the sleeve of his sweatshirt, then ran up the back steps into the doublewide. But now he can't help but picture her with blood in her hair. He can still feel his sweat running cold as the nose of that rifle rapped the glass of the truck's back window.

Harry walks a block down Poplar and tries to shake free of it, crossing the street to the library where the glass of the huge front door is covered in palmprints, and the muscles in his neck turn to cold wires when he remembers that his fingerprints—from both of his piss-stained hands—are all over that rifle, stock to barrel.

The computer terminals are all occupied and Harry decides to wait. John, the lanky librarian who's been helping him with his research about his mother, waves from the circulation desk. Harry gives him a nod, and John motions for him to come over. But Harry sees a woman get up from a computer and he nearly elbows her out of his way to get to the empty seat.

Bail had been set for a methamphetamines dealer who'd hidden drugs inside light bulbs. A new maternity ward at

Providence Hospital had seen the arrival of its first twins. Lightning outside Deer Lodge had struck a man's pickup and engulfed it in flames, but miraculously the driver had sustained no injuries. There was a picture of the guy standing next to his charred truck, a bemused look on his face. And somebody had butchered a cow in a field eighteen years ago, then fled to Oklahoma. Charges were being dropped due to lack of a speedy trial. Harry read these headlines, one after another, as cryptic prophecies of what lay in store for him.

The headline piece is still the wildfire raging through Glacier. The two-laner through the park, called Going-to-the-Sun Road, had been blocked off. A picture of massive flames juxtaposed with a separate photograph of a white mountain goat in a meadow of wild flowers with her kids huddled beneath her. The diptych seemed to suggest the fire was coming straight for them.

"Hiya, Harrison," John says, touching him on the shoulder.

Harry startles. "Hey. I'm kinda working on something here."

"No problem," John says. "I found the Alpha Phi yearbook you were asking about. Funny coincidence: my wife was in that same sorority as your mom back then. It was mis-shelved between some of the Kappas. And you'll be pleased to hear that there are a couple other things my friend at Providence managed to dig up too. Come find me up front when you're all done here."

"Five minutes, okay?"

Harry's scrolling and clicking through the *Missoulian* online and then he finds it.

There's a single item describing police called out to reports of gunshots and an altercation beyond Bonner-West Riverside, on Flagler Drive. Harry holds his hands behind his neck, lacing his fingers there, as he leans in to read it on the screen. No substantive details, no police sketch of the assailants or desperate quotes from any partygoers. It's a two-sentence dribble in the crime blotter: A young woman had been shot. No name given, but she was in critical condition. Suspects at large. No one in custody.

FOLLOWER

Harry needs to show his ankle to a doctor.

The skin around the four holes itches ceaselessly, and the thought of a nurse draining it and dressing the wound is starting to sound heavenly.

He rolls by the front of the ER in his pickup and it looks quiet enough, but he's too rattled after reading the squib on the library computer to stop and get out. He circles the block and makes another slow pass. He's not sure who might be in there, but he knows the big guy from last night injured himself toppling out of the truck. Again the woman with blood smeared down the length of her arm stumbles through his mind.

What if the police are staking it out? He's not sure if they even do stuff like that, but he doesn't want to walk into some snare. He's scrutinizing every passerby through the double lens of spying and being surveilled.

Harry pulls the truck into an empty spot next to a big pine tree, and he flinches when a squirrel appears, freezes, and then scrambles back up the trunk.

He shuts off the engine and watches the ER's main entry. An old man in a wheelchair is being pushed out by a pudgy guy in scrubs and is left there in the sun. The man takes out a brush and starts brushing his long, gray hair.

Harry pulls up his pant leg to consult the wound, on the off chance it has magically improved since he last checked. It hasn't.

He gets out of the truck and ambles through the lot, up to the crosswalk. That's when he sees Paul, Kristin's friend from last night. He'd come up to Harry when he'd arrived at the party. Paul had pointed at a cooler of beer, even offered him a scoop out of his tin of chewing tobacco.

Three or four cars pass by and Harry watches as Paul walks through the automatic doors with an older woman Harry doesn't recognize. The woman has on a gray Snoopy sweatshirt and pink sweatpants. Her hair is cut short, and nested badly at the back. When Paul disappears inside, the woman stops to look around—nervously it seems to Harry, though he might be hallucinating. He watches her take a long drag on a cigarette, then she throws it into the street. It sparks and rolls on the asphalt. When the automatic doors seal shut behind her, the crosswalk turns in Harry's favor, but he stays put to think.

Harry's already late to meet Calvin. He wants to turn back, head out to the river, but the wound on his leg throbs in protest. He pictures Paul running toward the jumble of people after the shots were fired. Paul knows what happened.

Harry's phone buzzes in his pocket, and he extracts it. Adrienne. He mutes it and decides to go ahead and cross the street. His leg spurting pain with each step.

As he comes through the automatic doors, Harry scans the waiting room. There's a lady holding her arm carefully, like an injured bird, watching a cooking show on the TV monitor. Some little kids are crawling around on the floor, smashing toy cars into a wall. Another guy's snoring with his chin on his chest, his head wrapped in a hood with the drawstrings pulled tight. No Paul.

Harry approaches the nurse on duty, a slender Native woman with white hair, lots of jangly bracelets on her arm.

"Can you tell me where those two who just came in went?" Harry says. "His name's Paul."

"And you are?"

"I'm Paul's brother, William."

Where the hell had William popped out from? Faulkner? The Bard? No clue, but out it flew.

"Down the hall on the left," she says. "Room four."

Harry passes a couple of nurses, smiles, and locates the door, glancing at the file in the plastic tray on the wall: *Tillett, Paul.* He listens for a moment but can't discern any voices. Harry taps lightly and lets himself in.

"Oh, hey man," Paul says. "Larry, right?"

Larry. William. He's anybody but Pat's kid Harrison in here.

"Good memory," Harry says. "I'm in the room down the hall and saw you pass by. Just wanted to say hey and make sure you were alright."

Paul introduces Harry to his mother, Tonya. Her eyes are puffy. And she appears to be in worse shape than either of them. Tonya takes this surprise visit as a chance to reunite with one of her menthols and she slips out of the exam room.

Paul's sitting bolt upright, like he's wearing a back brace. When the door closes again, he grins at Harry, showing his stained teeth.

"That was some crazy shit last night, right?"

"Seriously," Harry says. "So, what the hell happened out there?"

"No idea, man."

"You didn't see the fight?'"

"Nah, me and my buddy Curtis hid out in the garage," Paul says. "Till the cops finally took off."

Harry had had a few by then, but he could swear he'd seen Paul jog out into the field—straight into the melee. Something isn't right, but Harry lets the lie hang in the air to see what sort of path Paul might try to cut with it. Paul falls into a fit of coughing, and it sounds like there's a coffee can full of rocks in his chest.

"Do you know," Harry says, trying hard to sound casual, "who shot the girl?"

Paul eyes Harry. He's about to say something when the door opens and in comes the doctor. Short guy, salt and pepper beard, glasses. He looks like the uptight German scientist who gets eaten alive in every alien movie.

"So, Mr. Tillett," the doctor says, looking at Harry. "Ribs?"

Harry juts his chin at Paul, still sitting ramrod-stiff on the paper of the exam table.

"I got trampled, Doc. Can't breathe all the way in. Been coughing blood since I woke up." Paul's still wearing that easy grin, but his eyes are a little worried now.

As the doctor begins his battery of questions, Harry tells him he's heading out.

"Take care, man."

"Later, Larry," Paul says, and Harry glances back from the open door as Paul lifts up his t-shirt with both hands: there's a purple bruise the size and shape of a banana just under his heart.

When Harry gets to the fork in the road where they'd agreed to meet up, there's no sign of Calvin's truck.

Between the library, the ER visit, and a stop at the Grizzly Grocery for a case of beer, Harry's been gone well over an hour, but still. He didn't think Calvin would bail on him. Harry's got a bad feeling now, paranoid that somebody's followed him out to the exit for Rock Creek. He realizes he forgot to stop and talk to John at the library. He'd been in such a rush he'd hobbled right past the circulation desk in a daze.

Harry drives slowly down the river road and spots Calvin's blue Ford pulled up into some grass. Before he gets out, he can hear Herkimer barking through his open window.

The dog lopes up to him and lets out a big woof. He's wiggling and panting and dripping mud from his chin whiskers, like he'd found something good to eat in a puddle.

"Hey, Herky. Where's Calvin?"

Harry follows Herkimer down a path through the tall grass. The river's rushing noisily and there's a light breeze as they trod to the bank. Everything smells like dry flowers.

Harry comes through a grove of pine trees and can see Calvin's up to his thighs in the middle of the river. A plump brown hawk is perched on the branch of a dead tree, eyeing the horizon: ten thousand pines, rocky beaches on either bank, and the river elbowing up through thicker woods even greener beyond.

Herkimer barks again, but Calvin doesn't look over. He's whipping his fly rod back and forth, chewing on what looks like a slab of jerky in the sunlight.

"We waited," Calvin says, still casting. "But the fishies were calling, Harrison. Besides, I thought maybe you'd been detained by law enforcement."

"It's nice to know you'd have been out here reeling them in all day if I had."

"Yeah, yeah," Calvin says. "What'd you learn at the library?"

Harry pauses to look around. The combo of Calvin's brash attitude, honking-loud voice, and that wily-ass look in his eyes—Harry isn't sure what he can trust the guy with. But he doesn't want to keep lying either.

Calvin sloshes back over to pluck out one of the fresh beers Harry's picked up.

"Least you remembered these," Calvin says, opening one and sipping a gush of foam off the top of the can. "You don't look so good, Harrison."

"Yeah, I'm not feeling great."

"You want my advice, you lay low."

"Lay low?"

"Low and slow," Calvin says. "When the falcon's in flight, do the gophers throw a jamboree on the meadow?"

"I don't know, Calvin. I'm not up on gopher activity."

"I am," he says, "and they lay very low indeed. Burrow into the cool earth, and just...*crack a cold one*."

With that, Calvin fixes Harry up with a pair of hip waders, which Harry pulls on over his jeans. Calvin hands him a fly rod, points to a nice rock sticking out of the water not far down the bank, and tells Harry to start casting there.

Harry takes a beer and the fly rod and plods into the

current. Herkimer bounds out after him and Calvin whistles for him to get out of the river.

Harry opens his beer and drinks half of it down in one slurp, before setting it on the big rock poking out of the rushing water at his knee. He works his line clumsily, turning around every so often to see how Calvin's doing it, casting steadily with a methodical ease. The two of them fish through the late morning, and Harry catches nothing.

He gets a nice sunburn and the wound above his ankle itches nonstop, as he feels the cold river water squeeze at it through the rubber boots he's wearing. Harry tells himself to relax, that it's finally healing up. He'd handled it in the parking lot of the ER himself, with a bottle of rubbing alcohol he nabbed from the nurse's station on the way out. He pours many cans of cheap beer down his throat well into the afternoon.

It should be long gone, but Harry's trying to spit out the flavor of last night's tobacco into the river eddies. His tongue keeps tasting it there between his lower front teeth and the raw inside of his bottom lip. He spits again and again, over the rocks into the water.

"You'd better quit your dippin', Harrison, or a doctor's gonna come for that pretty jaw of yours, and you'll be doing TV spots about it through a hole in your face."

Somehow Calvin seems to notice nothing, but manages to see everything—and it enrages him. But Harry's gotten himself tipsy enough to have dampened the sting radiating from his wound to a dull undulation up his thigh.

He's watching a hawk glide from tree to tree when he tangles his line into some twigs and a clump of leaves. He tries to free it with two clean whips.

"You gotta cut that rat's nest, Harrison, and start her over."

Harry plops down on the rocks at the shoreline and winces. Calvin clocks this.

"You ready to tell me what happened to your drumstick?"

"Twisted my ankle. Over at the library."

"That's alright, Harrison," Calvin says, shaking his head with a tricky smile. "You keep fibbin' if it suits you, but the truth'll come sluicing out of you before long."

"I got bit."

"Not snake bit, I hope," Calvin interrupts him and goes into a lengthy tale about Calvin's buddy Pierre who'd been bit twice on the same trip and refused to let Calvin suck out the venom. "We decamped promptly, but Pierre had to amputate. I said, 'Don't you blame *me*, Pierre.' Now that fool won't go near an elk hunt with old Cal."

Harry leans all the way back against the cooler in the shade of the bank, eating pretzels out of a plastic bag, listening to the ravens caw at each other from either shore.

He can't stop replaying the scene from last night. Kristin running into the house. Paul jogging into the field. Harry had turned back and gone for the truck. Something wasn't matching up.

Harry pictures Kristin locked in the bathroom, terrified. The police pounding on the door, flanked around the house with German Shepherds and shotguns and flashlights. Maybe Paul doubled back and hid out in that garage like he'd said. But maybe he's hiding something.

Harry shuts his eyes in the bright sun. A fresh wave of

panic rolls through him. He takes another beer from the cooler and holds it without opening it for a moment, to feel its perfect weight in the palm of his hand. He brings the beer up to his sweaty temple and holds it there.

He can see the ambulance from the gas station as it's followed by all those patrol cars, whining through the highway's blackness. He's fucked up now, and everything from last night begins to fuse in his mind—each stray thought's another log tossed onto growing flames. It's starting to look like the Glacier fire raging next to those mountain goats huddled together in the grass.

Calvin's muttering and whispering to himself as he's whipping his line in and out of the river. Harry sits up when he hears something coming through the brush. Herkimer's barking.

Somebody's hiked down the herd path and emerges noisily from the bushes right behind Harry. Harry squints into the sunlight, trying to make out the guy's face.

"Howdy, Calvin."

It's a tall man with a lumberjack beard in denim overalls blotched with oil stains. He's out of breath. Spittle at the corners of his mouth, long scraggly hair all over his shoulders. He's about the same age as Calvin and Patrick—mid 50s is Harry's guess.

"Hey, Greg," Calvin says. "You playin' hooky from the shop?"

"Something like that," Greg says, wiping his forehead with a blue handkerchief he pulls out of his pocket. Greg stares at Harry.

"You'll never guess who that rascal is," Calvin says.

Greg's brow furrows. He says nothing.

"That's Harrison Stables. Patty's kid. He drove all the way up from Tucson to get his line tangled into a dog patch and drink up all my beer."

"Huh," Greg says. "You don't look much like your old man."

"Don't be rude, Harry. Toss him a cold one. The man looks thirsty."

Harry takes a beer out of the cooler, wet with ice. Greg lumbers over to him, blocking out the sun. He studies Harry's face with something like mistrust before reaching over and taking the beer. Greg pops it open, sucks it down in two huge swallows, and flings the can into the shrubs.

KRISTIN

"If I win?" Harry heard the woman say, "then you gotta dance to the Rolling Stones."

She chuckled at the enormous man she spoke to. The big guy took off his ball cap and wiped his brow sweat into the bushy tufts above his ears, replaced his hat, and motioned for another drink by holding the empty glass over his head even though the tavern was practically empty.

Harry was procrastinating on the afternoon he met Kristin in Missoula. Or distracting himself from what he'd come in here to do. He was half-watching this little scene from the far end of the bar, by the dartboard and toilets, writing in his notebook.

The décor inside of Child's Tavern was a lot of mirrors over wood paneling. One wall was covered with yellowed beer posters, featuring ladies with feathery manes. They were donning high-waisted bikinis and shiny pumps, each model raising a frosty mug adorned with the logo of the beer they were supposedly guzzling.

"And what if I win?" the big guy said.

"Then I'll do a strip tease," the woman said, rapping the bar hard with her knuckles, "right on this tabletop, Glenn."

Glenn pretended to spit out a mouthful of beer. Two of Glenn's buddies nearby laughed a low rumble. A football game was on the monitor above the bar toward which four or five other late afternoon drinkers were faced. The bartender was also the owner. Rod. Warm eyes, one of his two front teeth the color of coffee. His hair had receded way back on his head, only a thin wisp he didn't bother to cut remained up front, like a kewpie doll's.

It was time for Harry to write down what he knew—or what he thought he knew. Or just the questions he needed to find answers to. Then he'd piece it together and bring the completed puzzle back to his sister. But now that he was actually in Montana, Harry was getting closer and it was giving him that queasy feeling in the pit of his stomach. A single question dogged him: What if Pat had something to do with his mother's death?

John Dowd at the library downtown was excited to have a project like this, a little too excited Harry thought, but he was a nice enough guy. He had a crooked row of bottom teeth, and a long nose. He wore thick glasses and sweaters, and was happy to track stuff down for Harry.

John had directed him to the sorority house down on Gerald Avenue, but Harry had idled in his truck out front for twenty minutes, deliberating. Coeds came and went, and Harry pictured her there. He'd wanted to go knock on the door. But he just sat there with his stereo playing quietly, lurking outside an all-women's residence in the middle of the day like your run-of-the-mill creep.

Harry decided he needed a drink first. Then he'd head back over there and ring the bell at Alpha Phi. See if they kept any records. Old pictures, maybe.

He sipped his beer at the far end of the bar, away from the other patrons watching the game, whose laughter and chatter kept distracting him.

"No homework allowed in here, pal," Rod said. "We have a strict get drunk and fall down policy."

"Oh, it's not for school," Harry said, stuffing his notebook into his backpack.

Harry decided to lay a couple cards down, see if Rod knew her, or knew of her at least.

"Well it better not be your taxes, then."

"Actually, there's a woman in Tucson that I—"

"Just one?" Rod broke into wet laughter. Saliva landed on Harry's cheek.

"Well, shit," Rod said, shaking his head. He brought Harry a fresh beer, and placed a shot glass down beside it. Rod located a bottle full of what looked like reddish honey.

"My first wife?" Rod whispered. "She's from Yuma, buddy. And she's *dead*."

"I'm sorry to hear that."

"You and you alone."

The brown tooth rested there on his lower lip. Rod hovered, waiting. Then he leaned in toward Harry, putting his elbows on the bar. A light came on in the man's eyes.

"You think you can say the right thing and she'll come crawling back to you, huh? She catch you in bed with her friend? I have been there, pal, right where you're sitting."

"Wow," Harry said. "That's not where I'm sitting actually."

"You been over to Lotus Massage on Sherwood yet?"

Harry shook his head, sipped his beer.

"Too pricey if you ask me," Rod said. "Let me tell you something about women."

“Okay?” Harry said, lifting up the shot, holding it in the light. Flecks of glitter. He drained it in one go and it burned all the way down. Tasted like chemical cherries and Harry squinched up his face, coughing hard. “What the hell was that?”

“Women need little presents and surprises and crap like that. They’re like cats. You ever had a cat?”

Harry shook his head and chased the putrid acid in the back of his throat with a swig of beer.

“Just like friggin’ tabby cats,” Rod said again, finger-combing the tuft of hair at the front of his forehead. “Oh, yeah. They’re all lovey-dovey, going *meow-meow-meow* one minute, sure. But then it’s claws out and they’re hacking you up like a Christmas goose.”

“I appreciate your advice,” Harry said.

“Angel’s Cradle,” Rod said. “Cure for a limp dick *and* a broken heart.”

Rod broke into a big chuckle at this line he’d probably said a hundred times and then added, “Had that bottle since ‘88. Can’t get rid of the stuff.”

“Let me ask you something, Rod. You ever run into a woman called Elizabeth Stables? Her maiden name—”

Everybody at the bar suddenly howled at the TV. Rod turned around and they watched as the camera panned over the faces of screaming fans, gesticulating wildly, their mouths forming dark ovals of ecstasy.

“Get ready to cough it up, Glenn!” Rod yelled, and he sauntered over to watch the replay with the others.

An interception, a fumble, a yellow flag flung onto the

turf, and a stadium someplace tropical going nuts.

Glenn, the big guy, slid off his barstool and bounded over to the jukebox. "Jumpin' Jack Flash" came on loud, smothering the din of a Ruffles commercial. Rod watched Glenn dancing solo, and gave him a wolf whistle.

Harry turned on his stool to see that Glenn was performing a sort of rhumba, his hips and shoulders working against each other. The woman at the end of the bar whooped. She was clapping and gyrating in her chair, not getting up, waving her arms over her head, her cigarette hanging from her mouth, covering her face in a veil of smoke.

"Here we go, baby," she said.

Glenn capered around the bar, mouthing along to Mick Jagger, making up words in a loud slur to whatever the song actually said. When he began to fuck at the air—his t-shirt revealing his gut—two others lurched around on their barstools to root him on. A guy in a cowboy hat pumped his fist dreamily.

The woman was clapping. Her belly came over her waistline, and she was wearing a bright yellow tank top that read *TAMPA, FLA* in rainbow lettering. Diamond-like studs rippled down the outer seams of her blue jeans. Her thin eyebrows were electric.

Alone again, Harry reached into his backpack and pulled out his notebook. He turned to a blank page, his pen poised, and sipped his beer.

Late afternoon light ripped a hole in the dark bar and a young woman walked through the doorway with a library book in her hand. She was about Harry's age, maybe younger. Her black hair was tucked behind her ears and she had on jeans, an unzipped hoodie, and a white t-shirt emblazoned with some indecipherable silver scrawl.

She patted Glenn on his shoulder as she turned sideways to slip by him, evidently not minding the big man's foamy lather. Rod placed a beer in front of her, and she opened her book. She was close enough for Harry to smell her perfume, which was full on watermelon. He tried to stay focused on his page as she started cracking peanuts open.

The cover of her book featured a black rotary phone against a blood-red background. It looked kind of old-fashioned, but one end of the phone's receiver was the head of a black snake, coiled and ready to strike, with its thin tongue poking out.

The guitar licks and drum thuds of Van Halen's "Panama" came on and Glenn was still at it. Harry could see out of the corner of his eye that the lone dancer was sliding a pool cue back and forth between his legs like a towel. Then Glenn was riding it around the bar, bronco-style, as David Lee Roth screamed through the speakers.

"You writing your suicide note over there?"

Her eyes were sleepy. Freckles on her cheeks. A tiny fleck of red peanut skin was stuck to her lower lip. Harry wanted to reach out and dab it with his pinky. He closed his notebook.

"Yeah," Harry said. "But I can't figure out how to start."

"What's wrong with 'Goodbye cruel world'?"

Harry smiled. "Not bad. Keep it classic."

"I'm Kristin," she said. "What are you really writing?"

"Harry." He sipped his beer. "It's a letter to my ex."

"Gotcha," she said. "I got a couple of those myself."

"She's down in Arizona." What was he communicating?

Eligible but not unlovable. Desired, but distantly.

"Why? She in prison there?" Kristin laughed at that.

"No," Harry said, charmed. "She just, like, lives there."

Tampa and Glenn were seducing each other in some ritual they appeared to be improvising on the spot. Harry tried to block them out as they clenched each other and fused into one drunken mass—swaying and pressing. Tampa held her arms aloft, and the side of her breast slipped out from under her tank top. A boozy shudder spilled through Harry.

"Wow," Kristin said. "I love these two. They don't give a fuck, you know what I mean, Harry?"

Glenn's hands were lobster claws, pinching the smoky air around Tampa. Harry glanced down the bar. Cowboy Hat and Rod and the others were glued to the Dolphins clumped at the five-yard line.

"Don't tell me you aren't a little jealous," she said, and downed her beer.

She got up off the barstool, and moonwalked over the scattered peanut shells, snaking her arms seductively at Harry to accompany her into the writhing pits of boogie hell. Harry froze, watching her with a dumb smile on his face.

Kristin held his gaze, shrugged, then walked into the bathroom. His sister's words flooded into his mind with the battery acid of that shot of Angel's Cradle: "Women like it when you're decisive," Adrienne had told him.

Harry had thumped his chest like a gorilla. Adrienne shook her head.

"Not rude or controlling. I mean, be clear and honest. You can't just sit on the fence and wait, Harry. You have to make a move. As in, decisive action."

"Should I be myself too?"

Adrienne had smiled. "Let's not go that far."

Harry pulled some money out of his wallet and zipped up his backpack. Wrote his number on a napkin and slipped it into Kristin's book. *Beast in View.*

A short blond guy in an oversized yellow hunting vest strutted through the open doorway. Behind him, a much taller man with long, black hair under a Stetson followed him in and nodded at Rod. Stetson let his eyes come to a stop on Harry.

"Hey, Frank," Rod said. "Your little parakeet's not allowed in here anymore."

"I look like his keeper?" Frank said, cocking his head.

The little guy said he'd leave when he got what he came for. Then he asked where Kristin was at and that got Harry's attention.

Frank said, "High Life. Your wife still on vacation?"

"You see her," Rod said, "and you can keep her."

Frank's eyes had dark circles, like he hadn't slept in while. He looked at Harry again and nodded as Harry zipped up his sweatshirt, slung his pack over his shoulder. There was a little man, a figurine made of metal wire, standing upright by Harry's empty shot glass.

"I make 'em," Rod said. "You can keep that one, for luck."

Harry picked up the small sculpture. It was warm. The little man had no face, just an egg-shaped head of metal wiring. It was the size of a rubber eraser. He didn't want to be ungrateful and wrapped his hand around it.

"You can have it," Rod said again. "I got a million of 'em."

TRAPPER

Harry wakes up with a hot headache on the shoreline of Rock Creek and wipes a strand of drool off his shirtfront.

His erection presses through his jeans against a warm unopened can of beer in his lap. Calvin's still out in the sunshine, lashing away at the river's surface with his fly rod, mumbling to himself with a look on his face like he's working something over. He's getting his free hand into a bag of Doritos.

Harry sits up and watches Calvin: crunching away, casting the line back and forth in a perfect choreography matched up with that buzzy whipping sound. Half insect, half machine.

"Hey Calvin, who was that guy who came by?"

"Greg owns the foreign auto shop down on Purdy Street, why?"

"I thought he was gonna pull my head off."

"Well," Calvin says, "you're ugly enough. I'll give you that."

Harry tries to get up but stops and rotates his ankle before testing it with any weight. It's moist and pained. Feels like there's seepage down in the heel of his sock.

Harry had dangled his bare foot out of the truck and poured half the bottle directly onto his swollen leg. He had to sink his teeth into his forearm to keep from screaming. Dabbed at it with some Burger King napkins. But now it feels worse, somehow. It burns.

"You missed the bear during your catnap, Harrison."

"Very funny."

“It was licking the sweat off your chin like a lollypop before I noticed it.”

Harry stands up carefully, leaning on the huge boulder beside him, and wipes the drool off his cheek with the sleeve of his shirt. He staggers slowly up into the trees for a piss. The breeze makes the leaves quake all around him.

“Black bear yearling,” Calvin says. “Not a grizzly.”

“Fuck off.”

“I wouldn’t let a grizzly lick at you, Harrison.”

Harry comes back out into the sun and the sounds of the river. He’s rubbing the top of his head, which is sticky and tight, like he’s wearing a swimming cap under his hair. His mouth tastes like warm beer.

“Who was the girl you went to see out at that fracas?”

“You don’t know her,” Harry says.

Calvin looks at Harry leaning on the big rock, waiting for an answer.

“Just a friend. Her name’s Kristin.”

Calvin casts his line a few more times. Then he turns to face Harry again, the fly rod suspended mid-air.

“Kristin…” Calvin says.

Harry finds a beer in the cooler and tries to stay calm.

“Can we talk for a minute about what I’m gonna do? I mean, I shot some bottles with those guys last night. The same two I drove out of the party. I threw their gun into the road. My hands were all over that thing, Calvin. But I didn’t shoot anybody, I swear to god.”

His voice has grown shrill but he can’t help himself from spiraling.

Calvin's brow furrows and he starts scraping his teeth over his lower lip.

Harry's blood starts to heat up again. He stands there in the shade holding the cold unopened can of Coors to the back of his sweaty neck. Ravens are bickering over something above them. Calvin stares a hole right between Harry's eyes and one of his eyelids starts to dance, a tiny nervous fluttering.

"Truth's like taffy, Harrison. You don't wanna start pullin' at it wrong and get yourself all stickied up inside it. That girl is dead."

"Which girl? What'd you hear?"

Calvin wades back over in comedic sloshing steps with his fly rod and the Doritos, the can of Red Bull squished into his armpit.

"Greg heard it on the radio. They probably got squad cars all over doing a dragnet for you jackals by now."

Harry just stands there.

"Kristin," Calvin says again, studying Harry's face. "Oglala girl? Hangs around the Peacock and Child's with a little dingleberry?"

"How small is this fucking town?"

"Which one? Because Missoula's the second biggest *city* in Montana. Just about anywhere's smaller: Libby, Wolf Crick, Big Sandy…"

"Okay, okay," Harry says, holding his palm out.

"There's Anaconda and Augusta, and a little ghost town called Comet that hasn't got zero people in it where Barbie Todd popped old Cal's cherry back in '56."

"Wow. I think you made your point."

Calvin undoes the suspenders of his hip waders, "I fish with two of Kristin's brothers. She got a couple more back in Pine Ridge. Her mama's shacked up with a Blackfeet guy called Lionel. Lionel was in the soup with me and your dad. Had his pointer finger shot off. Though he didn't get purple-hearted out of Saigon until this doofus from Rhode Island named Ricky drove a jeep over his boot."

"Meaning what?" Harry says. "Kristin's my cousin?"

"Don't know about that, but it'd be alright with Cal if she was. She's a cutie, and she knows her way around a firearm. Like the song says, *She was a black-haired beauty with big dark eyes.*"

Calvin lets his appraising eyes go all over Harry as he steps out of his waders. Then he whistles loud to Herkimer who'd been napping in a patch of grass.

"Don't tell me you don't know Bob Seger, Harrison."

"Seriously, no more gopher shit. What am I gonna do?" Harry says. "Adrienne told me you worked for the sheriff in Whitefish, and my leg's not doing good—"

"What?"

"My sister," Harry says, quieter now, "told me you were a deputy or something?"

"Oh yeah," Calvin says, chuckling hard, "that's *right.*" Calvin's laugh is a cross between an owl's hoot and a series of stifled sneezes.

"You know what?" Harry says. "Don't tell me. I don't want to know."

"No, I used to get in little tussles, and your dad was always good for some bail scratch. After it happened a couple times, I just told Pat to tell you kids that if the sheriff rings from Montana it was because I"—he does nice big air quotes here—"*worked there*," and Calvin starts giggling again.

"Adrienne will be so pleased to hear this."

"But you're right about one thing: gopher time's over, Harry. Let's wrap up this picnic. We're gonna have to go see Silas out at the Trapper."

Harry follows Calvin's blue Ford back down the river road under all the trees throwing a lovely mosaic of shadows over their vehicles.

Herkimer is chomping at the breeze in the back end of Calvin's pickup, bounding from side to side, and the warm wind floods in through Harry's passenger side window. For a brief moment Harry has the fleeting sense that everything will turn out okay.

But when Calvin pulls into the dusty lot of a road saloon called the Trapper, Harry can feel that glump of tobacco smoldering in his belly again. The sense of being followed still nags at him, though there's nothing but a cloud of road dust and leafy trees in his rearview mirror. He wants to drive right past Calvin's rig, back out to the cabin to sober up, call Adrienne, and reassess.

But Calvin would know then that something was very wrong indeed. And even if the guy doesn't call the cops on Harry—which he might—Harry's pretty sure Calvin would be pulling into the gravel driveway himself, banging on the cabin door before dark.

In the parking lot, Harry uses the payphone to see if his

cell has any messages, praying there will be something from Kristin. But there's only one message, and it's from Adrienne:

"Harry, will you please call me back and let me know what the fuck is going on?"

An array of taxidermy animals adorns the tavern's brown walls. A bison head, two bighorn sheep, and many deer and elk, their great antlers fuzzed with dust. Harry finds the rabid-looking possum—its jaw cranked open in a scowl—the most disturbing of these. It's hard to avoid looking at it through the mirror behind the bar, floating there over his shoulder.

Calvin introduces Harry as the progeny of Patrick Stables to Silas, who leans back with his arms folded, considering. Silas has on a black leather motorcycle vest with various pins and patches whose insignias Harry doesn't recognize. There's something about the turnip-shape of Silas's skull that gives Harry the impression that he has no teeth. Silas is working at his own tallboy of something behind the bar, its can adorned with a red tiger, under which some kind of health warning in Asian characters is stamped.

"Why was your friend Greg looking at me like that?" Harry says under his breath when Silas turns around.

"Looking at you like what?"

"I don't know, Calvin. He was just *glaring* at me."

"Greg knows your old man. So, maybe he was checking for family resemblance, wondering if you belonged to the milkman."

Harry sets his elbows on the edge of the bar and puts his hands into his hair. He finds something above his left ear with two fingers and thinks it might be a cube of shattered window glass. It's a ladybug that must've hitched a ride from the river. Harry lets it walk from the back of his hand onto the bar's glossy wood surface. Calvin squishes it with his beer bottle and wishes it a Merry Christmas.

Harry gets up and locks himself into a stall in the men's room for a peek at his leg under the napkin wad he'd applied in the parking lot. Each step he takes sends out a wet throb of electricity through his kneecap up into his tailbone. There's a good deal of pus and it's gone from looking like four bee stings to about forty. The swelling's so bad now that the curve of what had been Harry's ankle bone is no longer discernible.

The holes themselves are geysers of mustard-colored ooze—and the Coors and pretzels turn over in Harry's stomach just giving it a peripheral sniff as he stretches the elastic of his sock away from it and pulls off the bandage gingerly with his fingers. There's discoloration and his leg hairs look to be burnt off. He'll have to settle up and head straight back to the ER.

"Well, they caught one of those boys," Harry hears Silas say as he limps back to the bar.

"Did they now?" Calvin says, taking a hummingbird sip off his whiskey.

Harry drains a fresh shot Silas filled for him, and a jolt of terror splashes down his spine.

"What'd I tell ya, Harrison? Silas doesn't miss much out here. The dragnet's in progress, baby. Score one for Hogan."

Calvin licks the tip of his index finger and draws an imaginary point in the air. Then he pats Harry on the back, downs his shot, and lets out a big belch followed by a chuckle. Harry looks at the TV mounted over the gin bottles.

"Son of a bitch who did the shooting is still on the loose though," Silas says.

"Have they released the victim's name?" It's the only neutral-sounding question Harry can think to ask.

"Nope, but those nitwits shot a girl. Died in the hospital this morning. Had too much Kool-Aid at a party last night up around Bonner. I probably served half of those little shits in here myself."

"*Hospitals*," Calvin says with disgust. Harry doesn't even bother with that one.

Calvin's yammering to Silas, but Harry's locked on the screen. The sound's off, but it cuts to a mugshot of the suspect they'd apprehended.

It's the big guy in the long white shirt who'd fallen out of Harry's truck last night. The one who begged not to be left out on the road. Donald Hunt. 33-year-old white male, from Coeur d'Alene, Idaho. Suddenly Harry feels bad for him, and now they're looking for his pal Tommy.

"Fuck heads," Silas says.

Harry asks if Silas wouldn't mind turning it up.

"Old Harry here was at that shindig when the lead started flying."

Harry glares hard at Calvin but keeps his mouth shut.

"Come on, bud," Calvin says. "Don't look at me like that or I'll have to call Patrick and tell him you been bad like Jesse James."

Silas reevaluates Harry for a moment, like he's trying to

discern if Pat's kid would be capable of shooting a girl and limping into his bar the very next afternoon to celebrate. Silas scratches at a faded green tattoo of a dagger piercing a red rose on his forearm and then gets up on a stepstool, adjusts the volume, and disappears out back for a smoke. Harry looks around and it's just him and Calvin now.

The broadcasters, a blond woman in a royal blue blazer and a black guy in a gray suit, exchange knowing glances and are replaced by an air freshener commercial's cartoon rainbow, which is springing all over this exasperated lady's house, her kids scampering after it and yelling "Freshie!"

Harry has not watched a television advertisement with such desperate focus in all his life. What did it mean—these children trailing a rainbow, whizzing out its replenishing colors onto whatever lay in its path? The kitty litter, the smelly work boots by the door, the sparkling toilet.

"Calvin, you know Tommy? Short guy, blond buzz cut, hangs around Kristin?"

"Sure, why?"

"He was the other one. With Donald Hunt," Harry says. "In the truck with the rifle. I'm pretty sure he's the one who shot the girl."

"Now that would've been handy to know earlier."

"Jesus. Why?"

"Probably that's good and bad. I mean, Tommy's dumb as a stump."

"Why bad though?"

"Family's in law enforcement. Which means Tommy has some *inappropriate sway* in matters of jurisprudence. That's why he marches around town like a toddler with a bellyful of milk and a fresh diaper on."

"When he told me his cousin was State Patrol, I just figured he was trying to scare me."

"He was not," Calvin says. "Although whatever else fell out of that kid's mouth was probably a whopper. Anybody see you drive off with Pipsqueak and Donny boy?"

"Maybe," Harry says. "I mean, it's possible. But I don't know."

"Well, Harrison, that sounds to me like a big fat *yes, definitely*."

Harry's now treading water in waves too big to see over. He sits there as the bottles against the mirror behind the bar start to pull away from him, like somebody's rolling it backwards on a movie set.

When the broadcast resumes, coverage shifts to a young reporter standing in the foreground of the fire at Glacier, followed by an eternity of still more commercials.

Then comes the finale: a local exclusive, which features a husky guy in plaid with flushed cheeks and a goatee looking awkwardly into the camera. He and his kids over on Beaver Street taught a ground squirrel to waterski behind a motorized toy boat in a kiddie pool on their front lawn.

At this, Calvin hoots so loud Harry recoils as if from a gunshot, and then Calvin claps Harry hard on the back, and breaks into roaring laughter.

BEAR

Harry lets Greta out into the yard when he gets home from the Trapper.

She trots a crisscross pattern out through the meadow grass, happily sniffing every scent. But he loses sight of her red fur immediately in the darkness. Normally, he would've walked out there himself, flashlight in hand. And with no moon, he'd have kept her on the long lead. But Harry is blasted drunk. He'd thrown up in the parking lot of the Trapper outside his truck.

His ankle is still seeping but the pain is more distant now, like an eerie horn blanketed by fog. Even in his compromised state, he's lucid enough to know that he can't get himself to the doctor until he sobers up, unless he wants to get pulled over again.

There's a message from his sister on the cabin's old answering machine: "Hi Harry, I got a call from your friend, Leah, or your girlfriend, whatever—anyway, she wanted to know where you are and she told me what you did to that guy's car. You're lucky you're not in jail, you dumbass. Unless you are, in which case have fun."

On his way out of Tucson that morning, Harry had gone by Ryan's place, located a nice desert rock the size of a football, and lobbed it onto the windshield of Ryan's Volkswagen Golf. It's not like Ryan was behind the wheel at the time and

Harry had doused it with gasoline. It was nothing if not *decisive action.* Ergo, Adrienne was overreacting as usual.

Harry thinks about calling his sister back to tell her that Calvin Hogan had been the Whitefish Sheriff's Deputy in roughly the same way that Harry used to have sexual intercourse with Angelina Jolie, but his sister would probably just scold him for letting her worry this long while Harry was getting plastered with Calvin.

He sits down on the edge of the bed to try and staple a few thoughts together. He's rankled and sunburnt. The spasmodic doses of panic coupled with Calvin's banter have wiped him out, and the lure of sleep is now luxuriously heavy.

When Harry yells from the bed through the cabin's open door out to Greta, she still won't come, and he's in no mood to go stand out there under the buggy porch lamp and holler at his dog.

But why hasn't Kristin called? The question sets whatever dregs of adrenaline Harry has left loose in his blood and he pulls himself upright on the bed.

"Fuck it."

He finds her number, saved in the contacts of his cell as "Kristin Missoula," and then hops over to the cabin's rotary phone on his good foot. But as Harry starts to dial, the room falls upward and spins hard around him. He's grasping a phone in each hand, and then a thick, oceanic blackness engulfs him.

After leaving Child's the afternoon that he met Kristin, Harry figured she'd use the napkin that he'd written his number on as a place to spit out her gum.

But Kristin had called to invite Harry out to some place called the Peacock Lounge. She told him her cousin Lucy was in town from South Dakota. That the place was a dive, but they had Karaoke. Well drinks were two bucks. Plus, they didn't card and Lucy was underage.

Harry got to the Peacock just before 8 p.m., but the place was empty. A couple old-timers perched on bar stools, nursing pints. Golf someplace dreary-looking, Scotland maybe, was muted up on the TV. Harry ordered a Budweiser and pulled up a stool, turning around every so often when some barfly came in with a newspaper under his arm.

When Harry ordered his second beer, he asked the bartender about Karaoke. "Thursdays," she said. "Not tonight."

Harry finished his drink, glanced at his phone, and drove back out to the cabin.

When he pulled into the driveway, it was dusky. He heard the phone ringing when he unlocked the cabin door. He reached for it, but stopped short, his hand over the receiver.

It could be his dad calling. Maybe Calvin finally got ahold of him and now Pat knows Harry's at the cabin.

He let it ring a third time, then a fourth. Greta barked at him to go outside, and Harry let it go to the machine.

It was Kristin, apologizing. She sounded upset and said she hadn't forgotten Harry. She sighed. They were headed someplace else for Karaoke.

Harry was in bed with the light out, not quite asleep when the phone rang again three hours later.

Kristin was calling from outside Child's, and wanted to

know if Harry could come meet her.

"Actually, I'm already back out in Rock Creek," Harry said. "In bed."

Kristin wanted to know if he'd sent the letter to his girlfriend, but her words slurred together, and her breathing was muffled on the phone. She'd had a few.

"Yeah," Harry said, "ex-girlfriend."

"What's her name again? How come you two split up?"

"It's a long story."

"You cheated on her, didn't you Harry." Kristin laughed. "I bet you did."

"I should probably hit the hay, Kristin."

Harry heard loud music, heavy metal on the other end, then it faded out.

"I'm not talking to him," Kristin said. There was another voice in the background. Someone had joined Kristin outside on the street.

"Kristin?" Harry said.

"No," she said, but not to Harry it seemed.

A woman's voice was pleading in the background, and Harry sat up in bed. Greta was sprawled on the floor, her eyes open, looking annoyed. The other woman stopped talking and Kristin was quiet.

"Everything alright?"

"Sorry, Harry. Lucy wants me to call Tommy, but I am not fucking *calling* that asshole."

Kristin and this Tommy guy were on and off again, and, after a muddled set of events that Harry couldn't track, Kristin had ended things, but Tommy wasn't taking no for an answer.

Now, Tommy was trying to convince Lucy, Kristin's cousin visiting from Rapid City, to get Kristin to meet up with him.

"Sounds like a fun dude," Harry said. "You should have Lucy point him towards Lotus Massage."

"Fuck off," she said. "You think I'm kidding?"

"I'm sorry," he said. "That was stupid."

Tommy had given Kristin that scar on her bottom lip. She asked if Harry had noticed it. He remembered the peanut skin he'd nearly reached out to remove. Before Harry could answer he heard her tell Lucy that she was going to get one of her brothers to beat the shit out of Tommy.

He asked Kristin if there was anything he could do and she let out a big laugh.

"You can't help me."

To make up for his joke about the massage parlor, Harry offered to head into town to give Kristin a ride home, but she refused. He asked her where Tommy was now.

"Fuck him," Kristin said. "*Fuck* that piece of white trash."

That one came out of the phone loud enough to get Greta to perk up onto her two forelegs like a sphinx.

"No offense, Harry."

"None taken?"

He sat up, patted Greta, and the dog stepped over to the door and looked back at him with those eyes. Harry let her out, flipped on the porch light, and Greta trotted into the far grass.

And then Kristin said sorry for calling so late, and that she normally doesn't drink and that Harry had to come see her at work tomorrow and that he should really go to some birthday party with her. It all ran together, but Harry told her he would.

She said, "Promise?"

And he promised her.

There was more commotion on the other end.

Lucy sounded upset and she was saying something to Kristin again, and Harry wasn't sure if the tavern door had swung open, letting music blare out, or whether Kristin had simply gone back inside the bar.

But the line went dead.

Birds are crying out.

Harry's head is a dull succession of wave-like throbs as sunlight spears into the cabin, piercing his eyelids. His clothes are sticky with sweat and he's feverishly cold in the morning breeze coming in through the open front door.

He'd passed out without removing the boot on his bad leg or the wool sock fused to the wound that he hadn't thought could become any worse.

It's worse.

If he wiggles his toes or rotates his foot gently at the ankle, his brain has no way of differentiating between what's skin, what's fresh or encrusted blood, and what's the fabric of the napkin wad he'd used to dress the injury—it's now all one sort of *encasement*. For reasons beyond him, the wound has somehow turned his wool sock a splotchy white color. Thoughts of gangrenous decay tumble through his mind in a fresh wave of dread.

Harry works himself upright, and pivots into the kitchen, clinging to the walls like a smashed roach, to gulp water directly from the faucet. Once he's gotten his fill, he takes the longest piss of his life, leaning against the bathroom wall, accidentally knocking the toilet paper out of its holder to unfurl across the floor.

When he lurches himself back into the kitchen, he notices that a box of Raisin Bran has been emptied out onto the yellow and gray linoleum. It's been smeared around. The strainer he'd filled up with fresh berries in the sink is empty and a musky odor hangs in the cabin.

Harry is so hungover that, instead of cleaning up the mess, he hobbles back to the edge of the bed and tips himself onto it, his temples pounding with hot blood as the morning birds chirp just beyond the cabin's open door.

This time there are dreams.

Harry is picking blackberries out of a great tangle of vines. There are many snakes and their lime green bodies are writhing up his arms. As he struggles to fling them off, he wakes up, shoving the knotted sheets off his legs.

His nausea is gone, but there's a dull pulsing behind his eyes. Wasps are cavorting inside his skull, drilling their way out. The rank scent in the cabin is some combination of wet fur and the hormonal odor of wild animal funk.

He hears a scraping noise coming from the garbage area out back. A light but determined scratching, maybe a squirrel at the trash.

But why isn't Greta barking at whatever's out there?

Harry swings his legs over the edge of the bed and agonizing seepage squirts free from his bandage at the least pressure. Whatever's foraging around out there keeps scratching.

He stands up trying to keep all his weight on his good foot, as Harry breathes through his teeth, his jaw clamped in pain.

Greta's not asleep inside the cabin.

She must be out back, starving, rooting through the trash herself, and, relieved, Harry chuckles and calls to her, letting her know that she's in very big trouble.

He gets one foot out onto the bristles of the doormat when a black bear at the garbage can looks up at Harry. The animal's long nose is stained with berries, its teeth purple.

Harry steps clumsily on his wrong heel and screams, falling backwards into the cabin, scraping his shoulder blade on the sharp corner of the desk. The bear turns and flies through the high grass, fast as a weasel, up into the forest line and disappears without a sound. Harry works himself upright and hops over to position himself inside the doorjamb and tears come to his eyes as he starts to yell for Greta.

GRETA

Harry was sitting on the sofa of the Sapphire Mountain Bed and Breakfast the morning of the party.

He'd picked up one of the magazines fanned out on the walnut coffee table called *Forever Smiles.* The cover showed a white-haired couple, arms interlocked, as they strolled over an ocean boardwalk, laughing at something marvelous.

"What are you doing here anyway?"

Harry set the magazine down. "You told me to come by."

Kristin was standing behind the reception desk, and she smiled at this. Her dark hair was back in a ponytail and shinier than Harry remembered from the bar.

"No, what are you doing in *Missoula*? I thought you were from Tucson or something."

He patted the magazine's cover. "Just trying to find some post-hip replacement golf tips in here."

Kristin cocked her head, raised her eyebrows. "I'm not into older men, just so that's clear."

She walked into the kitchen and came back a few moments later with a cup of coffee for him. But she avoided his eyes and looked nervous, like she'd regretted inviting him—or hadn't remembered, which might explain her confused expression when Harry stepped through the door and its little bell jingled.

She sat down beside him, handed him a steaming mug.

"Did I say anything embarrassing last night?"

"Not at all," Harry said. "I was a little worried though, when you hung up on me."

This brought down silence like a burlap curtain. Kristin was lost in thought and touched a fingertip to her bottom lip.

"That bad?"

"You mentioned someone named Tommy…" and Harry trailed off deliberately, narrowing his eyes, hoping she'd fill this part in herself.

Kristin's boss, a wiry woman with sculpted gray hair, came striding into the lobby, a vase of cut flowers in her hands.

The woman said good morning to Harry but didn't look at him. She was plucking at the flowers, arranging them on the antique table by the entrance. She turned, sighed like an actress, and asked if Kristin wouldn't mind disposing of a mouse that Jupiter left in the kitchen.

"Dead or alive?" Kristin said, wrinkling her nose.

The woman shrugged and went out. They heard the faucet in the kitchen, plates clinking.

Kristin whispered, "It's better than being a cashier at Walmart. That was my last job."

"What was before that?"

"Before that I was in high school and I worked the drive-thru at Taco Bell. I was sixteen. Insider tip: don't order the chalupas."

"Ahh, yes," Harry said. "The fifth basic food group."

Kristin put a finger into her open mouth and made a gagging sound, a gesture Harry hadn't seen since about seventh grade. He felt something. What was it precisely? He liked her. Simple as that.

"So, what did you come up here for?"

"I used to live here, actually," Harry said. "When I was little. So, I've been over at the library, trying to find records of where my mom and dad lived before me and my sister were born.

"My mom grew up in Helena, but she went to the University here. I figured out that she lived in a sorority house over on Gerald Avenue. She met my dad when he moved here after he got out of the army. From what I can figure out they got married and moved into an apartment south of campus, on Hastings. This would have been 1973? She was already pregnant with my sister by then so—"

"Pretty riveting stuff, Harry."

"Right. So, long story short, my mom died when I was a kid."

"God. I'm sorry."

"It's alright. I was two. Not even. I only have one memory of her, which is probably just from looking at old pictures and stuff my sister's told me."

Kristin put her hand on his arm and left it there for a moment. Harry regretted unloading so much of what he'd managed to find out, but it felt good to talk to somebody other than John about what he'd been doing in Missoula.

"I'll be right back," Kristin said, and she disappeared into the kitchen.

Harry hadn't told his sister anything yet. He wasn't exactly sure why he needed to do it alone, but he'd come up to Missoula imagining he'd solve the mystery of their mother's death and just unveil the whole thing to her wrapped up with a bow. Maybe it'd make up for all the dumb shit she'd bailed him out of these last couple of years.

Kristin came back in with two big chocolate chip cookies

and sat down next to Harry on the sofa, tucking one leg under the other. The hem of her dress came up a ways, and her bare thigh was a millimeter from Harry's. She offered him one of the cookies, wrapped in a napkin like a burger. Then she bit into hers, pensively, and he noticed the scar he'd mistaken for a fleck of peanut skin on her bottom lip now. It was pink, no wider than the stem of a cherry.

"How'd your mom die?"

"We don't know," Harry said. "My dad's told us different things over the years. A long illness. Her battle with such and such. He said it was a bone disease, then leukemia. Then cancer."

"I think leukemia *is* cancer," Kristin said.

"That's what I told my sister. But she's sure none of it's true—and she won't even speak to him anymore because of it."

"Because she thinks your mom was killed or something?"

"I can't say it hasn't crossed our minds," Harry said. "But I don't think so. We know only that my dad's hiding something, and refuses to talk about it now. But he's a quiet guy, so it might not be as fishy as Adrienne thinks it is. He came back from Vietnam all fucked up. He was pretty abusive, a heavy drinker, all that. When I was seven and Adrienne was ten, he sobered up and got re-married to my step-mom. But by then they never talked about my mother. It was like she had never existed. The other thing is that he married my mom's sister."

"Classy," Kristin said.

"Yeah," Harry said. "We always called her Aunt Sally, since that's who she was to us first, which is kinda weird. So, that's it. Here I am."

"Sounds like our dads would get along just fine."

"God, I hope not. Did yours get drafted too?" Harry said.

"No, but my step-dad Lionel did," Kristin said. "My dad never laid a hand on me but he used to kick my older brothers around. It made them tough, I guess. He didn't even drink, he just woke up pissed off. I haven't seen him in years."

"I'm sorry," Harry said, and he remembered the dead mouse in the kitchen, but didn't mention it. He didn't want Kristin to get up. They sipped their coffee in silence for a moment. Kristin's bare knee touched the side of his leg and neither of them moved. A heat washed through him. Yet talking with Kristin made him miss Leah so badly it burned.

"What about your grandparents. They still in Helena?"

"Both passed away. And my mother had no other family. Except my aunt, her older sister. But she's pretty much a vault. You know what a hoarder is?"

"What, she lives in a house full of junk?"

"Exactly. Raggedy Ann dolls and stuffed animals and Beanie Babies pouring out of all the bedrooms."

"Whoa," Kristin said. "That's spooky."

Harry laughed at that. Finished his cookie.

"I've been scouring old police records but," Harry paused, "I haven't found anything yet. I can only do a little research at a time and I get overwhelmed. End up taking my dog to the mountains or just head to the bar."

"There must be county records," Kristin said. "Downtown or something?"

"I haven't made my way over there yet, but yeah. Maybe I'm stalling a little."

"I'd be afraid of what I'd find if I were you," Kristin said. "I mean, what if your dad was involved?"

"It's not impossible," Harry said. "But I have to know—even though I don't want to know. If that makes sense."

One of the cats—maybe the mouser—a sleek black one with a pink nose, slipped between Harry and the coffee table, swishily seducing his shin bone with its tail. Harry moved his leg. The cat paused to yawn, then leaned down, and pressed its face onto Harry's shoelaces.

"Shit," she said, getting back up, "I need go find that mouse, which better be dead. But you should come to that party."

Cookie crumbs fell to the floor and she leaned down to dab them off the hardwood with her finger. The neckline of her dress fell open, watermelon shampoo wafted into Harry's face, and he saw the top of her breasts now in a black lacy bra, before looking off.

"Whose birthday is it again?"

His eyes kept finding the little scar on her lower lip.

"Who knows. Maybe it's mine."

"No shit? Happy Birthday."

Harry asked to use the restroom, and went down the hall. When he came out, Kristin was perched behind the reception desk, writing something down.

"You can bring your gun if you want."

"To your birthday party?"

She looked up, smiled. "Sure, why not? We always set up bottles and cans for target practice out in this field. What do you normally do you at parties?"

Harry pictured the frozen tendrils of the mop in the closet

out at the cabin, where Calvin thought a rifle might be.

"I don't know," Harry said. "Drink beer. Tell lies."

"It's at my friend Jesse's house, east of town. Here."

Kristin handed him a napkin. She'd drawn a sketch of a map and an address on Flagler Drive.

"*Kristin*?" her boss called from the kitchen.

"Shit. I'll see you tonight, Harry."

Harry is calling out for his dog from the truck's open windows, wincing slowly over potholes and stones on the dirt road, along the pine trees lining Rock Creek, where Greta liked to splash around in the sandy shoals of the river and dart after birds.

He hollers for her until he's all but lost his voice and drives home, clapping and whistling pathetically, as he shambles from the driveway back to the cabin door.

But Greta's gone.

He'd lost her to any number of fates up in the mountains beyond the river. He can almost hear Calvin telling him that Harry's spoiled city dog will be gored by the antlers of an elk if not maimed by a mountain lion twice her size.

That, or she'll run and run—and Harry will not see her again.

The sunlight dims as it fades through some monstrous clouds shrouding the nearby hills and soon it begins to rain. A soft summer storm at first, which turns the dry air's dustiness to a cool odor of earth and grass. Pretty soon the rain swallows the near distance of the meadow as the droplets become a thunderous downpour.

Harry stands out in the rain beyond the porch for a

while. It's hard to describe, but his foot now feels like a brittle stone inside his hiking boot. He's sure any weight placed on it will cause his swollen skin to rupture straight away, and everything below his kneecap will go to slush.

He decides to pour more alcohol on the wound, but when he fishes the bottle out of the truck, he sees what he's done. In his panic after leaving Paul at the ER, he'd grabbed the wrong thing from the nurse's station—and accidentally poured half a bottle of bleach onto his leg. Which would explain why his wool sock had gone white and why his leg hairs had been singed off.

Harry comes back inside and removes his soaked sweatshirt, turns the electric heater on, and puts a kettle on the stove for coffee. He looks the bear's mess over: Cereal and shit on the floor. The smell clinging to the musty walls.

He remembers Calvin in the river yesterday, sipping his Red Bull, and teasing that a black bear had licked the sweat off Harry's face as he napped on the bank. Nothing amused him about this coincidence now. It might as well have been a premonition, and it makes Harry want to rip the mustache off Calvin's face.

He remembers Adrienne's message on the cabin's answering machine, and decides not to call her. His "decisive action" for the morning would be to avoid his sister.

Harry had told every neighbor he could flag down about Greta having run off, but they'd all shaken their heads. George Willis across the road tipped his cap and pulled away before Harry had even finished describing her.

Now Harry can't shake the feeling that Tommy might turn up out here in his oversized hunting vest. The houses and doublewides along Rock Creek are spaced a ways apart. Many have locked iron gates over which cattle skulls hang. Others, like Pat's cabin, are exposed to the road, without a fence or partition of any kind. How many of them have a Toyota truck with a shot-out window and an Arizona license plate parked out front?

Harry keeps picturing Tommy up on the road, out where the bear had been scrounging around in the trash, or standing at the sink in the bathroom when Harry turns around in the kitchen and scares himself blind. Any slow vehicle out on the road, any flash in the corner of his eye, any stray sound was Tommy in his yellow vest training his rifle on the back of Harry's head.

He sits down on the bed to watch the kettle tick up to a boil when he feels something in his pocket. It's the napkin on which Kristin had written the directions to the party out east of Missoula, on Flagler Drive.

LOGBOOK

Harry is watching the rain come down through the open door when the cabin's phone rings and he hoists himself up and limps over to answer it.

"Hello?"

"Harrison?" Calvin shouts. "You sound like hell. What happened to your voice, you catch the grippe?"

"Just tired," Harry says. "What's the word?"

"Word's bad. The police chat with you yet?"

"I'm sitting in the cabin where you just called me, aren't I?"

"Testy, testy. *Sheesh.* Well, they won't be long to visit with you."

"What did you hear?"

"You meet a kid named Tillett the other night?"

"Tillett…wait, yeah, I remember him. Paul?"

"His dad's Greg Tillett. Same one who came by the river yesterday. Greg just phoned me. They clapped bracelets on junior."

Harry had known something was up with Greg, the way he'd stared at Harry.

"The cops think Paul shot the girl?"

"That's what Greg's fretting over. No charges yet. He's trying to raise the dough to get Paul out on bond."

Harry pictures the nasty black bruise on Paul's ribs. And Paul's mother had looked frantic, drained. Harry needs to figure out why Paul lied to him at the hospital, but still doesn't want to tip his hand and tell Calvin he'd seen Paul in the ER. Holding onto to this shred of info might be his undoing, but if Harry spills it to Calvin he feels like the whole thing will cave in on him.

An idea hits Harry—possibly paranoid—that Greg followed him out to Rock Creek somehow. He could've been parked in the lot next to Harry's pickup. Harry had staggered out of there as fast as he could, distracted by the searing pain coming from his leg, and could've missed the guy while Harry was accidentally bleaching his wound.

"Harrison?"

"Hang on a sec…I have to think."

"Well, don't bust your brain on it."

Greg Tillett must've known Harry had been at the party. Greg had to have been trying to sort out how Harry was involved and why the hell he'd been fishing with Calvin Hogan. If Paul pulled the trigger, then how come the big guy in the white shirt said to Tommy: *Why did you do that?* After Harry threw the rifle into the ditch, he'd heard him say, *You're so screwed, Tommy.* There's no way Paul was the shooter.

Did Greg Tillett think Harry shot the girl? Or is he just hoping to get the heat off his own son? And there was that banana-shaped bruise on Paul's ribs that Harry had seen before leaving the ER. Paul told the doctor that he'd been trampled, that he had trouble taking air.

"Earth to Harry…"

"What about Tommy?"

"You still worried about that squirrel dick?"

"As a matter of fact, I am still worried about that squirrel dick."

"I chewed the fat for a while with Silas after you blew chunks and wandered off last night. Tiny Tommy strolled into the Trapper with Frank Keene. I heard him boasting that he'd lawyered up, stonewalled the cops, and they let him dance."

"Tommy told you that?"

"I'm not saying I *believed* him. I'm just relaying the data as it came in to old Cal. But as of last night, Tommy was undetained. And Paul Tillett and that big Coeur d'Alene boy, Donny, were still behind bars. Now Greg's trying to get a bead on who shot the girl."

"Did Greg say anything about Kristin?"

"No, but Silas heard she's back in the Dakotas—fled."

"*Fled*?"

"Skedaddled, lit out for the territories, ran for—"

"Calvin, I know what *fleeing* means."

"Okay, okay. Well your little valentine's gone, Harrison. How's your doggie bite doin'?"

"I accidentally poured bleach on it."

"Whoopsie! Well, they do some pretty good titanium prosthetics now. Get you set up like the Terminator, and you'll be back on your rollerblades in no time."

"Thanks, Calvin."

"One more thing, bud."

"I'm scared to know."

"Think it's time you went in for a chat with the fuzz, don't you?"

John Dowd had a peculiar expression on his face when Harry came up to the circulation desk at the public library after visiting Kristin at the Sapphire.

"You found something?"

John took off his glasses, glanced over to the children's area. There was a pretty middle-aged woman there reading to a bunch of preschoolers. She looked familiar.

"Looks like your father was right, Harry."

"About what?"

John told him to come around the desk. Harry followed him down a hallway of offices, back to a windowless conference room. John shut the door and motioned for Harry to take a seat at the table.

"I did some snooping around," John said, lowering his voice. "Outside the library."

"What do you mean?"

"Evidently your mother *had* been in the hospital," John said. "Several times, in fact."

"How do you know?"

"I can't tell you everything. But I have a friend at Providence, and she managed to locate the hospital's old logbook from '79."

"Do you know what she'd been there for?" Harry said.

"I gave my friend your mother's name and date of birth, and she said a number of dates popped up on the computer. But the files are old enough now that they haven't been digitized. The thing is, everything before 1984 was only recorded by hand if the—" John broke off, looked down at the conference table.

"If what?"

"If the patient was deceased," John said. "Apparently, they only added older records to the computer system if the patient continued to receive care past '84, if that makes sense."

"Sure," Harry said. "So, can your friend get access to the files or…?"

"She thinks they're located at an offsite storage facility, which is out near the airport, halfway to Wye. But it might take her a few days. Why don't you leave me your number, and I'll call you when she locates the records. *If* she locates them, I should say. Perhaps, if she's willing to, she can talk with you herself…"

John got up and found a notepad in a drawer and drew a pen out of the breast pocket of his shirt. Harry wrote down his cell phone number and added the cabin's just in case.

"Cell phone?" John said. "Pretty fancy."

"Not really," Harry said. "But it's nice to have on the road. I really appreciate your help, man. Will you thank your friend for me, even if she can't get to the files?"

"Of course. I should get back to work," John said and slipped the pen back into his pocket. He extended a hand to Harry and added, "I'll call you when I hear from her."

There was a skinny kid—long dark hair, maybe sixteen or so—sitting next to a vacant computer in the bay of terminals in the library when Harry came out from the conference room after meeting with John.

The kid appeared to be muttering to himself, looking out over the top of his computer, laughing every now and again. Harry sat down beside him. The young guy was deep in conversation with somebody who wasn't there.

Harry logged on and opened up his email account. There was still nothing from Leah. Or anything else of interest, for that matter. He clicked on the draft folder and opened the story he'd been writing to her, little by little, and thought it might be time.

It was a story about a bear that had lost her cub and wandered into a tiny town called Augusta to find him. The townspeople were hysterical, because the huge grizzly was not deterred by the clanging of their pots and pans and even gunshots fired into the air. The bear wouldn't leave without finding its baby, but the people didn't understand that. They told the sheriff he had to do something.

So, the sheriff—a tall man with a nice smile and gray mustache—came down thinking he was dealing with a rabid or wounded animal. He saw the enormous grizzly sniffing around some cars near the dumpster behind the one diner in town. And he cocked his rifle and he shot the animal many times. The bear reared up, nine feet into the air, her black paws splayed out, and she roared and fell down dead.

The sheriff's men gathered behind the diner to haul its body off. One of them called dibs on its head. Another wanted her thick fur for a rug. They joked about making it into a Halloween costume and smoked jerky. The sheriff himself wanted no piece of the grizzly and said nothing to the men as they cracked jokes and squabbled and heaved it up onto the bed of their police truck.

Two days later, the sheriff was sitting up at the counter in the same diner. His scrambled eggs and toast were getting cold as he read about a record snowfall in Vilnius. He was looking at a picture of icicles hanging off the roofs all over a city he'd never been to, when a little girl in a high chair with food on her face squealed and pointed out the window and said, "Doggie!"

The sheriff turned to the street and saw a bear cub waddling through town in the sunshine.

The sheriff got up and went outside and watched the fuzzy thing amble right down the boardwalk, the newspaper jammed under his armpit where there was a perfect half-moon of sweat on his gray uniform. And the sheriff knew then that he'd orphaned the defenseless animal and he couldn't stand it. He didn't think the sow had been likely to harm the townspeople, but he'd shot her anyhow. Men under his watch had bickered over her carcass, like so much roadkill.

The sheriff was in bed that night and he couldn't sleep, so he got up for a glass of milk in the kitchen. He took a big swallow and saw that there were two grizzly bears in his back yard, watching him, waiting for him to step outside. The sheriff was in his long underwear. And the moon was huge like I don't know what, Harry wrote. Like an owl's eye. Like a coiled-up white garden hose. Like a *something.* And the sheriff unlocked the deadbolt on his back door and opened it.

One of the bears roared silently. Its lips quivered, but it was almost a dream—and no sound came from the immense animal. The sheriff, in his underwear with milk in his mustache, stepped out into his yard through the doorway with a long silver flashlight gleaming under the moon.

And he walked all the way out as if to say, *Okay*. And the bears turned and headed into the trees at the edge of the man's small yard. And he clicked off the flashlight and let it fall to the ground, and he followed them into the woods.

Harry came out of the Grizzly Grocery holding a bouquet of yellow irises to take to Kristin's birthday party.

He got into the truck and felt his phone buzzing in his pocket. He thought it might be John calling with news about Harry's mother but it's wasn't John.

It was Leah calling from Tucson.

Harry's mouth went dry and a big Coca-Cola truck churned around the corner, hissing as it blocked out the sunlight for a moment. Harry didn't want to let it go to voicemail, but he was too afraid to answer it. It hadn't occurred to him that Leah could just call him up out of the blue. That they could simply talk at that moment, in real time. He held the phone in his hand, but waited too long. When he clicked to answer it, she'd hung up.

No wonder you haven't been able to write anything.

He wanted to prove to her that he wasn't a failure or stuck on his dead mother or whatever it was she thought that had made her unsure about him.

He glanced over at the irises for Kristin, sitting there on the passenger seat, wrapped in crinkly cellophane. Some were exploding open with orange crumbs of pollen on their petals. Others were still closed up like slender green alligator mouths.

Suddenly the flowers seemed garishly beautiful, old fashioned, and Harry had no idea what he was doing.

He put the key in the ignition and glanced down at his phone.

Leah had left a voicemail.

Seventeen seconds. They hadn't spoken in over a week. What could she possibly say to him in seventeen seconds? She'd be furious, of course. Harry had taken Greta with him in the dark hours of the morning, leaving only a note on her counter.

Sorry I said that.
xo Harry.

He took a deep breath and brought the phone to his ear.

"Harry, it's me. I got your story. So, yeah. I'm sorry if I hurt your feelings but you put me in a weird spot. Anyway, Ryan told me what you did to his car. Obviously, I had to tell him about us—so, that's that. I hope you and Greta are okay."

He punched the steering wheel. Then he punched it again and again and again and again.

Harry hadn't socked anything since he'd punched Ryan Edwards in the mouth back in Tucson.

LEAH

Ryan and Leah were already together by the time Harry showed up for school in Arizona.

The two of them had been dating for almost a year, but Ryan had gone to Nepal for three months, and Leah had broken it off with him.

Harry and Leah started seeing each other a couple weeks into the sweltering Tucson summer. They had been friends, in classes together. But Leah had been with Ryan. Harry just hung back, tagging along sometimes to the bar with the two of them and Leah's younger sister Annie, to shoot pool and share pitchers of beer.

Ryan was searching for a yoga guru, traipsing around Kathmandu in flip flops with his long hair tied into a bun on the top of head. That's how Harry had pictured it anyway. He rang his sister for advice.

"I think I like this girl," he said. "No, I do like her."

"Call her up. Ask her out on a date."

"But," Harry said, "she was just dating this other guy."

"Do you have her number?"

"Yeah."

"Do they have a farmer's market in Tucson?"

Harry sighed. "Adrienne, if I knew the answer to that, would I really need your help?"

"Call—what's her name? Leah?—call *Leah* up and ask her

to join you on a hike with Greta."

"That sounds too easy. What's the catch?"

"There's no catch, dummy. If she says no, then fine. You never ask her out ever again. Got it? Just be easy going, but get to the point. What's the big deal?"

"So, the stakes are monumental, yet I should be completely casual?"

"Decisive action, Harry. Hang up the phone and call the woman. Get off the fucking fence. And don't overthink it. It's not calculus."

"I'm hanging up."

"Call me back. Let me know what she says."

Harry called Leah. And Adrienne was right. It worked. He invited her on a hike up to Sabino Canyon and she said she'd love to go. That she'd been wanting to meet Greta. Everything else was like falling water and Harry heard nothing more and had already hung up, grinning like a doofus.

Leah had this way of saying *hi* like she was happy he'd called—not as though she'd been waiting by the phone but like she was a little surprised. He loved that *hi* immediately. Her voice sounded better in real life than he'd been imagining it—warmer, but a tiny bit raspier, too.

"I like that you just called me up," Leah said.

"My sister told me to," Harry said. "I mean, I wanted to all by myself. But she told me what to say."

"All by yourself, huh?"

"That sounds like I'm eight years old. But I just turned nine."

Leah laughed. It was a pity laugh but he took it. Harry heard that first *hi* in his head for three days—in the shower, walking Greta around the neighborhood at night, brushing his teeth in the morning.

After their first hike they started hanging out. Leah fell for Greta instantly, and the three of them started to go on excursions together, to escape the city's blistering heat. By late August, school was back in session. First week of their second year, and everybody from the creative writing program was at the Hawthorn after a meeting on campus. Ryan, too, was back from his Himalayan pilgrimage.

Ryan had hugged Leah, which was fine. Why shouldn't they hug? They were all playing pool together, like old times. Harry was privately congratulating himself for being so chill about it.

Ryan looked good, Harry thought. His teeth were whiter. His long hair had grown longer. He was really tan, and Ryan seemed to listen more and move more deliberately. Harry thought he and Ryan might be friends, though not right away maybe. And Ryan, too, was acting very cool about Harry and Leah being together now.

Until, that is, Ryan kissed Leah on her neck.

The two of them were at the bar getting more drinks. Ryan was buying a beer for Harry at the time. Harry was shooting pool with Annie, Leah's sister. Harry looked up from his shot and saw Ryan's mouth on the side of Leah's neck, just above her necklace. Leah didn't push him away. She put her hand on Ryan's arm and Harry looked at Annie. Annie looked down at the floor.

So, Harry set the pool cue down on the table and went up to the bar.

He said, "What the fuck are you doing?"

He shoved Ryan.

"Whoa. Hang on, bro—"

Ryan looked at Leah, but her glass of wine was all over the front of her dress and she and Annie started for the door.

Ryan said, "Don't be an asshole, man. I think this is a misunderstanding. So, let's—"

Harry started yelling and called Ryan a "Piece of shit hippie scumbag freak."

Ryan pushed Harry, not hard, more like a *just-stay-back* kind of the thing, with both hands. Harry didn't care. He wanted Ryan to swing at him so he'd have an excuse to beat his head in. He glanced over to see Leah and Annie crossing the street through the front window of the bar. He heard Adrienne's voice then: *Get off the fucking fence, Harry.*

Then he socked Ryan in the mouth.

Ryan was quicker though, and he hit Harry one-two—right then left. Harry moved out of the way of the first one, but the second one caught Harry on his eye.

The bartender leapt over the bar, their fresh beers were knocked over, a stool clattered to the floor, and everybody in the bar corralled Harry and Ryan through the front door out onto the street.

Ryan took off running down Congress Street, the direction that Leah had gone with Annie. Harry just stood there in the hot darkness of the night, a hand over the side of his face, as cars passed by. Ryan had given them all a ride to the bar in his Volkswagen. A couple other people came out to ask Harry what happened and if he was alright. He looked through them, took his hand from his eye, and told them to fuck off.

Then he walked home two miles in the dark, his eye pulsating like a smacked wasp.

The next morning, Harry got a call to let him know that he'd been removed from the graduate program. A formal letter of expulsion would come in the mail, but they were notifying him that he was no longer allowed on campus, effective immediately. It had been a clear violation of the code of conduct. Harry said they couldn't do that. It was just an argument between friends, and it had happened *off* campus.

The program director said that in fact, the graduate school maintained a zero-tolerance policy, and it had indeed occurred at a school-sponsored function, organized by the creative writing program (they'd all gotten a single, measly drink ticket), and there was no choice but to see to it that Harry was out. He was sorry, but it was settled.

Harry asked if Ryan had been kicked out too, but the director wouldn't say and Harry told the guy he'd better watch his back.

"Are you threatening me, Harrison? Because if this is going to be a police matter—"

Harry hung up.

Then he punched the wall in his kitchen. Then he punched it again, harder, screaming in rage when he felt a small bone in the knuckle of his middle finger split.

Harry called Leah to tell her he'd been kicked out of the program. She was sobbing. He went over to Leah and Annie's apartment later that morning, after icing his eye with a frozen TV dinner. He decided to bring Greta, hoping that would soften things between them.

Greta was thrilled to see Leah. She ran through the door and leapt up on the couch. She was wiggling and barked twice, thinking they must be headed up to the mountains.

Leah tried to touch Harry's eye, but Harry wouldn't let her, raising his arm and pulling away. Annie was sitting on the couch, playing with Harry's puppy. He and Leah took a walk around the neighborhood.

Leah hadn't told Ryan about Harry. In fact, Leah hadn't broken it off with Ryan. Not exactly.

"We just said we'd see."

"See *what*?" Harry said.

"I didn't know what would happen with you and me."

Harry stopped walking and turned to face Leah on the sidewalk. It was blazing hot, not yet eleven, and already over a hundred degrees in the sun. Harry's eye stung and the sweat from his forehead wasn't helping.

Leah said, "Ryan was halfway across the world. I didn't want to put my life on hold, but it's not like I could call him up in the Himalayas and tell him you and I were kind of starting to date."

"*Kind of*?" Harry said.

She mentioned that she'd gone out with Ryan for coffee after he'd come back to Tucson. Twice.

"You slept with him?"

"No," she said. "I mean, not since he's been back. We just met to catch up. He was in Nepal for three *months*. We hadn't resolved anything between us."

Harry hated the way she kept saying *we*.

"So last night at the Hawthorn. He didn't know anything

about you and me?"

Leah shook her head.

"I should've told him. But you said you weren't looking for anything serious."

"I said that on our second date. That was almost two fucking—"

"Don't yell at me, Harry."

He sighed.

"You and I didn't define anything," she said. "Which was okay, since I knew that you knew that I'd been with Ryan, and that he was coming back after his trip."

Harry didn't know what was worse. Ryan seemed like less of a dick, but he was stunned by Leah's hesitation. Worst of all: she was right. The two of them hadn't technically defined anything. It's just that Harry was staying over with Greta two or three times a week. He wanted Ryan to be back in Kathmandu. Or just dead in a ditch, any old ditch would work great.

"It's too hot out here," Leah said. "I need to get back."

"Do you want to be with him?"

"No..." Leah said.

"Alright then."

After a pause, Leah added, "Harry, I don't know."

They walked back in silence to Leah's apartment. Leah opened the door, and Greta leapt onto her, her tongue falling out the side of her mouth. She barked and went down into a play bow, then barked again and ran in a frenzied circle. Annie was sitting on the floor with Greta's goofy rubber elephant toy in her lap. She covered her mouth, trying to stifle a laugh, when she saw Greta go nuts for Leah. And Leah was crying.

Harry took the dog's leash off the kitchen counter, snapped it onto Greta's collar, and said, "Come on, let's go." And they left.

Leah called Harry a week later and asked if they could talk.

"About what?"

"Can you come over tonight?"

Harry took Greta over to Leah's that night. His eye looked better. It was still yellow at the corner, sort of brownish at the bridge of his nose. But the ugly plum-colored swelling was gone.

When Leah opened the door, she said "Hi" in that way. Not happy, or surprised. It was this matter-of-fact sort of we've-seen-each-other-naked-so-greetings-are-a-little-awkward-since-we-should-be-past-ordinary-human-stuff. It was just Leah's *hi*, and everything inside him unfroze when it hit him.

They walked around her neighborhood after dark with Greta. They made dinner. Annie wasn't around, and Harry didn't ask Leah about her.

Leah said nothing about Ryan. Neither did Harry. He just wanted to be near her. Look at her face. Hear her voice.

They had sex that night and slept together in Leah's bed. They had sex again in the morning, which Greta interrupted, scratching on Leah's bedroom door.

Leah missed her classes for a few days and they slept late and went out for breakfast. They hiked in Madera Canyon with Greta a few times, though the monsoons had started in the afternoons and it wasn't quite as stifling in the city—highs of 99 degrees, instead of 112 downtown. Then the flooding rains came: electrical storms, which spooked Greta and she whined and tried to wriggle herself under Leah's bed.

Harry still had his student loan money, so he didn't need to tell anyone about getting kicked out of school yet. He was relieved not to have to ask his sister for cash. He'd have to get a job, but he'd have enough for rent, bills, groceries, and dog-food for a couple months, maybe till Thanksgiving.

On one of their afternoon hikes, Harry even told Leah about his mom. She couldn't believe he'd let it go this long without finding out what had really happened to her.

"Aren't you dying to know?"

"Of course I am," Harry said. "But what if Adrienne's right?"

"You mean that your dad might have been involved?"

He looked at her, said nothing.

"Harry, that's all the more reason to find out what the truth is. It's no wonder you haven't been able to write anything since you got here. I'd be blocked too."

It hurt him, but he knew she was right. Harry had written next to nothing after a full year in the program.

In the letter that arrived from the program director, he'd said Harry could appeal the expulsion, and be put on academic probation, but that he'd have to see a counselor if his appeal wasn't denied. They wanted a formal letter of apology, letters of recommendation speaking to his quote-unquote character, and "a written commitment to counseling for anger management strategies." He threw the letter out. He told Leah he was done with grad school, writing—all of it.

It was a Sunday night and Harry and Greta slept over at Leah's again after a long hike up to Bog Springs, where Greta had flushed a bobcat up into a tree, and they'd driven back to town slowly in a flooding monsoon. Greta had a bed out on the couch and Harry was happy after they'd showered and made dinner.

They'd come through something. He was thinking about his mom and his sister, and he decided to show Leah the photo he kept of the three of them in Montana: Harry naked, not quite two. Adrienne about five, dancing around the sprinkler spray, and their mother in the foreground, sitting next to her friend, in profile, watching her children, a cigarette smoldering between her fingers.

Leah took the picture from him. "She's beautiful, Harry. That's your mother? She was so young."

"Twenty-eight, I think."

"Who's this other woman?"

"My mom's friend? I'm not sure. I don't even know her name."

"It's so sad. You two are really cute. Look at your sister, how happy she is."

"Maybe I'll write about it," Harry said. "Once I find something out."

Leah handed him the photo and Harry put it back in his wallet.

"Let's go away," Harry said in the darkness of Leah's bedroom that night.

"For the weekend?" Leah's voice was sleepy, raspy.

"No, let's leave. Me and you. We'll take Greta. Get the hell out of Tucson."

"I need to finish school, Harry. I only have a year left."

"Let's get married then," Harry said. "I want to be

with you."

"Harry..."

"What?"

"That's not a good idea."

And that was it. After a while, they fell asleep. Or Leah did. Harry couldn't even keep his eyes shut. At about four, he saw the screen of Leah's cell light up. He went to the bathroom and was going to try and lie back down, but he picked up her phone and saw the message from Ryan: "Everything alright? Missed you in classes this week."

The next day Harry and Greta were in his pickup north of Flagstaff, outside the Grand Canyon, before Leah would even be up. He taped the key to his apartment to a note he left on Mrs. O'Brien's door across the street, telling her that he'd had a family emergency, and would she mind keeping an eye out.

On his way out of town, Harry stopped for gas, and seethed. It was bad enough that Ryan was missing Leah—and writing to her at four in the fucking morning to say so—but it also meant that only Harry had been expelled for their fight at the Hawthorn.

Harry replaced the fuel nozzle, got back in his truck, and drove over to Ryan's apartment complex. He found a good-sized rock, raised it up with both hands over his head, and smashed it into the windshield of Ryan's VW. It didn't go through the safety glass, but it had shattered. It was stupid, brutish even. Then again, it was nothing if not decisive action.

Harry didn't know what Ryan knew. He and Leah never talked about him again. He left the rock there, like a big stone stuck in a frozen pond. He found a Sharpie in his glovebox and wrote *MISS YOU TOO* in big letters on the driver's side door.

Harry got back in his truck and headed north toward Phoenix. And he was talking to Calvin Hogan on the payphone outside of the Grizzly Grocery in Missoula two and a half days later, coaxing his way into Pat's cabin out on Rock Creek.

If I stay here trouble will find me
If I stay here I'll never leave

— The National

PART 2
THE PARTY

DARKNESS

It's the middle of the night and very dark in the room where Harry finds himself many hours or perhaps days later in a bed that is not the cabin's.

His wrists are cuffed to the bed frame's aluminum handles, and when he discovers the plastic restraints Harry assumes that his infected foot has been removed and that he's in some prison hospital.

He starts to scream and then stifles it—his throat a dry creek bed. When he tries to swallow, his Adam's apple gets stuck on the way up and comes down dragging. Nobody answers his half-scream, or maybe they didn't hear it—but for a few minutes, he stays quiet to let the possibilities parade through his mind. They all end up at the same place: Tommy must have put the killing on Harry.

He hears footfall in the corridor, and the door to the room opens. A man appears at the foot of the bed, empty-handed. He is quiet for a moment and then comes to Harry's bedside, clicks on a lamp, and asks in a soft voice if he's awake. Harry stays silent, keeps his eyes shut. Many more lights—or one massive central one—come on above the bed and Harry blinks, trying to take in his surroundings.

A man dressed in nurse's scrubs. Black hair and a scar across his upper lip. Something is tattooed on the inside of each of his wrists. Symbols, foreign characters. Harry tries to make out the designs on the man's arms, but the room is still blurry and Harry's pupils are now flooded with too much light. Crumbs of sleep in the corners of his eyes he can't get at.

"Do you know where you are?"

"Jail?"

"You're at Providence Hospital, Mr. Stables. You've had a nasty infection and fever."

He says his name is Denis and wants to know how Harry's feeling.

"What did you do to my foot?"

At this, Denis actually laughs. Harry struggles to get out of the plastic restraints but can't. And he lays there, breathing angrily.

"We left your foot on," Denis says. "We thought you might like to keep it."

Something heavy is inside Harry's chest. He squirms himself up in the bed and can see that Denis is tapping gently on the tips of Harry's toes, but Harry can't feel it. He blinks and shakes his head at the nurse. Denis smiles. His teeth are small, with a black gap between the front two uppers. Harry's foot is bandaged in gauze under the sheets.

"I can't feel a fucking thing down there. Is that normal?"

"You can ask the doctor in a few minutes," Denis says. "Do you know who the president is?"

Harry sits there for a second, staring at the scar over Denis's lip.

"George Bush."

"Which one?"

"W.," Harry says. "For fuck's sake, how long have I been *in* here?"

"A little over twenty-four hours."

"Why am I handcuffed to this bed?"

"You pulled out your IV in the middle of the night. And when we managed to get it back in your arm, you did it again. In your sleep. Then you gave Maryann, the morning nurse, a big scratch on her throat."

Harry says that he doesn't remember doing that.

"You were screaming for somebody named Greta," Denis says. "We looked on your cell phone but—"

"That's my dog."

"Then that would explain why we had such a difficult time getting in touch with her."

The scrap of a dream comes to him: Greta encircled by a dozen raccoons in the woods. She was cantering and turning and barking with her lip pulled up over her teeth. And the ring of raccoons—up on their haunches, their tiny black claws open—was slowly clsoing in on her.

"She's missing," Harry says.

Denis makes a pouty face and Harry wants to strangle his fat neck.

"Is she a purebred? Sometimes purebreds get stolen around here."

Harry tells the nurse that she took off running. Then he asks him how he got to the hospital.

Denis tells him that he'd arrived badly dehydrated and exhausted. And that he'd been hallucinating. That his leg wound was infected, suppurating, and the skin was becoming necrotic. It had given Harry a fever, with a temperature of a hundred and three. Harry had collapsed getting out of his pickup in the hospital parking lot. With the engine running. Apparently hitting his head on the concrete in the pull-through where some nurses were smoking.

"I don't remember any of that," Harry says.

"Oh, and we found this," Denis says, and pulls Rod's little metal figurine out of the pocket of his scrubs and sets it on the night table under the lamp.

The wire man's empty oval face looks out at the room.

"Fantastic."

"Question for you: how'd you burn off your leg hair?"

"Bleach."

"Ah-ha," Denis says. "That one stumped us."

"If only that was the dumbest thing I've done lately."

"Harrison…" Denis is looking at the computer. "Was your mother a *Star Wars* fan?"

"Can you take these things off now?"

"We'll have to ask Maryann. She's the one who wheeled you in and got your leg out of that *boot*." Denis sticks out his tongue and widens his eyes. He says that Harry's hiking boots should be incinerated but as a policy they have to keep everybody's personal effects, so they were double-bagged, on a shelf in the wardrobe by the window.

"Seriously, can we…?" and Harry lifts both of his chafed wrists up at once and shakes them, forces a smile.

Denis leans over him and Harry watches him unhook the plastic restraints, which had been fastened with ridiculous simplicity, preventing only an infant or Hallucinating Harry from unhooking them. Harry tries to read the symbols on Denis's wrists.

"Is that Blackfoot?"

"Black*feet*," Denis says. "And no, it's Chinese. My brother did them with a sewing needle and India ink one night. *Long* time ago."

Harry rubs his wrists and Denis reaches over and holds out a bottle of lotion and gives Harry a squirt in his hands. He slathers it onto the chafe marks, which burn.

"They were supposed to say *danger* and *opportunity*, but one of our residents is from Beijing and she told me they're closer to *moment* and *awry*, which doesn't really have the same ring to it. I was fifteen."

Harry sends a signal to his foot down there in the sheets, but nothing is coming back, and even though his hands are now free, he still doesn't want to look.

"It's numb down there."

"I'm not surprised. I saw that bite. It was ugly. I'll let the doctor know that you're awake, so she should be in to check on you soon."

Harry sits himself up and Denis brings over a stray pillow. Harry leans forward so that Denis can slip it behind him and Harry's upright now.

"We would've called your parents, but we couldn't find them in your contacts. So, we called the last three numbers dialed on your mobile phone. One of them was the Sapphire Mountain B&B, but the lady I spoke with said you weren't a guest there."

"Fucking Christ," Harry says, trying to think of what the other two numbers must have been. "Who else? Where's my phone?"

"Somebody named Carlton? But we couldn't tell him much. You were still unconscious."

"Calvin, right…did he come by?"

Denis shakes his head and goes out.

By the time Harry found the intersection of county roads, he wasn't sure he wanted to be at Kristin's birthday party.

Dusk was killing the blue sky slowly and a translucent half-moon was beginning to glow. It was quiet and all the lights of the rambling doublewide trailer were off when he pulled in, though he could make out silhouettes through the front window. There were no house numbers visible, no other neighboring homes around at all.

Kristin had drawn Harry a map on his napkin at the Sapphire that morning and told him to go around back where everybody would be at the fire.

He parked his pickup where another seven or eight cars and trucks were pulled up in the front yard. When he shut the engine off, he heard voices and laughter. A sinewy feather of smoke came from behind the house, which he saw in the rear-view mirror. And then he heard what sounded like a gunshot.

Harry sat in the truck with the bouquet in his lap, with Kristin's map resting on the empty cup holder. The stems of the irises were still wet. He removed the cellophane wrapping and the thin rubber band. He held them there as he stared through the mirror at the house and watched the smoke rise, goading himself to either open the door and get out of the truck or drive back out to Rock Creek and call it a night.

He rolled down his window, and the truck ticked to silence. It was only the second week of September, but as night fell, it was the first time he got that smell of autumn—crisp air with wet smoke in it. He picked up a Santana song on a far stereo.

Harry got out and walked around the side of the house through tall grass growing up against the garage. It was filled with junk—a small motor of some kind, all manner of tools in various states of use and rust, and there was a child's blue wading pool, which had apparently been used to mix concrete.

He stopped to let his eyes adjust before joining the crowd of people gathered around the fire. He flinched at another rifle shot, and followed the sound out to the field, where two figures were drinking and having target practice.

The taller one, wearing a white t-shirt, ambled farther out through the grass to set up more bottles. The shorter of the two had on a bright yellow vest, and he rested the gun on his shoulder like a big game hunter. Even at this distance, he recognized him from Child's a few days earlier. The parakeet called Tommy.

Harry wanted to remain a shadow to soak all this in, surveying from afar, but something was moving behind him in the grass. An animal sniffing around the truck, though he could make out only its shape. A dog or a coyote, maybe.

He was antsy. The news that his mother had been in the hospital several times before she died and the call from Leah put him in a hostile mood. He wished he could somehow unsend the story he'd written for her, delete it altogether.

He wasn't sure what he was doing at Kristin's party, but when he recalled sitting next to her earlier that morning at the Sapphire, something like calm trickled through him.

Harry walked over to the group of people, fifteen or twenty, sitting and standing around the big flames. He scanned their faces for Kristin's.

"Hey," a guy's voice called. "Is that Matt?"

He came in closer, felt the heat of the fire on his face and hands, and everybody turned to look at him.

"No, I'm Harry. Is Kristin around?"

A woman in a lounge chair sat up and said, "Who?"

Her legs were crossed as she scratched the head of a white mutt that looked like an enormous puppy. She brought a cigarette to her mouth and pulled in a long drag.

"Kristin?" Harry said again, now certain he'd misremembered her name, wandered into the wrong party, or made her up entirely.

"Tommy's girlfriend," somebody said. "She ain't here, man."

The young guy who'd mistaken Harry for somebody named Matt came over and introduced himself as Paul. Paul was wearing a Broncos hat, a dark fleece, and had a bulge of chewing tobacco in his lower lip. His cheeks were ruddy. Paul offered him some chew and Harry declined with a shake of his head.

"I'd take a beer, though."

Paul pointed to an ice chest at the bottom of the back steps to the house, and Harry went over and pulled out a bottle of High Life.

"Yeah, they were fighting earlier. She'll be back though."

Paul spat a stringy coil of brown saliva down, a strand of which strung over his arm like fishing line. "You wanna shoot?"

"No, thanks," Harry said. "Maybe later."

They turned to watch the shooters out in the field. The two men were little more than shadows in the failing light, but dusk seemed eternal this far north in the late summer, as the first stars poked through the western sky, still a deep blue.

Paul wanted to know where on Rock Creek he was staying and whether Harry had been fishing. There was a pause as they drank and watched the men take aim and fire.

"What are you doing up here?" Paul asked. He'd heard Tucson had excellent weather year-round.

Harry sipped his beer, decided to tell him he'd come up here to look for his mom.

"She run off with the mailman or something?" Paul said. He laughed.

Harry smiled at this, but didn't look at him, as they stood side by side. Harry drinking, Paul drinking and spitting into the grass at their feet.

"She died," Harry said. Just like that. "But I don't know how and I don't know why, so here I am."

"Shit," Paul said.

Harry was playing it up. He didn't like Paul's crack about the mailman, though the guy probably hadn't meant anything by it. Harry was happy to be able to say that she was dead, and then that washed through him like dark clouds blocking out the sun.

"So, who's your old man then?"

"Patrick Stables."

His name sounded familiar to Paul and Paul wondered aloud if their own fathers might have known one another, back in the day. Harry mentioned Calvin Hogan's name, that

Patrick and Calvin had been in the war together. Paul lit up.

"No shit?" Paul said. "I know Cal. Though he's hard to miss."

Harry wasn't sure if this was good or bad. After that first night, Harry had managed to avoid Calvin. Definitely didn't want word getting back to Pat in Denver. Harry had been deleting the messages on the cabin's old cassette tape answering machine. Its little red light flashing when Harry got home from the library with a bag of groceries and a six-pack. Greta leaping all over the place to get outside and run down to the river.

Paul said everybody knew Calvin Hogan, since he'd guided various rivers and streams in the region for decades. He'd talk tourists and frat boys into weeklong hunting expeditions for mule deer and elk. Probably birds, too.

"Lolo, Hogback, Seeley Lake," Paul said. "Depends on what you want. But me and my brother Walt used to go out to Bob Marshall or Scapegoat. Unless we were hunting whitetail, then we'd trek way up into Pattee Canyon for them. That's one of Cal's spots."

Harry missed many of the names Paul was tossing out, as he flipped through a slideshow of images where this was what Harry would've grown up doing. He might be wearing a dirty ballcap and have a big wad of Skoal in his lip. Getting fucked up on High Life and shooting discarded objects in a field every Friday night for the rest of his life. Going to some place called Hogback to point big guns at wild animals.

Paul walked over to the cooler and fished out another couple beers. Harry was scanning faces, wondering why Kristin wasn't here. He looked into the house to see if maybe she was inside with friends.

Paul handed Harry another beer and asked how he knew "Kris," as he called her, when a younger, stumpy guy in a denim shirt joined them. He spoke to Paul but kept glancing up at Harry with nervous eyes. Harry nodded at him. His cheeks were chubby and clean-shaven. His eyes were bloodshot, wrecked by drink or amphetamines, and he wore a faint mustache that made him look even younger.

"Hey, I'm Harry."

"How ya doin' there, Harry?" He looked down at the irises Harry had forgotten he was still holding. "Those for me?"

The stumpy kid shot a glance at Paul and smirked.

"Yeah," Harry said. "Happy birthday, fuckface. You want me to sing to you?"

It slipped out before Harry had realized how pissed he'd gotten. Paul coughed at this and was smiling, watching the two of them. Harry's heart was pounding. He switched his beer to the hand holding the bouquet, to free his right one, which he brought up to rub along the stubble of his jaw—showing Stumpy the shape of his fist.

Harry got that old friendly feeling of wanting to smash this kid right in the mouth. It came back into his blood like a shiver of wind over a field.

Paul and the other guy broke into nervous laughter. The kid said, "Just fuckin' with you, man," and he spit onto the grass.

Harry smiled and took a swig of beer to steady his nerves.

Paul's stumpy friend uncapped the thin lid from a tin of Copenhagen and held it out. Harry looked at him, pushed his finger into the moist tobacco, and scooped some up. It felt like wet coffee grounds.

"Doesn't this shit have fiberglass in it?" Harry said, bringing his finger to his nostrils, inhaling its earthy menthol stink.

Paul laughed and said, "Let me have some, too, Curtis."

Curtis stared at Harry, then took another big pinch himself, adding it to the black wad already covering his lower teeth. Curtis muttered something completely unintelligible. Harry looked at him, and then Curtis shrugged as he let fall a stream of brown juice out of his mouth by simply turning his head to the side as if to sneeze. Curtis's lower lip protruded out cartoonishly like he'd been stung by a bee.

The three of them stood at a distance from the bonfire as Paul and Curtis talked over each other about where the better trout fishing had been lately.

Harry was trying to sip beer without swallowing tobacco juice. He watched as Tommy in his yellow vest jogged back in toward everybody at the fire. Same blond crew cut, same big attitude. Tommy shouted at everybody to drink up so that they'd have more bottles for target practice. He looked to Harry like the kid who pisses in the swimming pool the moment he's waist deep in the shallow end. Even at this distance, he didn't look old enough to fire a gun let alone purchase beer.

Harry watched him walk hurriedly back out to the field with an armful of bottles and cans. And then the shooting resumed.

Harry looked over and saw Tommy's friend from Child's: Long black hair, tangled under a Stetson and acne scars. What had Rod called him? He was wearing red flannel and dark work pants, his legs were crossed, dusty black cowboy boots sticking out, one on top of the other, and whatever they were made of—snakeskin, cheap vinyl—was starting to peel off.

Hey, Frank. Your little parakeet's not allowed in here anymore.

Frank's fingers were interlaced behind his head. His hat tipped downward, like a man reclining in a Marlboro ad.

Frank was staring at Harry from a lawn chair near all the others. Even as he murmured to those around him, he kept his gaze locked on Harry like some sort of psychopath, biding his time, spitting out sunflower seed shells.

Harry wanted to be rid of the irises now. He wished everybody would look away for a second so that he could lob them into the crackling fire. He couldn't figure out why Kristin had invited him to her party and not even bothered to stick around long enough to say hi.

But it had only taken Harry a half hour and three beers before he was out there in the field with the butt of a hunting rifle wedged into the crook of his shoulder, missing each bottle he aimed at.

The tubby guy in white and Tommy were ribbing Harry, and then cursing like they'd never seen a worse shot. Harry was their entertainment for the evening. The big one kept saying, "Just move closer, dude." But Harry didn't feel like putting his back to these two.

The kick of the rifle was eerily mechanical, and Harry knew the muscles of his shoulder would ache in the morning. But even missing and missing again, Harry was half drunk and feeling at one with every sound out there: the reloading and cocking of the rifle, the springy tension of the warm metal trigger of the Ruger, the jeers and hooting of Tommy and Tubby, outdoing one another, taunting and chiding him, and the echo of the shots into the hills.

There was part of himself that Harry had not met before, a part that was right at home out here, and it had emerged with disturbing ease. Harry felt like Leah would capture this perfectly in a story, this gradual and then all-of-a-sudden feeling of being in something brand new and familiar at once. Harry missed her. He hadn't heard her voice in so long that it stung to recall her message out in the field.

Ryan told me what you did to his car. Obviously, I had to tell him about us–so, that's that.

Tommy's white face was lit up in the moonlight, his yellow vest the brightest thing out there. His eyes big, and his voice hoarse and high-pitched.

Harry was trying to reload the rifle, dropped a bullet into the grass, and Frank emerged from the darkness and pulled the weapon out of his hands.

Frank said, "Here, hold my *flowers* while I shoot a gun for the very first time in my fucking life." The other two broke into wild laughter. Harry stepped back as Frank took aim, and a bottle splattered to shards.

The irises were on the ground beside Harry's beer bottle. He didn't even remember setting them down, thinking he might need to slow down on the High Life a little.

Harry turned to look back at the fire, as Joe Cocker played on a boombox holding court in its own lawn chair, and everybody was talking over the music. From this distance, Harry watched somebody Frisbee a pizza box into the fire like a big white disc, and the flames took it and turned it blue and then orange, and it warped in on itself like a sheet of paper.

Harry picked the bouquet up off the ground and walked back toward the house, leaving the three of them to it, and he watched another pizza box skim into the flames and land on the other side of the firepit to loud laughter. The white dog barked and barked at this, clearly distressed.

Harry found Paul and Curtis where he'd left them, when the screen door at the back of the doublewide opened and Kristin appeared there, in jeans and a dark hooded sweatshirt. The hood was over her hair, she had ahold of something long Harry couldn't make out, and for a split second she looked like Leah, which sent cold fireworks through his chest.

Kristin was smoking a cigarette, and she set what Harry could see was a rifle down in the back room of the trailer, a laundry area where a stroller, a battered rocking horse, and a colorful kind of playpen with animal toys attached to it had been tossed.

Harry was so relieved to see her that he had to stop himself from laughing. She paused there a moment to look out over everybody from the top step at the door. And as she scanned the faces at the fire, her eyes passed right over Harry's like he was no one.

For a second Harry thought that maybe they hadn't met. Maybe she hadn't invited him to this party, and that napkin in his fist jammed in the pocket of his jeans held his own scribbled notes for some story he had failed to write.

One of the women on a lawn chair yelled up to her and pointed over to Harry all at once, and said, "Flowerboy over there was looking for you, Kris."

Her eyes found Harry in the dark, and she smiled sadly,

dragged on her cigarette, and started down the steps.

"Hey, Harry. I didn't think you'd really come all the way out here."

She was shaking her head, grinning, and it was the Kristin Harry recognized. Her eyes were sleepy, kind. In the moonlight he thought he could make out the tiny scar on her lip.

Harry opened his mouth to speak but choked on some tobacco juice, which had formed an unfortunate pool over his tongue. He spat down hard, a gob of it splashing his boot. Then he wiped his sleeve across his face and raised his bottle to her as she came over. Harry badly wanted to extricate the wad of chew, but it had sealed itself to the inside of his lower lip, and the moment he started to hook it out with a finger he'd have a messy situation on his hands. He'd need a sink and some Kleenex to do it right. Plus, he didn't want to retch in front of Kristin, so Harry squeezed it in there a little tighter, pretending he'd done this a thousand times.

Kristin greeted the other two, and Paul tipped his cap, said, "Hello, Lovely." She squeezed Paul on his arm. Curtis spit down a blob of tobacco and grinned at her.

"These boys got you dipping chew, huh?"

Harry smiled at her with his lips sealed shut so as not to lose more fluid. Without a word, he held the flowers out to her, but she glanced at them like he was just doing a show and tell, and didn't take them. Emptiness flooded through him.

"I have to tell you something. Come with me."

"Oh, don't worry about it," he said, relieved to spit out his load, and he wiped his chin with the back of his hand. "It's all good."

Kristin took Harry by the arm, and they walked away from the other two, toward the shadows of the open garage. Paul and Curtis continued talking, but Paul was watching them, his eyes all over Kristin.

"Harry, it's not my birthday."

"Ah ha," he said. "That makes this bouquet even more special."

"I was kind of joking earlier. I don't even know why I said it. I'm sorry."

"That explains why there's no cake."

"This is probably TMI, but I'm—" and she made a face like she was too afraid to say it.

"Back together with Tommy?"

"No," she said, looking out at the field. "I'm pregnant, actually."

Harry wasn't sure why she felt compelled to confide in him, who she'd known less than a week. But he saw that things were not as they had been when he'd stopped by the Sapphire that morning.

It was time for Flowerboy to hit the trail. He didn't want to make things worse for her by being seen with a big bouquet of yellow irises from a stranger. Harry looked back to Paul and Curtis. Paul was still staring at Kristin.

Before Harry figured out what to say, one of the shooters started hollering. Among the silhouettes out in the field he could still make out Tommy's vest, Frank's Stetson, and the tubby guy's long white shirt in the moonlight. But there was a fourth figure with them now too. And one of them was saying, "*Stop! Stop it!*" And that was followed by a high, tittering laugh from Tommy.

Drunken child-like laughter and it cut across everything.

Kristin turned to look out at the commotion, but Harry was staring at the side of her face. Up close, he could see that her eyes were red, like she was high or like she'd been crying. Harry didn't want to trouble her with the stupid bouquet, but he wanted badly to be free of it.

"Same old everything tonight," Kristin said. "Tommy and Frank with a rifle and a case of beer is a bad recipe. At least they didn't get you shooting out there with them."

"Yeah, no," Harry said. "Totally."

Kristin bumped her hip into Harry's. She tossed her cigarette down and stepped on it.

What Harry will remember later is that he hadn't cared about what was happening out in the field. Or whatever was about to happen. It had fuck all to do with him. And Kristin and Harry were alone for a moment, like the evening had colluded to pull everybody away from them. He wanted to leave. He wanted stay. He wanted her to hit the road with him. He wanted to be alone in bed. Or be having sex with Leah up in the mountains. Harry had furnished that nice, warm buzz he had earlier with two more beers and he was drunk. Not sloppy, but a coagulating mess of mixed signals gushing from his brain to his gut to his heart and back in new streams.

"I take it Tommy doesn't know yet," Harry said.

"No, I told him."

"What are you gonna do?"

But Kristin didn't answer him.

"Those stupid motherfuckers," she said.

She was staring out in the field at Tommy and the others

now, where there was more taunting and laughter. There was a shot. Then another. And another two that went *pop-pop*.

Harry couldn't make out what was being said, but everybody at the fire had fallen silent and was turned to face the four men, who were arguing about something in the tall grass beyond the yard's edge. A young woman got up and ran out to the four of them and the four became five.

"Lucy," Kristin said, "don't go out there."

But Lucy was off, running.

"Is that your cousin?" Harry said.

"How'd you know that?"

"The other night…on the phone."

Harry had asked what the fuck Tommy's problem was. He'd had a mind to drive into town to beat him half to death. He remembered Kristin telling him that Tommy's dad used to wake him up in the morning if he'd slept a minute past 6 a.m., and take a bike chain to him. "What was he going to do, call the police? His uncle *was* the police. So's his cousin."

Harry and Kristin watched as eight or nine others got up from the fire pit to jog out to the field. A bag of potato chips was knocked over in the dirt, and the two dogs went at the mess. More hollering and confusion followed.

Harry heard Tommy laughing and then there were another two reports from the rifle.

Three women—the one with the white dog and two others who might have been sisters—stood up at the fire to watch, frozen. All three had their arms folded. One of them yelled at somebody called Kevin to be careful out there. And by then just about everybody at the party had joined the cluster.

Harry and Kristin were watching, but Harry asked Kristin again what she was going to do about the baby, about Tommy.

"He says we have to get, you know…"

Then Kristin looked at Harry, and her face suddenly seemed much younger.

"Get what? An abortion?"

"That's what Lucy said, too."

Harry looked into her eyes, shook his head.

"*Married*, you dumb-ass."

"Married," Harry said under his breath. "Jesus."

The absurdity of this struck Harry twice—picturing Kristin having to go through this ceremony with Tommy—and the fresh shame of having proposed off-the-cuff to Leah in bed the night before he'd just taken off. What the hell had he been thinking?

More garbled yelling came from the field. Somebody shouted "*Tommy, stop*!" And then another rifle shot that the evening siphoned right up.

Harry and Kristin watched as Paul jogged away from Curtis out toward the altercation. Just a nonchalant traipse into the high grass. A routine thing, like here we go with this old game again. Paul dropped his bottle of beer into the grass, and he may as well have been a shadow puppet getting dragged out into the melee.

The beer was in the front of Harry's head, seeping down under his ribs out to the tips of his fingers with a delicious feeling of being alive. He was so relieved, suddenly, that Leah had had the sense to tell him it was not a good idea. She was absolutely right. He'd been so embarrassed at her response that he'd had to flee. But now he recognized how absurd it had been to spring it on her like that. They'd dated for a few months. She hadn't even really only been with him. Harry wanted to laugh, and apologize, and revel in the good fortune of Leah's level-headedness.

He inched toward Kristin and could smell the cigarette smoke from her clothes, and they watched the figures out in the field form a kind of murky huddle apparently trying to undo whatever had started.

It was quiet for a moment and Harry could see that they were wrestling as shadows over the rifle, which looked like the branch of a tree in the moonlight.

When Harry looked at Kristin, she was squinting her eyes at the mess of clumped shapes. He opened his mouth to say he was going to take off, but two or three people were running back toward them and this was the first moment that things felt truly out of joint. The fifteen or twenty people in the melee beyond were then a smear of jostling shadows.

The boozy blood inside him picked up speed, and Harry spat out a spear of tobacco juice onto the ground, taking care to miss his boot this time.

Somebody—it sounded like Paul's voice—shouted, "Get the fuck off me!" and a clear shot from the rifle rang out, followed by another and the guitar solo to "Hotel California" on the stereo was blanketed by everybody shouting and screaming.

The jockeying mass was dispersing quickly as everybody came running toward Harry and Kristin, where the light from the bonfire and the back of the house shone onto their terrified faces. Several people were hunched over, running low to the ground, their silhouettes made into something ungainly and monstrous.

The dogs sprang up happily from the spilled food, in on whatever game this was becoming, and everyone was yelling then. And they were hollering to get out.

Kristin pulled on the sleeve of Harry's sweatshirt, and then she ran toward the back of the house and leapt up the stairs, taking two at a time, into the laundry area of the doublewide where Harry had seen Kristin leave her rifle.

He hesitated and watched her disappear into the house with three others clambering up the back steps behind her. Everybody else was running past Harry to get around the house to where their vehicles were parked out front.

When Harry looked back out to the moonlit field, there were only three or four people left in the throng of the figures. He heard a final shot from the rifle and that person, just a shadow, really, seemed to fall into the grass.

Harry dropped his bottle, and started running back toward the truck through the uncut grass between the house and garage.

A crowd of people was in front of him now, shouting and retreating from whoever had the gun.

Harry ran as fast as he could around the side of the house, after everyone, ducking down. He let the stems of the flowers fall from his clenched fist without realizing he'd even had a hold of them still, until his fingers came free and touched the evening dew of the uncut grass.

The white dog had gotten ahead of Harry and was panting heavily right at the door of his pickup. Harry clapped to shoo it off, but the dog leapt up on him, thinking this to be more happy fun, and nearly knocked Harry down. The dog was nipping at the air around him, like a puppy in play, with big, gleaming eyes, and its spitty tongue flapping loose.

Harry flung the door of the truck open and pushed the mutt's head back with the door's sharp edge, harder than he needed to—it shrieked—and the dog then slipped its suddenly ferocious head in a sleek undulating maneuver up under the door.

The animal opened her mouth on Harry's leg, biting down deeply just above his left ankle.

Harry kicked the dog's face hard with the heel of his boot, and he let out a scream and managed to get the door partly closed and the key into the ignition.

The engine turned over. Harry put the truck in reverse and looked up, but the rearview mirror was filled with people now scrambling to escape, and he couldn't budge without plowing into them or running over the white dog, still leaping and bucking boisterously among the terrified people.

Then Harry felt the bed of his truck dip down.

DETECTIVE

Harry's alone in the hospital room and looks over at the IV bag which has a long tube stretched into the crook of his arm, where it disappears into a vein under an X of white tape.

His head hurts, but other than having no feeling whatsoever in his left leg, Harry thinks maybe he's alright. He doesn't know if it's painkillers or saline solution or something else flowing into his arm, but he wants to pull the needle out, throw his clothes on, and get back to the cabin.

He can see rain falling through the streetlight beyond the room's window. He pictures Greta out on Rock Creek, starving to death, shivering in a ball on the cabin's muddy doorstep.

He starts clawing at the tape on his arm, to try and peel it back and yank the IV out. The door opens and Denis is back with the doctor. She looks like she got out of med school last weekend.

"That must've been some raccoon."

"Yeah. It was a dog, actually," Harry says.

"A what?"

"A white shepherd, husky mix. Some kind of mutt."

"When did this happen to you?" she says. Her hair is dark and her big brown eyes are peering right into Harry's. Suddenly he feels naked.

"Couple nights ago. Did I get a tetanus shot or something?"

"You're thinking of stepping on a rusty nail," she says. "What you got was a shot for rabies. I take it you don't remember that?"

Denis pours him a glass of water and waits for the doctor to finish examining Harry's leg. She's unwrapping the gauze, then peels back a stained bandage.

She looks up and asks Harry how it feels now. Harry says it feels like nothing.

"Good," she says. "Nothing is good."

"*Nothing is good*," Harry says. "Okay. So, can I get going or what?"

"You need rest." She's writing something down in her file. "You had a serious infection and fever."

Harry tries to imagine tying the bed sheets together to climb out the window into the rain. Or maybe there's an elevator.

"What time is it?" he says. "Where's my stuff?"

"It's 2:45 in the morning, Mr. Stables." And she tells Harry about the medicines she's going to prescribe and asks how his head is and looks into his eyes with a penlight and has Harry do some deep breaths. She places a bare palm flat on Harry's chest with her stethoscope and says, "Sorry my hand is cold. It's always freezing in here."

Harry shuts his eyes and the doctor says, "Deep breath, Mr. Stables…And let it out."

"Do you know where my phone is?"

"Again. Deep breath in. Okay, let it out."

"Do you know who the nurses spoke with?"

"You should rest here until at least the morning, and we'll reassess then."

She doesn't answer any of his questions before walking out of the room.

He's so tired, but he can't stop thinking about Greta. He wants to get back in his bed. At home. In Tucson. With his dog, and just sleep for days.

It's wet and windy and horrible outside. Harry watches silent flashes of lightning in the distance through the window. Denis returns with a tray of hot food and sets it down beside the bed. Another nurse comes in carrying two aluminum crutches. She sets them against the foot of the bed, glares at Harry, and slips back out, bumping her hip on the doorjamb.

"So, nobody came to see me?"

"Actually," Denis says, "a detective came by this evening and asked what you'd come in with."

Harry sits up again. He lowers his voice. "What'd you tell him?"

Denis laughs. "I told him the truth. That you'd been bitten by a wild animal."

The rain's eased up a little, but it's nearly 4 a.m. by the time Harry gets back to the exit for Rock Creek.

Denis had been right about Harry's boots. One was fine, and Harry had gotten it on all right. But the other one smelled like a pus-filled sock, so Harry wrapped the plastic bag his clothes had been in around the gauze of his injury and left the boot behind.

After hopping over to the aluminum crutches, Harry wrangled himself out of the room—down the elevator and out through the automatic glass doors into the rain—and tossed the crutches into the back of the truck, which he located with help from a friendly security guard after a twenty-minute search for it in the storm.

Harry's drenched and sweaty, but more or less alive. He doesn't know what sorts of drugs he's on, but they give his senses a euphoric dreaminess. The truck's steering wheel feels massive and smooth under his hands. The windshield wipers fling the rain off with frightening power.

There's so much water on the passenger side of the truck that the seat's now discolored by rain. Harry feels pretty sure that he's escaping something now. He has to get back to the cabin to see if Greta has turned up—and with or without her he'll be gone before the sun's up.

He wants to call Kristin, but his phone's dead. Its charger is back on the cabin's oak dresser. He asked Denis what he'd missed in the world before pretending he was going back to sleep, but Denis said that nothing ever happened in Missoula, and that it was boring here and that he wanted to relocate to a hospital in Seattle, where his brother and some friends had gotten jobs as dockhands last spring.

When Harry asked Denis if he'd heard about the shooting, Denis said he knew one of the nurses who worked in the ICU where the victim was and had tended to her. They'd airlifted her to a bigger hospital in Billings, where she later died. But Denis couldn't remember the name of the woman, only that she wasn't from Missoula.

Before Harry reaches the muddy driveway, he can see from the road that the lights inside the cabin are on.

Harry can't remember if he'd left them on himself, in his delirium. But all that comes to him is having yelled at that bear in the garbage before tripping backward into the doorway, scraping his shoulder blade on the desk edge as he came down.

Harry slows to a stop in the middle of the road, still not feeling much more than a dull clod where his lower leg is. Then a shadow in the cabin moves across the window facing the road. The figure is between the end of the bed and the kitchen. Something else is in front of that window, blocking it, but Harry can see clearly enough that there's at least one person inside the cabin.

He waits there in the cab of the truck, but clicks off the windshield wipers. His heart starts thwapping hard. He kills the truck's headlights, but it's too dark to see anything with no moon through the clouds. He doesn't want to flip them back on and draw attention to the road, so he lets the engine idle while he thinks over his next move.

Again the shadow moves across the frame of the window, starker this time.

The bathroom light flips on and Harry watches the figure disappear. He turns the high beams back on and puts the truck in gear, driving slowly over the deep divots and puddles. The rain's spattering in the wind and blobs are smearing up the glass as Harry lurches forward under all the dripping trees shrouding the road.

When Harry gets as close as he can to the cabin—without turning into the driveway—he flips off the headlights once more.

The bathroom light goes dark. And the shadow moves back into the main room of the cabin, where it stops and looks out the window to the road, straight at Harry's pickup.

The gravel driveway's still out of view on the other side of the cabin so it's not possible yet to see if a police car is parked out front.

Harry sits in the darkened cab for a moment and reaches down to find the Maglite in the truck door. He clicks it on, though its beam is dim if not quite dead. Everything reasonable inside him says to leave now.

But Harry will never forgive himself for abandoning Greta up here.

He shuts off the truck's engine and opens the door in the rain, right there in the middle of the road.

He hears frog sounds and trees creaking in the wet wind overhead. His foot is no longer searing with pain, and he can finally feel it—strangely tender—below the wound itself. He listens to the sound of rain dripping onto the hood and splashing the puddles fused up with the amphibian chirps. Harry's senses are magnified to something superhuman, and he thinks he'll be able to use his bare hands to overpower whoever's waiting for him in the cabin.

Getting his plastic-wrapped foot onto the ground is the issue, so he swings his right leg around first, slips onto his knees, and that foot sinks into a deep puddle. Harry mashes his balls on the seat edge and has to keep from crying out. With both feet planted in the muck, he props his elbows onto the seat like he's using the truck as a barricade after some botched heist.

Then, gently, he pushes the door closed behind him, and the dome light on the cab's ceiling goes dark. He gets hold of the back end's wet steel to hop himself around and retrieve the crutches from the bed of the pickup. When he gets each one wedged into his armpits—managing to hold the flashlight awkwardly in the three bottom fingers of his right hand—it's right about then that Harry realizes what an enormously stupid idea this is.

He hears a dog bark. It sounds familiar, but not like Greta's. One of George Willis's Weimaraners up the road, maybe. The monotonous woof gets louder. And for a second—leaning against the bumper—he thinks the white mutt from the party has tracked him out to Rock Creek somehow. The barking continues like some bleating alarm.

Harry's crutching himself like a smashed crab down toward the back of the cabin into the wet grade, below the road's edge, when the rubber-tipped end of his crutch slips over the surface of a stone and he spills forward, face first, into the grass and hits his cheekbone hard on a rock.

He lets go of the Maglite to steady himself back up with one of the crutches. But he hasn't even got himself halfway up before the barking dog is upon him, and Harry turns over like a beetle in the weeds, fumbling idiotically—not knowing whether to guard his injured leg or his face. When the dog lurches closer its angry barking grows ferocious, but it stays back three or four feet. And the animal leaps from spot to spot, smashing the grass down but seems to be held back by an invisible force.

Harry can see the flashlight's beam obscured by the tall blades of grass. One of the crutches has been bent in the tumble. The dog keeps barking as Harry struggles to get himself upright, trying to keep the weight off his bad foot, when he hears someone out back of the cabin.

"Who's there?"

That voice. Harry reaches over to the flashlight and takes it up in his muddy hand. By some miracle, the fall has realigned its batteries and its dim beam is now bright as a spotlight. Harry tries to shine it at the dog, still barking insanely and thrashing in the wet foliage to point the intruder out to whoever's coming out of the cabin.

"*Harrison?*" and then comes Calvin Hogan's hooting laughter.

"Calvin, you motherfucker."

"What are you doing out here in the shit salad, bud?"

The incoherent shriek that comes from Harry's deepest bowel only produces more yodelingly high-pitched giggles from Calvin.

Harry aims the Maglite's beam on Calvin's face as Calvin plods waist-high goose steps in his rubber boots through the rainy grass and bushes—and everything around Harry shrinks when Calvin's own enormous hunting lantern dwarfs the beam of Harry's flashlight.

"Get that laser beam out of my eyes, Harry. You alright?"

He tries again to prop himself up with the squished crutch.

"Where's your Hungarian pooch, bud?" Herkimer's barking like mad and Calvin kicks his dog back.

"She's not inside?"

"Nope," Calvin says. "Give me your hand—"

"She took off."

"Drop the torch, Harrison. Grab onto my shoulder. Took off where?"

"For a sleigh ride with Santa Claus—how the fuck should I know?"

"Okay, okay," Calvin says. "Let go of the twig, too. That

thing ain't helping you none."

Calvin pulls him up out of the mud, and Harry gets his arm around Cal's shoulder to steady himself. Calvin smells like B.O. and Coors. Harry wants to hug him and cry and beat him to death with his hospital crutch. Calvin's still chuckling and tells Herky to quit yapping at Harrison.

They trudge into the cabin—Calvin steadying Harry, crutchless now and sopping with filth. Before they're even through the doorway Harry can see the place has been ransacked. Somebody's been out here and turned the place upside down. All the furniture's been kicked over, the drawers emptied.

It was the bed's flipped mattress that Harry had seen blocking the window from the road.

RANSACKED

Calvin goes back around the cabin to get Harry's truck out of the road and Herkimer trots out after him.

Harry dries himself off and splashes his face with warm water in the bathroom. He needs a hot shower, but he'll have to chat with Calvin first. More feeling's returned to his leg, though it's still pins and needles. He can wiggle his toes now in the damp gauzy stuff hidden in the plastic bag rubber-banded around his shin bone.

Harry leans against the doorjamb, looking over Pat's cabin. Plates and bowls broken into shards on the floor. His clothes scattered about and evidently stomped on. The dresser's tipped over onto its front and the mattress has been flipped up to expose its empty black bedframe, which had been concealing a vintage *Playboy* and some mice droppings.

Somebody, maybe Tommy and his pals, had had some fun in here. Harry wraps himself in a blanket, and sits on the edge of the bed to eat some stale Corn Pops out of a chipped coffee mug.

"You remember Paul Tillett?" Calvin says, coming back inside with his mud-spattered dog.

Harry freezes. He still hadn't mentioned running into Paul and his mother at the ER, seeing that nasty bruise on Paul's ribs.

"Yeah, why?"

"Well, Paul Tillett's dead."

"*How*?"

"Somebody ran him over when he was coming out of his house this morning, after the coppers set him loose."

"The police thought Paul shot the girl?"

"Could be. But they never pressed any charges if they did."

"Who ran him over?"

"Unknown. But whoever it was knew Paul was back home, because they staked the place out. Whacked him in the street like a doe and peeled off. Nary a witness."

"Calvin, I saw Paul and his mom at the ER. Before I met you at the river."

"Well, Harrison," Calvin says. He's started cleaning up the broken plates and bowls. "Aren't you full of surprises."

"Paul told me he'd hid from the police in the garage. But I'm virtually positive he ran into the swarm of people after the fight started."

"Virtually positive, huh? What was he doing in the hospital, anyhow?"

Harry describes the nasty bruise under Paul's heart. Calvin nods, gives Harry that wily look.

"What?"

"Banana-shaped?" Calvin says. "How about *butt-of-a-rifle*-shaped?"

"Meaning Paul had a hold of the gun?"

Calvin gets up from his squat and comes over to pantomime turning around a long rifle, and jams Harry in the ribs with it.

"He said he'd been trampled."

"Trampled? You ever been trampled, Harry? I have. And

you'd have more than a single contusion on your thorax to show for it."

"You're right. He looked fine otherwise. He said he hid out."

"Sounds to me like something's not lining up," Calvin says. "So, who was Paul covering for then—Tommy?"

The only two people Harry had seen Paul talk to were Kristin and himself. Then Harry remembers Paul's buddy Curtis: that stumpy fucker with bloodshot eyes and a fat lip full of chewing tobacco. Harry had just about busted him in the mouth after Curtis had made fun of his flowers.

Calvin pauses a moment from sweeping the busted dishes in the kitchen into a paper bag.

"Who trashed this place, bud?"

Harry shakes his head. "The nurse said a detective came by my hospital room."

"Oh yeah, the *hospital*. You were asking for it, weren't you?"

"What?"

"What'd this so-called detective look like?"

"I didn't see him."

"And you didn't think to ask Nurse Ratched for a description? Harrison, what's a detective doing nosing around a hospital wing?"

"I don't know, Calvin," Harry says and sighs. "Somebody shot a girl. There's gotta be police out looking for clues, right?"

Harry hadn't thought to question it when Denis told him that. He lays back on the mattress and shuts his eyes. Herkimer comes over and starts nudging Harry's arm with the top of his skull to get Harry to scratch his ear.

"Did you think I was a rattler out there in the mud, Herky?"

Calvin's dog gives out a muffled whine, rotating his head to get the right itch.

"Riddle me something, Harrison."

Harry keeps his eyes closed. Places his hands over his belly like a satisfied dead person.

"Why'd that male nurse say you were staying at the Bread and Breakfast downtown?"

"*Bed* and—never mind," Harry says. "It was on my phone. With my Arizona ID, that must've been what they assumed. Kristin works there."

"Well, I popped in over there before coming out here to see what was what. Lady with a boy's hairdo at the desk said she met you."

"Kristin's boss. What'd she say?"

"Not much, but we had a convivial exchange. She had the sparkle for Cal."

"Isn't she like *seventy*?"

Calvin laughs and mutters something about staying out of the henhouse.

"Kristin came into work, though. So whatever Silas heard about her going back to Pine Ridge must've been bunk."

"You saw Kristin?"

"No, but apparently she's worked all her shifts. Innkeeper said she switched to nights."

"I'm lost. I mean Paul Tillett's dead?"

"Very much so," Calvin says.

"And why would Kristin be working the night shift now?"

Calvin shrugs. "Yeah, it's a pickle. But we'll get it figured out before they put a sack on your head and march you to the gallows."

"Thanks, Calvin. Wait, didn't you come try to find me at Providence after the nurse called you?"

"Nope," Calvin says.

"Why not?"

"Cal don't do hospitals, bud. Setting foot in one of those things is begging for ghastly luck. Nothing personal, Harrison. It's a plain phobia I got."

"You'll electrocute a puppy, but hospitals are out of bounds?"

"Bad juju, kid. Cesspools of mutilation, malady, and communicable sickness. Meanwhile, Harrison, go to the authorities. First thing in the morning. Tell them what you just told me. It's your only viable play."

"I know," Harry says. "But won't it look too suspicious?"

"Possibly. But that mongrel nipped your tendon. Doctor's note might be as good as a get-out-of-jail-free pass. That's probably the best alibi you could've hoped to've had in this quagmire."

"What happens if they don't believe me?"

"Thing is, Harrison, if they have witnesses who seen you plinking cans with those boys and screeching down the road with them in your Toyota Tacoma—that's bad."

How many people had seen Tommy and Don in the back of Harry's truck? Ten? Twenty? Harry put his hands into his hair and started working his fingers over his scalp.

"I can tell you that you don't wanna abscond into the night like a cat burglar. Won't look favorable on you. Tiny Tommy might be trying to slip Paul's killing onto you."

"What possible motive would I have to kill Paul? I didn't even *know* Paul."

"Harrison, you're looking at this thing all wrong. If Tommy's trying to skitch out from under a murder charge, in order to do that, he's got to nudge somebody else into the lamp light. Whatever he tried to hang on Paul Tillett"—again Calvin mimes jabbing the rifle into Paul—"Well, it didn't stick too good. Now he's looking for another playmate to finger."

"Your way with words is really astonishing, you know that?"

"Stay focused, kid. I'm trying to pull you out of a fresh hole in the graveyard here."

Harry doesn't want to talk to the police. But he doesn't want to run either. Both paths seem like irreversible mistakes. He lays there on the bed, petrified.

"Harrison, I reckon it's safe to say that whoever it was that tore this cabin apart doesn't need to check the directory to find you next time. So, take your pick: you want tire tracks on your carcass, slumped in a ditch like Greg's kid? Or chat with Missoula's finest over a cup of Juan Valdez?"

"But I didn't do anything."

"Happy days," Calvin says, and he sits down on one of the plastic chairs, stretches out his legs, and begins picking between his two front teeth. "And you shouldn't have a thing to fear. I mean, so long as you get your story straight. You were into this thing a bit deeper than you let old Cal in on over our flapjacks, weren't you?"

"I should've told you everything. I should've never gone fishing with you. I'm sorry about that."

"And what about the Ruger that the cops snarfed up in the ferns?"

"I threw it out of the truck. Into the ditch." Harry makes a throwing motion with both hands, like he's bailing water out of a boat. "Wait, Silas told you that?"

"Last night's evening news, kid. So, let's try this again: Why'd you have a hold of their weapon?"

"Because we *grappled* over it. I had to get the rifle from them after they threatened me with it in the truck."

"Okay, okay. But the sheriff's gonna wanna know why you helped these guys make a getaway from the fracas in the first place."

"I didn't know they were in the truck."

"See, that part right there, Harry? Starting to sound like horse dung wrapped in a cow pie."

"I knew they were *in* there. I just didn't know that they'd shot somebody. I was trying to get away like everybody else. And I'd been bitten by a fucking *dog*."

"Sheriff's gonna put it like this: Now then, Mr. Stables, you mean to tell us that you casually drove Tommy with his Ruger Medium Sporter along with his sidekick, Dipshit McDonald, away from the rumpus for an evening pleasure cruise without the remotest wherewithal of what had just transpired only moments before at the party thirty-seven people can verify you'd been shooting a loaded weapon at?"

"Calvin, I panicked. I got on the road and drove the hell out of there. Kristin saw me leave alone."

"Bud, come on now. You said your gal pal ran back into the house. Plus, you *didn't* leave alone. You just said so yourself. So, better to not plant a falsity in your own mind"—Calvin taps his frizzled temple here—"as to something the young lady couldn't have seen because it didn't happen to happen. Time's up, gopher boy. It's your play."

Herkimer is barking outside the cabin door.

It's light out when Harry opens his eyes. He doesn't try to move his bad leg, as he'd finally gotten comfortable and his head's no longer pounding for the first time in days. Harry can wiggle his toes and senses the whole fleshy contour of his ankle and shinbone. It feels sore, but it's no longer a ghost foot below his knee.

There's murmuring outside and it sounds like Calvin's talking to somebody about three feet from the entry. Before Harry gets his leg swung over the edge of the mattress, the cabin door opens and Herkimer bounds inside. Calvin peeks his head in and says, "Merry Christmas, pal."

All the furniture has been righted, and the broken bits and legs set on top or nearby. Calvin's even piled up Harry's clothes onto the end of the bed without waking him.

"Who were you talking to out there?"

"Thinking aloud. Trying to wrap my head around this debacle you tumbled into. We got a lot of peculiar pieces that don't appear to fit."

"It's okay, Calvin. I can handle it."

"I have my doubts about that. Anyhow, Pat called me before you landed in Rock Creek. I promised him I'd keep you out of trouble. And I owe him a lot more than that from…any number of things."

"He told you I was coming?"

"He mentioned you might be looking to get info on your mother," Calvin says. "I wasn't supposed to let on. Did I have you fooled?"

"Jesus Christ. What about my mother?"

"We can discuss that another time," Calvin says. "Anyways, it's not my place—"

"You didn't tell my dad about the party, did you?"

"Nah," Calvin says. "But if he asks I'm not lying for your butt."

Calvin looks grave, pensive even. His crafty, river-guide brashness has thawed into a mask of worry.

"You know what happened to my mom," Harry says. "Don't you."

Calvin looks away. He turns for the sink and slurps some water direct from the tap. Then he wipes his mustache with a dirty dishtowel.

"Well?" Harry says.

"Harrison, I don't wanna get in Pat's way on this one. I'll have to check with him."

"You know he's lied to me and Adrienne about her for years?"

"Tell you what, if you call your old man and let him know what kind of dog patch you got yourself into then, maybe we can talk about your mother. But first thing's first. You have the law to contend with presently."

"Calvin?" Harry says, scootching himself upright. "What are you wearing?"

Calvin has changed into a puffy hunting onesie patterned in snow camo, a digital vomit of pixelated gray and white. Evidently, it's a furnace too, as Calvin has the front unzipped halfway to his navel. Nothing underneath. Just a thatch of chest hair taking in the breeze.

"Nice, right? It's a coverall loaner from the dry cleaners while my other one's gettin' sudded."

"I don't want to know what could've brought you to a dry cleaner."

"Elk blood. Sawed into a major artery between the heart and a lung before this bull was all the way out, and it came up like Old Faithful, baby."

Calvin snickers at this, squinches his eyes, and bobs his head around to avoid imaginary blood splashing his face.

Harry asks if there'd been any sign of Greta while he'd been passed out, and Calvin quits laughing, shakes his head.

"She could be any number of places. There's been so much rain, that water won't be limited to the crick so, only the Vizsla knows where the Vizsla goes. I betcha she'll be back though."

Calvin holds open the old *Playboy* to show Harry a young white woman wearing a feather headdress. She's doing a pouty thing with her mouth.

"That isn't mine."

"Says she's a poet. You might glean a few tricks of the trade from Ms. Lana Wood here."

"It was under the bed."

"Oh, *sure*..." Calvin says, holding his palm out as if to slow a car. "I already got this issue anyhow. Simone Hammerstrand in a Jacuzzi full of bunny-shaped bubbles? Classic."

Harry imagines Paul run over in the street outside his own front window. He remembers that man in the *Missoulian* article, the one who'd butchered a cow in a field under the cover of night then fled to Oklahoma. Nearly twenty years had gone by and they still wanted that asshole.

"You know what? You're right. I need to talk to the police. If I leave town I'll be extradited or some shit. Whatever the cops do across state lines. Especially if this thing has become two killings."

"Atta boy," Calvin says.

"Yeah, well, it was nice knowing you."

"I'd escort you, but I got a thing with this gal Marilyn going on a little later. Keep me posted, Harrison. You're doing the right thing. If any of those flatfoots give you the side eye just demand to see the top hog—and keep your lip zipped till he shows. Whatever happens, stay out of that hospital. Should've called up Cal at home on Old Pond Road. I'd have stitched you up like a caddis fly myself before dropping you into that septic hole."

"You're making a chat with the police sound better by the second."

"So long, Harrison."

TROUBLE

Harry gets everything packed up to make sure that he can leave right after he goes to the police.

He locates his passport and wristwatch, still in one of the dresser drawers. Then he calls Kristin's cell, gets her voicemail again, and hangs up.

And there was that scraggly-ass Frank in his black Stetson. Harry could still hear Donald Hunt saying *Why did you do that?* And Tommy saying, *You go to the cops and you're fucked.* Tommy had to have been the shooter, so what had Paul had to do with any of it? And what could've been worth killing Paul for?

Harry's twice-folded hundred-dollar bill is still tucked into the back of his passport along with the snapshot of Harry in a wading pool, Adrienne parading around. His mother smoking a cigarette with her friend on the porch. Harry looks at the photo for a moment and considers calling Adrienne.

He dials from the cabin's phone and gets her voicemail. Harry tells her he's alright. That he hadn't wanted to say anything until he found out more, but that their mom had been in the hospital before she died. John, this librarian downtown, has been helping him, and John has a friend at the hospital who's digging up the old records in storage. Then Harry says Calvin knows something too. He hangs up and looks at the photo again.

More than two decades his mother has been gone.

Harry stands in the warm cabin and studies the picture, its white border, its matted otherworldly look, the high, full light of late morning or early afternoon summer over Harry and his sister out in the mown grass. And Harry's eyes go from his own nude little body to Adrienne's frozen stance—like a figure-skater posing in the spray of the sprinkler—and back to their mother, Elizabeth, where he lingers on a stray lock of hair beside her lovely ear, a thin thread of smoke, barely a line of whitish-gray, that coils up her arm from the cigarette between her fingers.

Harry looks at his bare leg in the picture and glances down to the monstrosity of gauze encased in a filthy plastic grocery bag below his knee. His jeans have been scissored up the outer side-seam by one of the nurses at Providence. Now it flaps open like a joke.

Harry remembers something.

He hobbles over and pulls out the old Yellow Pages from the kitchen cabinet, where he finds the phone number he's looking for. He picks up the phone and dials.

"Providence Hospital—how may I direct your call?"

"I'm looking for a nurse. He treated my wound. His name's Denis. Blackfeet guy, heavy set, maybe early 30s? Tattoos on his wrists…."

"Hold, please."

There's a long wait as Paula Abdul sings in his ear, and Harry remembers that little metal figurine Rod had given him at Child's. Harry's not sure if it's bad luck to have left it in the hospital room, but it gives him the creeps to think of it now, perched there under the lamp, looking out blindly from its empty face.

"Hello?"

"Denis, it's Harrison Stables. I was in yesterday and—"

"I remember, Harrison. You snuck right out of here, didn't you? How's your leg feeling?"

"Yeah, sorry about that. It's doing better now, thank you. Hey, do you remember that detective who came in?"

"Sure," Denis says. "What about him?"

"Do you recall his name? What he looked like?"

"He was only here for a second."

"Little blond guy, yellow vest?"

"No, he was tall. White man. He was in street clothes, in jeans I think."

"Long hair—scraggly? Cowboy hat?"

"No, no hat. He did have long hair, it was tied back in a ponytail. He was a little scruffy, but I just figured he was undercover or something."

"Did he show you his badge?"

"I don't think he did, actually. I guess I should've asked him—"

"Boots?"

"Yeah. His boots were peeling apart, like they'd been melted."

Late in the night, Harry hears a faint crying outside in the darkness.

It's a peculiar sound he doesn't recognize—a sort of warble, throaty and lucid. It wormed its way into a dream he was having about a bear asleep in the back of his pickup. Harry had been driving as slow as he could to keep it from waking up, but the truck hit a pothole on the road, and the bear got up and Harry was talking to it through the cab window he'd pulled the rifle through. He was telling it in this friendly way to lie down and go back to sleep, and he heard himself saying *we're almost there*. Next, they were parked on the side of a sunny road, and the bear started making a whining, awful sound like it was badly hurt and Harry woke up, certain that the police were in the cabin's driveway, and that the cry was coming from a siren.

Not having a gun seemed particularly stupid to Harry at this moment in the middle of a wild valley. He grabs the mop out of the closet and takes it in both hands as he peeks out the bathroom window onto the front where his truck is parked.

Harry had left the porch light on and his pickup was alone out there—no cars, no Calvin—but the terrible crying continues intermittently. He knows that it might be Greta, though it doesn't sound like anything he'd ever heard come from her. Harry sees a flayed coyote, a buck gutted by razor wire, a bighorn sheep mangled by a vehicle in the road—this carousel of slashed animals, much worse than his nightmare—and he's wide awake.

Slowly he opens the door to the darkness outside and steps into the cool night air. Nothing. He stands there a moment to listen and hears the cry once more, farther off. He grips the black length of the flashlight. He can put weight on his injured foot again, which is still sore, but no longer numb.

"Greta?"

Harry takes two steps out and stops when the awful sound

comes again, this time from the other side of the cabin. The night air brings the goose bumps up on his arms and the back of his neck. Harry's heart starts thumping.

He hobbles out around back—the plastic grocery bag rewrapped around the dressing of his wounded leg—and he follows the beam of his flashlight and hears it once more, but it's fainter now, a clipped whine of some kind. An uncanny sound—something Harry knows in his blood but much stranger.

He waits there and listens under the stars. Something rustles out in the weeds, but it's a ways off, and he casts the flashlight's beam in that direction. He sees only the undulating grass being pushed by the wind.

When he hears the cry again he staggers more quickly in its direction, casting the light toward it and hobbling up and down faster now. Again the cry comes, but it's lower and more guttural, anguished even.

"Greta?"

Only wind, the river rushing in the distance, soft tree sounds. An owl hoots. He stops in the grass and looks back. The light in the cabin is a hundred yards behind him, maybe more. When the sound comes again it's a cry of rippling pain. He turns to face it, his eyes squinting through the beam opening the grass edge before him where a dark forest lays beyond. Then a familiar bark. He shines the light on it.

Greta is pacing there. She's crazed, shaking. Immune to the Maglite's beam in her frantic eyes. Something is all over her head and face. Harry calls to her again, softer and can now see that she's got sticks or twigs in her fur. He hobbles himself closer, slowly, fearing that she'll bolt. He speaks to her, and she barks again and follows it with that wincing howl that draws up every hair on his arms.

Harry takes her by the scruff of her neck, her collar long gone in the woods, and he manages to get ahold of her, gripping her fur with one hand and aiming the flashlight into the muddy grass with the other. Together they stagger, hunched over awkwardly, back to the far light in the cabin's window, which guides them down to it like any other pair of summer insects out here mistaking it for the moon.

Greta stands in the cabin's entry and turns in a circle and then lets out another stabbing whine.

In the light, Harry can see that there are twenty or thirty porcupine quills in her face and ears and neck. He puts a fresh dish of water in front of her, but she can't touch it with all the slender spines coming from her long nose. She's filthy, covered in layers of mud and dust and excrement. Her eyes search everything and nothing in the cabin and she shivers.

Harry goes into the bathroom and locates a pair of tweezers. The quills are long and each no thicker than the tubing that houses the ink in a ballpoint pen. Greta lets out an agonizing shriek and turns again in a circle like she has to pee. The quills stick out like long, bowed hairs. Harry tweezes out the first one and appraises it in the light. It is striped and rigid. Beautiful. Greta barks once, a terrible goose-like squawk that he does not want to hear again.

He speaks to her softly, pushing her rump down, and she looks away from Harry's work—showing him the many quills in the side of her face. A tiny broken one hangs from her blood-matted ear, no longer than a wooden match.

With his left hand, Harry takes her again by the oily scruff of her neck. She's docile now. Greta won't meet Harry's eyes. But he goes to work, singing Neil Young under his breath, and gently pulling the quills out, one at a time, inspecting each thoroughly like a living animal itself. Harry sets them down, one after another, on the nightstand under the lamp as though it's a surgeon's metal tray.

Greta glances at him balefully when a spine comes out, but she stays quiet. And Harry keeps singing "Harvest Moon" as he plucks them free, which doesn't seem to calm her, but helps to steady his hands.

When he's got them all out, he looks her over, still holding her by the scruff. Again she pulls her head away from him, and Harry glances at the cabin's closed door, takes a deep breath, and lets her go. Greta steps over to her water bowl and drinks and drinks. There are flecks of blood on her snout and in spots around her neck, but nothing deep. He pours her some kibble, and she just sniffs at it and sits down in her bed and then curls up in the warmth of her blanket on the cabin floor.

Harry gathers the quills and holds them like a bouquet of tiny spears. When he brings them to his nose, they smell like Greta. Just rangy dog odor. A smell he happens to love. He thinks he should wash her snout to disinfect it, though Harry knows she'll resist. He wants to let her rest, but he's afraid of infection, given his own recent exploits in animal-inflicted wounds and self-treatment.

Harry warms the kettle up and brings over a bowl of

soapy water. He lets it cool as he strokes Greta's belly, though she's eyeing him warily now, on her side. He sets the bowl on the floor and dips a clean kitchen towel into the water. Some warm steam comes from it, and he dabs the wounds as best he can. But Greta keeps turning her face away from him, like it's a game she's too tired to play.

"Greta," he says. "Let me get these. Come here."

It's too much to battle her. Seeing her eyes like that is worse than pulling out the quills. Yet he can't shake free from the thought that now that she's actually safe in the cabin, she'll die in the middle of the night, wracked by fever.

Harry finds the number for a 24-hour veterinary clinic in Missoula in the phone directory. He dials and brings the receiver to his ear, watching Greta breathe, her ribs rising and falling, in the lamplight. The woman who answers must have knocked the phone over when its ringing tore into her sleep. Her voice is like wet rocks. Harry apologizes for bothering her so late at night. He tells her what Greta had gotten herself into. The vet says it happens all the time out here.

"But she won't let me touch her snout…"

"Well, I wouldn't either, bucko." And the vet laughs a husky laugh, which rattles into phlegmy hacking. Harry holds the phone away from his ear as she coughs something up.

"She'll be fine. Just make sure to get every quill out."

Adrienne called twice yesterday and once more tonight, each time leaving a shorter message on the cabin's old answering machine.

She was frantic over the voicemail Harry left about their mother.

"Call me the moment you hear something, Harry. And I swear to God if Pat had something to do with it, I'm going to fly to Denver and murder him. Just so we're clear."

Harry's relieved to have a bone to throw Adrienne. It's wrecked the big surprise he'd planned to bring back to her, but at this point he could care less. Anything but having to tell her that he'd nearly lost Greta, that the cabin had been trashed, or that another guy from the party had been run down and killed in the street.

It's well after midnight by now, too late to call him, but Calvin picks up—just like always—on the very first ring.

"Hey, it's Harry. Any news?"

"Not on my end. I've been waiting on you. What'd the uniforms say?"

"I haven't gone in yet. I decided to get packed up then take a little cat nap, but it turned into a nine-hour coma. Greta's back though."

"The return of the red hound. She alright?"

"She smells like a dead cow, and I just pulled about twenty porcupine quills out of her face, but she seems okay."

"Herkimer loves going after those critters. She'll be fine. Matter of fact, Herky loves some dead cow. I had to pull him out of a donkey carcass one time and he—"

"Calvin, there was a guy at the party who was out in the field with Tommy. Not Paul Tillett, and not the big dude from Idaho they locked up, Donald Hunt. Another guy. Frank Somebody. Tall, long dark hair. Cowboy hat. Mean looking and he—"

"Sounds like Frank Keene, what about him?"

"Who is he?"

"One of the wastoids who hangs around Tommy. He was with him the other night at Silas's when the tater tot was bragging about slipping through the dragnet. Why? He come peeking in your window?"

"Maybe," Harry says. "I think he was playing detective at the hospital."

"You'll think twice about settin' foot in one of those germ troughs now, won't you?"

"You know, I don't really think that's the moral of this story."

"You check your wallet?"

"Why?"

"They figured out where the cabin is, didn't they?"

"Hang on a sec," Harry says.

He reaches for his wallet on the dresser. Everything's in there—cash, credit cards—except Harry's driver's license. In its place is a scrap of paper folded in half: *GET THE FUCK OUT OF MONTANA*.

SAPPHIRE

Harry's not going to bed.

It's after 2 a.m., and he's slept all day and now he's in bad shape. He doesn't know why Frank and Tommy want him out of Montana, but he's not in the mood to locate their doorbell to ring it and find out. Harry remembers Calvin saying that Kristin was working nights for some reason at the Sapphire, so he tries her there now. She picks up.

"Kristin, it's Harry."

"I can't talk. I'm hanging up."

"Hang on, can you just tell me what's going on?"

"Go fuck yourself."

And the line's dead.

Had Kristin taken Tommy's side? Was she protecting him because he'd gotten her pregnant? Harry can't square it with that last conversation they'd had before everyone fled the party.

He looks over at Greta and doesn't want to move her. She's sleeping soundly, the tiny spots of blood on her muzzle look like black flies as they dry. Harry's got everything sorted, and he goes over and picks Greta up and carries her out to the truck, where he's made a nest of blankets for her. She sits up in the seat, alert as a goose, looking through the open passenger-side window out into the cool darkness.

Harry hobbles back into the cabin, shuts off the lights, locks the door, and pulls it shut behind him. He leaves everything packed and ready by the oak dresser. He would've loaded his stuff into the truck, but with his window missing, he doesn't want to risk having what remains of his belongings swiped while he sits across the table from a handful of cops.

Cold air from the river sweeps in through the open window, and Harry and Greta get on the road to head to the Bed & Breakfast. The clock in the truck reads 2:35 a.m.

There's no one behind the desk when Harry pulls up outside the Sapphire on Poplar.

He comes up the front steps, and sees Kristin sitting on the couch, drinking a Diet Coke, paging through a magazine. He happens to glance down and notices a dead field mouse, tiny, on the doormat. One of the cats must've left it. He peers in at Kristin, and a chill lifts up the hairs on the back of his neck. He hasn't seen her since the moment they parted ways at the house. It's only been a couple days, but it feels like a year's passed.

Harry taps lightly and she stands up, shaking her head at him as she walks over. She's wearing a black Nike sweatshirt and a striped skirt over dark tights. No shoes. Kristin furrows her brow, and cracks the door.

"I can't let you in here, Harry. You need to leave. Now."

"Can you please just tell me what happened?"

"What do you mean, what *happened*? Everybody saw you."

"What are you talking about?" Harry looks over his shoulder. Greta's head is framed in the truck window, watching him at the door.

"Don't lie to me. I know you drove those two out of the party."

He stammers about not meaning to, that he'd panicked, that he couldn't get them out of the back of his truck, that they had the rifle, that a dog had bitten him. Harry kneels down on the stoop of the B&B and pulls his pant leg up to show her the plastic bag around the gauze on his ankle. She makes a face like he's trying to sell her a busted watch he found in the street.

Harry says, "I ditched them on the road. Why would I do that if I was trying to help them?"

Kristin's eyes are puffy, dark bags beneath them. Her eyes search his, considering.

"Tommy's been telling people that was your plan. So that you could all split up and head separate directions."

"*Plan*?" Harry says. "He's lying. I hardly knew who Tommy *was*. I spit in his eye and got the rifle from him and threw it into the fucking weeds. I bet he forgot to tell you that part. And that guy Don begged me not to leave them out there. Did Tommy mention that—Don whimpering and falling into the ditch?"

"Keep your voice down."

Harry turns again. Still no cars on the street. It's the quietest he's seen downtown Missoula. The traffic signal at the intersection of Taylor and Poplar just shifts through its colors for nothing.

Then Kristin speaks quietly, articulating each syllable with anger, "One of those assholes killed my cousin Lucy. So, I don't give a shit if you didn't *mean* to help them. I don't care if you all end up in jail together."

“I’m sorry,” Harry says. “I didn’t know. And Paul’s dad was following me. And then Paul was run down and—” Harry stops himself.

Kristin has tears in her eyes and she sighs. She opens the door and steps aside to let him into the warmth of the Sapphire’s lobby.

“Just for a minute. You can’t stay. I’ll get fired if I wake the guests. There’s been too much commotion around here already.”

One lamp is lit by the green sofa where Kristin’s been reading, two of the cats are curled up together on the pillow beside her spot.

“Did you tell Tommy where I was?”

“Why would I do that, Harry?”

“They trashed my dad’s cabin. I think that guy Frank figured it out somehow. He stole my ID when I was over at Providence for my leg.”

Kristin looks at Harry, but his words don’t seem to be landing. Her cousin is dead. Paul Tillett is dead. So what if they tipped over Harry’s dresser and smashed a few cereal bowls in his dad’s shitty cabin?

“I’m sorry about Paul,” Harry says. “And your cousin, Kristin. I didn’t know that.”

“Yeah well,” she says. “Me too, but…”

Her voice is hollowed out and small. Harry knows he should just give her a hug and leave, but there are still too many questions to answer before he can make his next move.

A red hatchback appears on the street outside, its stereo blasting Guns N’ Roses. Kristin and Harry both turn to look, and there’s a dull thump against the door, then a second louder smack. Harry's ducking down on the carpet. Kristin creeps over and peeks out. She opens the door.

"Kristin, what are you *doing*!?"

The car speeds off. Harry watches Kristin lean over and come up clutching two newspapers.

"That scared the living shit out of me."

"Every night that asshole bangs the door with these." Kristin pulls off the rubber bands and set the papers out on the coffee table.

Harry looks at the clock. Almost 4 a.m. When he glances outside, Greta's paws are up on the edge of the open window, like she wants to leap out.

"You should get out of here, Harry."

"You don't think Paul killed Lucy, right?"

"Fuck no," Kristin says. "But Paul had been arrested after Tommy and Don were. Tommy got out first because his uncle and his cousin Ian work for the state patrol. I guess they were all fighting over the gun after Tommy started waving it in people's faces. Everybody was telling him to stop and Tommy kept turning to whoever said anything and was pointing it at them, firing just over their shoulders. Finally, Paul tackled him, and there was a struggle over the rifle to get it away from Tommy. That's when everybody else rushed back toward the house."

"I saw Paul and his mom in the ER the morning after the party. Paul was lying to me for some reason. He said he'd hid out in the garage, but you and I saw him run into the field, after he'd been standing with that other guy."

"Curtis Beard," Kristin says. "He's a loser, but harmless."

"But why do you think Paul lied to me?"

"I don't know, Harry. I don't want to talk about this anymore." She sounds less angry now than exhausted. "You need to leave. I can't keep going over this shit with you."

Kristin looks through Harry's eyes to something else. He stands up from the couch, makes to go, but has to ask her:

"You think Tommy killed Paul?"

There's a long pause. Kristin sighs, finally meeting Harry's eyes.

"I saw Frank's shitty black Mazda out front, right where your truck is parked," she says. "He's been coming by here and just watching me through the window. Anyway, I hadn't heard about what happened to Paul yet, but I noticed Frank's headlight was smashed, the side mirror was hanging out of its socket. Then I heard that somebody ran Paul over in the street."

"If Frank and Tommy have been stalking you, why the hell are you working nights now?"

"Harry, the door of my apartment's like cardboard. Tommy's tried to kick it in before, and it opens right onto the street. I can't be alone there at night. Not that I can sleep anyways, so I might as well be getting paid. Here at least there are security cameras"—and Kristin points them out now, one by one—"on the porch, over the counter, in the stairs, out back, and a couple of others. Just in case."

"Fucking Christ. I gotta go to the police."

"Don't do that, Harry. Just go home. I know you don't think you did anything—and I believe you—but Tommy's lying about what happened. And the police already let him go. Who knows what kind of story he made up when they had him in custody. But if you drove them out of there, and if he and Frank killed Paul, which I'm pretty sure they did, then—"

"You're right," Harry says. "I'm just tired of hiding out and running."

Harry goes to the door and looks out in the street. Greta sees him and barks.

"What the hell are Tommy and Frank creeping around here for?"

"Somebody told Tommy," Kristin says, "that I'd been with you at the party, *Flowerboy*. But I guess that's my fault for telling you it was my birthday."

"It's not your fault," Harry says. "I'm sorry I left you there."

Kristin walks over and takes Harry's arm, squeezing it the same way she'd squeezed Paul's at the party, after she'd come down the back steps of the house.

Harry looks at Kristin. He doesn't want her to let go.

"They're just trying to scare you, Harry."

"I gathered that," he says, and hesitates. "Kristin, were you and Paul…?"

"No," she says, and she lets go of Harry's arm. "But we used to go out. Before Tommy."

Harry doesn't know what to say. He reaches for the door and the night air outside hits him. Kristin hugs her arms across her chest, shivers.

He looks into her eyes. "I'll see you later, okay?"

"I hope so. But, Harry, watch out for Frank Keene. That guy's a psycho."

BETSY

Harry knows that Flo-Ann's Diner opens at 5 a.m. to service the fishing crowd, and by the time he's walked Greta along the trail down on the Clark Fork and gotten over to Lester Street, all the lights are on in the restaurant and it's a quarter of.

Harry swaddles his dog up in her blankets on the front seat of the truck. When Linda spots him in the parking lot, she waves from inside, and unlocks the front doors.

"It's cold out here. Get inside, Harry."

He wants to hug her when she touches his shoulder as Harry comes in through the entry. He finds a booth in the back of the empty diner, gets his leg propped up on the plastic leather bench. One of the cooks he'd seen Calvin talking to the other day gives Harry a nod from the kitchen, as the cook yawns, covering his mouth with a fist.

Linda brings over a menu and a cup of coffee. The smell of her cigarettes and perfume floats over Harry, and he warms his hands over the steaming mug. He's trying not to rehearse what he'll say to the police, resolute that he'll go ahead and answer the detectives' questions as simply and as accurately as he can.

No hedging, no bullshit, no lies. And no more hiding out at Pat's cabin. No running away from what he needs to face up to. Maybe Kristin's right, but he can't keep staggering around like this—at some point he's going to lose his hold and sail his pickup over a cliff.

Even an animal has to give up eventually and confront whatever's hunting it.

Harry will tell the truth, exactly as everything transpired—regardless of the consequences. He's learned all the lessons he needs about sitting on the fence waiting for the right moment to lay his cards down.

And Calvin, Harry now prays to God, is correct: that, by volunteering his testimony to the officers across the table of some smoky interrogation room, Harry will be set free. Thanked profusely for cooperating with their investigation and aiding them in bringing the killer—or killers—to justice. Maybe he'd even have a claim to the reward money himself.

Harry pictures Tommy in his yellow hunting vest, screaming and thrashing the cabin's wooden furniture. Frank Keene kicking things over with his peeled boots. They either wanted to kill him or scare Harry out of town—perhaps they didn't really care which. Maybe they'd seen Harry with Paul Tillett. If they'd staked out Paul's house, they might've watched Harry follow Paul and his mother right into the Emergency Room. For all they knew, Paul had told Harry everything that had happened out in the field—and they have only to whack them both in order to kill the prosecution's flimsy case against Tommy.

Harry's whole body fills with a quick and passing doom, like a wind that spools through an alley, sucking up leaves and scraps of trash into a cyclone. The gust rearranges everything in the pull of its funnel and then, like that, it's gone. Some shit kickers get trigger-happy, kill a couple people, smash your life to pieces, and then vanish after the police collude behind locked doors.

"You want something to eat?" Linda says.

"Think I'll wait and see if Calvin shows up. I just called him on my cell."

Linda rolls her eyes and smiles.

"It's nice you've been keeping him company. He's had a rough go lately."

"Calvin?"

"Since everything with Lorine."

"Who's Lorine?"

"His wife. She took off with Randy Owen, one of Cal's fishing buddies. He's been down in the dumps, but embarrassed probably, so you didn't hear any of this from me."

"Gotcha."

"When Cal told me that your daddy asked him to look after you up here, it was the first time I'd seen him back to his old self, joking around, gabbing, telling tales."

"I had no idea."

Linda shakes her head. "We're no cakewalk, but men—you guys are clueless, aren't you?"

"Pretty much."

"What'd you do to your foot there?"

Harry's leg is still propped up on the booth, the bulk of the gauze exposed from his cut-open pant leg.

"I got bit by a puppy and fell in the mud."

"Lordy. You need something stronger than coffee? You look like shit—no offense."

"How about a shotgun and a bottle of bourbon?"

"Better ask Santa for those, if you've been good. If you haven't, then stay away from my daughters."

Linda snorts at her joke, and the bell on the diner's glass door jangles as Calvin Hogan, dressed in his snow camo one-piece and black combat boots, comes in, and spots Harry. Calvin's hair is wild, like he'd blown it dry and gave up half way through the job.

"Well, well, well…I don't know about you, Harrison, but I reckon it's time to wrap this debacle up and say *Feliz Navidad* once and for all."

A waft of Calvin—wet earth, Old Spice, and Herkimer—comes over Harry as Calvin slides into the booth. For a moment, Harry feels that he'll make it out of Montana with his dog alive, and with all his limbs more or less attached.

"Now what debacle would that be?" Linda says, pouring Calvin a cup of coffee.

"Can't tell you, darlin'," Calvin says. "Not unless you know the secret handshake."

"I got your secret handshake right here," she says and flips Calvin the bird. "Did you find your mom yet, Harry?"

"What was that?"

"I said, '*Do you need a warm up there*?'" And she refills Harry's mug without waiting for his answer.

"Sorry, I must've misheard you."

"Get your mind out of the gutter, young man. Been hanging out with Calvin Hogan too long, by the smell of things."

Calvin taps his temple. "You do *not* wanna know what goes on up in this playpen, pretty lady."

"Put a cork in it," Linda says, and walks back into the kitchen.

Harry glances out to the parking lot where a family of four has parked their minivan next to Harry's truck. Greta pops her head out of the open window as a boy and girl come over to talk to her and pat her head. Their father has a bushy goatee and wears a plaid shirt. He looks familiar to Harry.

"You recognize that guy?"

Calvin makes a big show of turning around as the family comes into Flo-Ann's, and the hostess leads them to another booth.

"Never seen him before in my life—why?"

"I don't know," Harry says, trying not to stare.

Harry lets Calvin know what Kristin's told him about the party, Tommy, Paul and, Frank's smashed black Mazda, the dangling side mirror—all of it.

"Yeah, well, I think Kris might've shot the girl."

"Calvin, the dead girl's her cousin Lucy. And anyhow, I saw her run into the house. It wasn't Kristin. I was with her."

"You don't think Paul died protecting Kris? She say anything about Paul being in love with her?"

"She mentioned they used to date before Tommy. That was all."

Calvin shrugs. "Tonya Tillett said Kris was her boy's one and only true love. So, she might've been in this sandwich somewhere closer to the meat."

But Harry had seen Kristin's eyes. They weren't the eyes of somebody lying, he knew that much. Harry is hoping that Calvin's just heartbroken himself, and that he wants a woman to be the one responsible for all this.

"Calvin, before I head over to the police station, I need you to level with me and tell me whatever you know about my mom. I found out that she was in the hospital. A few times before she died. I just don't know what for."

"Yeah, I talked to your old man last night. He's not doing too good, Harrison. You might give him a ring yourself one of these days. Just FYI. Sounds like he's back in the hospital himself. Hasn't been let home in over a week. Says your, um, Sally's not doing so hot either."

"Shit. I'll give them a call."

Calvin lets out a big sigh, like he doesn't want to go on, looking around the diner.

"Actually, now's not really the time, Harry. It's just—"

"Please."

"Alright, don't bite my head off. Remember, you *asked*."

Judging by the look on Calvin's face—some mix of trepidation and defeat—Harry's not ready, but he thinks of Adrienne. And it's more than enough reason to insist that Calvin spill what he knows now.

"Basically, your mother was driving us home. She was stone sober, but the rest of us—Pat was up in the front and I was in the back with Ginny—and we'd been dog paddling up to our earlobes in Mai Tais and jungle punch and just nasty stuff at the Brunswick, where your dad had the night off.

"Your mom and Pat were celebrating with us after me and Virginia tied the knot. It was Halloween of '79, but already there was ice on the roads, especially at night. I think you and your sister must've been with Betsy's friend Carol. I don't recall.

"Anyways, it was dark on the interstate, but the headlights picked it out standing right in the road—a small fox, not even full-grown. And the fox went this way and then, I don't know why, it decided to do a U-turn, and doubled back.

"So, your mother swerved to miss it, then must've overcorrected, and we went through the guardrail and turned over a couple of times in the Malibu. Slid into the ravine, down to the Clark Fork, stopped in the trees about twenty feet shy of the water. Your mother, well, you know what happened. We were all three of us drunk as shit, and that was how come we took the impact okay, I guess. Just dumb luck. Your dad broke his leg so bad the bone popped through. But Ginny and me in the back were fine. We felt truly awful, Harry.

"When Ginny and I clambered back up to the road for help, we saw the animal struck down in the road. Your dad must've noticed it too—but we never said anything about it, given the circumstances with your mother and what not. Anyways, they got the jaws of life down there. Managed to get Betsy out of the Malibu, god knows how. She was scratched up pretty bad. Spent a night on life support over at Providence. But there was hemorrhaging from the impact. Nobody wore seatbelts back then, Harrison. That was it. We thought she'd pull through, but we had to let her go. And she died in the hospital."

For a second Harry thinks there must have been a mistake. Her name was Elizabeth, and he'd never heard her called anything else.

"Betsy?" Harrys says.

"Yeah," Calvin says. "She—we smashed into a couple of cottonwoods as the Malibu turned over and she got crushed behind the wheel. Your dad stayed down in the ravine with her, until the paramedics arrived—but it was another hour probably before they could saw her out of the wreck. Harry, you know, brain-wise she probably didn't survive the collision, if you get me."

Harry hadn't even known it was a car crash, never mind the fact that it had happened half-way down the road to Rock Creek, a few miles from where Harry had been pulled over on the interstate after leaving Marty's Mart after the party.

He hadn't known that his dad or anybody else had been with her. Nothing. Pat had told Harry and Adrienne that he'd gotten the scar on his leg in the war.

They called her Betsy, though. Not Elizabeth.

"Is that it?"

"That's all I got, bud. I'm sorry."

"She'd never been sick before that?"

"Not to my knowledge, but I steer clear of hospitals, as you know. They're vectors of putrid—"

"Thanks for telling me. Seriously."

Calvin blows his nose into a napkin with a terrific honk.

"You might look up that gal Carol. She knew your mom from her school days."

"Carol who?"

"I'll try and remember for you, bud. I'm sorry. You got me a little frazzled here."

Calvin dabs a napkin at the corner of his eye and glares out the window. Harry downs the rest of his coffee and gets up, and rests his hand on Calvin's shoulder.

"Thanks, Calvin. I mean it. I can finally let Adrienne know."

Calvin says nothing, just stares off into the parking lot.

Harry hobbles through the diner, now filling up with all the morning locals. He decides to save the battery on his cell, so he uses the payphone by the toilets to call Adrienne, but it's barely 6 a.m. and she must be sound asleep. Still dark in L.A., where it's an hour earlier. Harry leaves her a short message, that Calvin said their mom had been in a car crash, and it wasn't some disease. That she can relax, that even if Pat had lied, he didn't have anything to do it with it. And Calvin was in the crash himself, so they could trust him. Before he hangs up, he says he's going to go talk to the police, and that he loves her.

When Harry limps out of the bathroom a few minutes later, he's feeling better. At least something—bad as it was—had surfaced. Been released, even. And he knows Adrienne will be grateful to find out. Harry doesn't know why Pat lied to them, but he's just grateful it wasn't his dad's fault, as he'd come to fear. And she *had* died in the hospital after all. That must've been what John discovered after his friend dug up the old files out in some storage facility. But John said there'd been a few dates prior to the crash—or was it several?—Harry couldn't remember. Regardless, it was over.

Betsy, Harry thinks. *Betsy.*

For some reason just hearing his mother's nickname settles something deep in him—and if he's not happy, exactly, he feels relief. Like he'd gotten to know her a tiny bit. He wants to study the picture of her in his wallet—his mother sitting next to her friend, smoking on the porch, watching him and Adrienne play in the sprinkler—but it's back in the cabin, tucked inside Harry's passport for safe keeping.

Limping back through the diner, Harry realizes who the guy with the bushy goatee is. It's the same one who'd taught the squirrel to waterski. He and Calvin had seen him on the evening news with Silas over at the Trapper.

Harry's grinning now, thinking Calvin's going to love this, as he's shambling past the booths, but Harry sees that there are two men sitting with Calvin in Harry's spot now. At first he thinks a couple of the cooks have just slid in to chat up Cal on their break, but it's Tommy in his yellow vest and Frank Keene, his dark hair drawn back into a ponytail under his Stetson.

Harry wheels around, and moves through the front doors, staggering quickly across the parking lot. Through the windows, he sees both Tommy and Frank get out of the booth and walk at a clip toward the front entrance. Calvin gets out to the lot before either of them do—he must've slipped through the kitchen out a back door—and Cal's shouting as Harry fumbles with the truck keys.

Greta's spooked and barking like mad now, and it keeps Harry from hearing whatever Calvin's shouting other than the word "police." Tommy and Frank emerge from Flo-Ann's, but just stand there watching Harry put the truck in gear.

As he tears out of the parking lot, Harry sees a black Mazda with a smashed headlight through the open window. But its side mirror isn't dangling. It's gone.

Harry rolls his truck to a stop out front of the police precinct on Ryman Street to stall for a minute.

He's not ready for this, but he knows he doesn't have much choice. There's nobody in his rearview mirror now. It's just after six in the morning, and the sun's come up. Two women, one in jeans and a sweatshirt, the other in black pants and a yellow blouse, are making their way up the steps, chatting. Harry studies the women, thinking the one in jeans might be Paul Tillett's mother Tonya. He remembers Calvin saying that Tonya thought Kristin was Paul's true love, and he'd seen how Paul had looked at her when Kristin came down the back steps of the house, just before setting her rifle aside.

Hello, Lovely.

A black police van appears behind his pickup and beeps twice. Harry flinches.

He pulls around the block and again comes up in front of the quiet building, the two women he'd seen now gone inside. Harry eases into one of the twenty-minute Visitor Parking Only spots and puts the truck in park. Greta sits up in the seat and looks out her window.

There's no sign of Frank's Mazda. And Harry's nestled in right up front, next to a patrol car. So, if they're going to try and run him over, this would be a fairly conspicuous spot to do it. But those two hadn't even tried to get out of the parking lot to give chase.

There are police cruisers and unmarked blazers and a big white and blue paddy wagon in adjacent spots all around Harry's truck. Greta looks at Harry and he puts his hand on her warm neck, but he keeps the engine on. He sits there watching the front of the precinct building, its boxy hedgerow outlining the black steel and glass entrance that looks as if it leads into the drab lobby of a local bank.

One police officer comes out of the main entrance. He pauses on the steps to answer a call on his mobile phone. The officer stands stoically, parted black hair and blue uniform, listening. He doesn't appear to have noticed Harry watching him, and Harry decides to wait for him to go back inside and then Harry will follow him up the steps himself. That will be Harry's cue to end this thing once and for all.

The cop is young, maybe twenty-two—much too young, Harry thinks, to be a police officer. He's clean-shaven and has the pleasant yet eager-looking smile of somebody who hasn't seen much bloodshed but who's anxious to jump into a squad car and flip on the lights.

"Stop dithering, Harry. Get off the fucking fence and go inside."

Harry watches as the officer on the steps draws the back of his free hand along his clean-shaven neck, perhaps feeling the recent growth that's come in. The kid looks off into the distance, immersed in whatever the caller's saying. Harry begins to mime the policeman's actions and puts the back of his own hand to his neck this way, and when Harry grazes his face he finds several days' worth of heavy stubble.

He reaches up and draws down the visor, finding himself in the small mirror there. His eyes are hollowed out, glassy. Harry's face appears both puffy and sunken somehow—like he's been inflated and then popped after having over-swelled. And he looks to have aged about five years in as many days.

"Okay, Greta, I gotta go face the music."

She's nestled into her blankets, and Harry gives her a few parting scratches behind the ear. He reaches over to unbuckle his seatbelt, when he hears the young cop on the steps begin to laugh.

The cop looks over at Harry for the first time as he chuckles easily, his shoulders quaking with laughter. Then he's doubled over. The guy's laughing so hard he can barely hold the phone to his ear. Harry watches this young cop come apart at the telling of some hysterical joke on the other end. He actually has to draw the tears away from the corners of his eyes, switching the phone to his free hand to do this with both of his forefingers, one and then the other.

The cop's just standing there now, his cheeks flushed from raucous laughter, wearing the serene and galled look of a person who's been dismantled by the hilarity of some magnificent story. The cop again looks at Harry, but this time he keeps looking.

Harry watches as the officer slips his phone into his back pocket and begins to walk toward the truck. At that moment, Harry knows: this is Tommy's cousin Ian.

The cop's jogging down the steps, right toward Harry, watching his black shoes and glancing up, and he raises one of his arms up into the air, his hand waving, flagging, but he doesn't call out. Harry feels that old flare of tobacco juice catch fire in his stomach, and all the blood goes into his fists.

Harry opens the door and swings out his bad leg, and then he lifts it back in and re-closes the door and freezes for a moment. The young cop's shuffling down the last steps and starts yelling. As he nears Harry's truck, the cop unhooks the black CB radio fastened to his shoulder and brings it up to his mouth without taking his eyes off Harry.

Harry puts the truck in reverse, turns around, and pulls out of the parking spot too quickly, smashing his rear bumper into a parked police cruiser on the opposite side of the street.

Greta sits up and barks out of her open window. Harry puts the truck in drive, and speeds against gravity up to the traffic light ahead. The signal's red but the intersection is empty, and he passes right through it. Then Harry floors it to the next signal, where he again slows toward its red light down to a guarded roll, and feels as though he's floating dangerously out of control now, as if in a dream of flying. When the cross traffic's cleared, Harry veers around a white sedan in front of the truck and proceeds through that red light also. He hears the driver shout from her car, which is followed by the long blat of a horn.

The next two lights are green, and Harry speeds through them going close to fifty. He then turns hard, cranking the wheel, onto the interstate ramp and speeds up to the empty highway, heading east, back to Rock Creek. A gleaming silver semi lumbers up behind him in the same lane, blocking out everything else in his mirrors.

There are a few cars beyond Harry's windshield, but no police.

No lights. No sirens. Not yet.

It's still early for much traffic, and the freeway's open. Harry knows the route well, and soon enough he's flying past Marty's Mart where he'd washed out his bite wound in that grimy sink.

Harry keeps hearing sirens behind him, but none appear in his mirrors. And he remembers the police cruisers burning by that night as he stood with those kids next to the stacks of firewood. Now there's only an occasional Mack truck in the opposite lane, and Harry keeps his eyes glued to the rearview mirror.

He has time now to mentally rehearse his next movements exactly and to solidify their precise order: He'll pull into the gravel driveway of the cabin, and—with the truck running—he'll grab Greta's food and dishes and his duffel bag, which is packed by the entry. Then Harry will quickly swing the door shut, lock it, and replace the key under the bucket outside, not forgetting to turn down the dial of the pilot light on the old water tank out by the trash cans.

He'll then hop back into his truck, reverse onto the creek road, and speed out to I-90, vanishing down some oblique southern route to avoid suspicion on the interstate where most of the patrol cars should be lurking.

As Harry approaches the exit for Rock Creek, he feels his foot easing off the gas, the truck slowing, and he glides up onto the ramp that leads to the road out to the cabin, clocking the spot where that coyote had been struck down shortly before he'd arrived—its carcass replaced now by a faded stain. The wind eases through the shot-out window as Greta monitors everything from the bed Harry's made for her on the passenger seat.

FRANK

Harry feels that clump of tobacco acid burning in the pit of his stomach as he and Greta roll over the muddy road out to the cabin for the last time.

It's started to drizzle again, and he can smell diesel as they pass the muddy lot of the Trapper. There's wet pine, too, and that clean, almost metallic scent from the river beyond the trees Harry keeps getting flashes of through the rain and foliage.

About halfway out, at a turn below the cliffs of a rocky ledge, a herd of bighorn sheep is in the road, grazing the wet grass on either side. There must be twenty-five or thirty of them. Their eyes strange slits, horns curled around the heads of the males beautifully. Mouths white, like they'd been eating out of yogurt cups. The kids—sand-colored, with tiny black noses—are huddled close to the females, as the mature adults stand sentinel, still as lawn statues, eyeballing Harry through the drizzle.

He honks three or four times, but they don't budge. To his left, sits an abandoned log cabin, the meadow grass high around a dilapidated riverboat, its tarp puddled with rain.

With the road blocked—and still nobody behind him—Harry has a moment to remember the first evening he'd driven out to the cabin, when Calvin told him if he was on the road early enough, he might see a few up on the boulders above.

Dawn. Right.

They'd called his mother Betsy, and she'd sustained life-ending injuries within a few miles of where Harry's idling. He gets the sudden urge to locate the spot where the four of them had gone through the guardrail in the Malibu, to bring flowers to it, to climb down into the rocky ravine, poke around for an old bracelet, a shard of glass—anything. Harry could sit down on the bank of the Clark Fork River, and say goodbye to his mother.

Greta must've smelled the bighorns. She's sitting up on the passenger seat to sniff the rainy air carrying their odor into the truck through her window. She barks twice, wanting to get out. This spooks the sheep, and they trot off quickly, all at once, and the road is clear.

When Harry pulls his pickup into the driveway, the black Mazda is there, waiting.

Frank Keene emerges slowly from the driver's side and Tommy opens his door and waves at Harry, like this had all been arranged, and they can go ahead and start their picnic now. Harry reaches for his cell to call the police, but there's no service out here and he sets it down.

There are many things Harry can do, and they fly through his mind one after the other: Smash their car and perhaps maim them both. Pull back out and drive down the road as fast as he can. Run over to George Willis's place and see if he can clamber over his iron gate and scream at the old guy for help.

But these two have probably already killed one person with that car, and it would be foolish for Harry to assume that the rifle he himself had thrown into the road wasn't also waiting inside the Mazda, or tucked under the length of Frank's black coat. And if Harry did manage to get down the road a ways, they'd have no problem running his truck off the highway, nudging him and Greta down into the same ravine the Malibu had crashed through. And Frank and Tommy would probably make it look like an accident anyhow.

As he sits there in his truck next to Greta, everything stills inside him. He doesn't want to scream out or plead with them. He doesn't even want to kill them or run.

He wants to talk.

And he wants this all to end, even if it means getting shot in the rain only to bleed to death right here in the muddy driveway of his dad's cabin.

Frank's wearing his peeling boots, his Stetson, and his long hair sticks to the sides of his face. Tommy has on his yellow vest and jeans. His hiking boots are filthy, rimed with mud. Through the truck's foggy windshield, Tommy's vest looks stained with something, blood maybe. Greta's quiet now, breathing with her mouth open, and she's looking out the window, back at the road for some reason, and she starts sniffing the air again.

Harry shuts off the engine and gets out, remembering his wound suddenly as he sets his boot into the gravel. Tommy takes a step forward, eyeing Harry.

"My cousin called and said his buddy watched somebody smash right into his cruiser. Was that you, Harry?"

"I don't have much to eat," Harry says. "A bear came in the other night. Got my food."

Tommy grins and looks at Frank and shakes his head

at Harry. Tommy's younger than Harry remembered. But there's something sad and unhinged about him. Like Tommy didn't particularly want to have to kill what he touched, like it was some curse he was trying to figure out how to live with. Harry remembers Kristin telling him that Tommy had been pointing the rifle at people and firing it just over their shoulders for a laugh.

"That was your truck, wasn't it, Harry?"

"Must've been somebody else," Harry says. "I was at the library. Checking my email."

Tommy fakes a little *ha-ha* laugh, which is scarier than him actually laughing.

Frank says nothing, just leans against the back of his wet car, crosses his legs. Harry makes a motion to follow him and he starts limping toward the cabin door.

"Come on in, fellas. You want some coffee? I don't have any cream or sugar. Bear got those too."

He walks by Tommy, avoiding the little guy's eyes, and takes in the smell of something wretched off of him, like human shit and putrefaction.

He gets the cabin door open. Harry's bag, passport, Greta's bowl and food—everything's right where he'd left it, ready to go.

Tommy pops his head in, looking around for the ambush. Harry recalls the mop clumped together in the closet and actually smiles to himself.

"You're all packed up, Harry. Where you off to?"

"I'm not kidding. A little black bear got in here the other day, tore this place up. Scared the hair off my head. I'm from Denver. We don't have shit like that in Denver."

Harry hobbles into the kitchen to get a glass of water, and when he turns, the two of them are both standing inside the cabin—between him and the door, which Tommy pushes shut and leans himself against. There's a bluish bruise under his eye, a scab on his jaw.

The bad smell coming from Tommy is now inside the cabin.

"You roll around in something dead?" Harry says.

"You ever been to jail, Harry?" Tommy cocks his head to one side.

"What can I do for you guys?"

Frank tips his hat back, looks around, and then sits down on the edge of the bed, opens up the *Playboy*, and starts paging through it. He still hasn't uttered a word.

Tommy picks up the passport and dangles it at Harry, as though he's holding a dead bird by its wing—the hundred-dollar bill and picture of Harry's mother both flutter out like leaves.

"I know you killed that girl"—and Tommy pauses to read—"Harrison Patrick Stables, born Christmas Eve, 1977, in Missoula, Montana."

"Did I kill Paul Tillett too? Because then I'd be in some real trouble."

Frank looks up at Harry, and over at Tommy. He sets down the magazine. Tommy drops the passport to the floor.

"If you're so innocent," Tommy says, "then why'd you smash your pickup into a cop car? You think they don't have cameras outside the station? My cousin told me they got pictures of you in your truck. Says they can see your red dog in the seat right next to you."

"What does that prove, exactly?" Harry says, the heat rising from his chest to his face now. "That I'm bad at merging into traffic from an angled parking spot?"

"Harry, when you ran from the party, Don and I tried to jump into your truck—to apprehend the shooter making his getaway."

"Okay, here we go," Harry says. "Then what?"

Tommy unzips his yellow vest and zips it back up to his neck, nervously, but he has a boyish smile on his face now, his pink gums visible.

"Then you ditched the Ruger—the one they've discovered with your fingerprints on it—and you've been on the run ever since."

"That rifle had ten people's hands on it," Harry says.

"Who was the last one to touch it though? Who tossed it into the bushes?"

Tommy keeps zipping and unzipping his vest, and Harry wants him to stop doing that.

"Go fuck yourself, Tommy."

"You think me and Don were dumb enough to handle that rifle after you winged it out of your truck? Harry, listen to me. You screwed up this morning when you smashed that cop car. So, now you're gonna do me a little favor, and I won't have t—"

Frank gets up and looks out the window. Harry hears Greta start to bark from the driveway.

"Won't have to what?" Harry says.

Tires over wet gravel. A silver truck is pulling in behind Harry's pickup.

"Who is it, Frank?" Tommy says. Frank is peeking out the

other window now.

"The muffin man?" Harry says.

Frank walks over and ducks himself into the closet, pulling the door shut.

Harry considers the bathroom, but stays put. He doesn't want the cops to gun him down at an accidental flush of the toilet.

The cabin door opens about half way, and Tommy takes a few steps back, bumping into the bed frame.

Greg Tillett—with his big beard, and brown hair all over his shoulders—pokes his head in. He's holding a very long shotgun in one hand.

Greg has red welts under his eyes and a wad of tobacco protrudes from his lower lip. His orange flannel shirt is wet with rain, and he has on sagging gray sweats tucked into knee-high rubber boots coated in mud. Harry sees his eyes squinch up at the smell in the cabin. Greg wrinkles his nose, and looks Tommy over with revulsion.

"Who drives the Mazda?" Greg says, his voice throaty and low.

He looks at Harry. Harry shakes his head and says nothing. He wants to tell him Frank's in the closet, but doesn't want Frank to shoot if he's got a gun in there with him. Greg turns to face Tommy and pushes the door all the way open with the shotgun's long barrel, and then Greg tilts his head toward the driveway, like he's trying to get water out of his ear.

"That your black car right there?"

Greg spits out into the driveway, a long rope, landing with a splash, and wipes his beard with the length of his arm. Harry's stomach is full of moths, battering to get out.

Tommy says nothing, but his mouth hangs open.

"I said: *Whose car is that*?!"

"Not mine," Tommy says, softly. "That's Frank's car."

Tommy points to the closet with his finger. The door of the closet swings open, like Tommy's done a magic trick. This spooks Greg. And he turns and levels the shotgun at the door, as Frank steps forward. Greg Tillett shoots him in the chest and then again in the head, splitting open his face. Frank's brain spatters onto the cabin wall. His body slumps down and then tips over like a cow's carcass slipping off a hook. Its thump brings the mop out of the closet, the long handle of which falls in slow motion, landing across Frank's twitching leg.

There's only a chin and a neck there now. Blood on the wall, the mattress, splattered onto the *Playboy*. Some fleshy part of Frank—his cheek or ear—is in Greta's empty food dish.

Tommy leaps over the bed and flattens himself down to get under it. A waft of Tommy's shit odor comes out into the cabin, effulgent. Without realizing it, Harry had evidently just sat himself down on his ass in the kitchenette, frozen, unable to take air.

He hears Greg Tillett turn and go out, crunching over the driveway's gravel, leaving a vapor of gunpowder in the cabin. Tommy is hyperventilating under the mattress, and after a moment Harry gets himself up and limps slowly to the open door, peeking out at the vehicles in the drizzle. Greg's behind the wheel of his pickup and rolling backwards up onto the road.

Harry looks back, and sees his emergency hundred-dollar bill under part of what must be Frank's scalp. Tommy gets out from under the bed and his eyes are all over his friend's corpse.

Harry reaches for the mop, takes it up in both hands and breaks its wooden handle over his knee. It splits unevenly in two, making splintery blades where it's cracked on either side, and Harry drops the mop-half back to the floor. He takes a deep breath, squeezing the spear-half of the handle in his fist, and turns toward Tommy, who's now gotten up onto the bed, to make himself taller than Harry.

"Harry," Tommy says. "Hang on a second, man. We can both—"

Harry shakes his head. He aims his weapon at Tommy.

"Say one more word to me and I will run this thing through your fucking throat."

Harry's gripping it overhand now, ready to drive it in like an icepick. His knuckles are white and he stares into Tommy's shifting eyes.

Tommy stands there on the mattress, with his arms out, his smile gone. Harry sees tiny flecks of what must be Frank's blood spatter on the side of Tommy's face.

Not taking his eyes off him, Harry leans down and, with his free hand, grabs his passport and the picture of his mother off the floor, and slips them into his back pocket. Then he gets ahold of his blood-dotted duffel bag by the door, and—still brandishing the splintered mop handle in his good hand—hobbles backward out of the cabin. He turns and limps over the muddy driveway and sees that Greta's still sitting up in the front seat of the truck.

Greg's silver pickup is long gone. Harry squats down by the Mazda's rear wheel and stabs the sharp end of the mop handle through the rubber tire. It ruptures with a farting hiss and the back end of the Mazda sags down as the tire deflates. He leaves it sticking out like a knife and staggers over the gravel to his truck.

Harry throws his bag behind the seat, climbs into the cab, and pulls the door shut.

Tommy appears in the cabin's doorway as Harry gets the key into the ignition, and he watches Tommy scramble to his knees, then yank the mop handle out of the Mazda's flattened tire.

Harry puts the truck in reverse, and Greta begins to bark and bark and bark through her open window as Tommy runs toward the truck. Harry rolls back up to the dirt of the 102, and they head north out of Rock Creek, Tommy shrinking on the road in Harry's rearview mirror.

We often meet our destiny on the road
we take to avoid it.

—Jean de La Fontaine

PART 3
ON THE RUN

DARBY & TENDOY

Harry slows through the towns of Lolo, Victor, Corvallis, and stops for the first time in the hamlet of Darby when his truck is nearly out of gas.

He'd taken a sleepy highway off of the interstate out of Missoula to head south toward Pocatello. He hasn't even made it over the Idaho border, and the tiny service station in Darby is so rustic, there are only two pumps on either side of its ancient metallic gauges. The glass is a spider web of cracks over the meter. Its numbers lurch up like one of those vintage alarm clock's flipping digits.

A bald man in bib overalls comes out from the lamplit insides of the station garage. He appears to have been working on an engine block of some sort, though there's no vehicle in sight, only the rusted-out shells of old-timey cars sleeping in the big weeds, which grow up around their pillowy-looking fenders.

"I'll pump it," he says, his voice quick and nasal, like a preacher's.

"That's okay," Harry says. "I don't mind."

The man comes over, licking at a cut on his bottom lip, and sets his hands on his wide hips. Harry furrows his brow, and then simply turns his back to him to look in at Greta who's stood herself up in the front seat. Harry studies the black dots of dried blood on her snout and she lets out a happy bark. Harry glares at her. When he goes for the squeegee in a bucket, Harry can feel the man behind him, waiting.

"Go on, let your doggie out," he says. "I'll do your windows."

Harry avoids his eyes, but thanks him and then walks Greta across the road where she shits merrily into the drainage ditch.

"He had to go!" the man calls to Harry, eyeballing.

Harry nods, curses under his breath.

He begins to think that maybe he's slipped free of Missoula, and that young cop at the precinct is suddenly a flailing joker in Harry's mind. He imagines the cop slipping on the steps, summersaulting like Buster Keaton down the stairs. And the gore in Pat's cabin—that thought alone sends adrenaline screaming through his blood. But he pictures Tommy suspended like Rod's tiny metal figurine on the road. His arms out. Frank's blood on the side of his face.

A sigh like an evening glow comes out of Harry then, and he shakes his head in the sun, which he hadn't realized had emerged from the heavy clouds. He tugs on Greta's lead after she bites at a hunk of tree bark. When they come back over, the station attendant's holding the squeegee, mid-windshield.

"What do you call him?"

Harry tells him Greta and the man asks to hear it again. His belly is pressing into the side of the pickup as he washes the glass. Harry notices the man's white shirt under his overalls coming up to reveal long scars on his gut as Harry opens the door and Greta jumps back up onto the waterlogged seat he's recovered with blankets. When the man finishes, he leans in to pet Greta, making a babyish goo-goo sound that puts the hair on Harry's neck up.

Bells jangle on the door and the man holds it for Harry with his elbow. A car passes on the highway, and Harry turns to watch it disappear into the distance.

The man swipes the credit card on one of those manual sliders, and Harry studies his oily fingers and nail beds, which must have been fiddling with wrecked engines for half a century. Greta's head is poked out of the open window, her tongue lolling free. Harry tells the man that he couldn't help noticing the scars on his belly and asks him what happened, if he doesn't mind saying.

The man wets his fingers in his mouth by drawing his lower lip down and works at separating the duplicated charge card receipt.

"Rudy," he says. "My uncle's pet bear over in Dillon. Uncle Jim bought him at auction after they retired Rudy from the state fair in Great Falls. Called him Rudy Blue Bear, but he was a regular brown. They used to spray his coat with some kind of dye. Smelled like a bad onion.

"Anyhow, when I was about ten years old, me and my baby brother were teasing Rudy. And Rudy Bear thought that wasn't much fun. I was waggling my jelly sandwich at him."

"He swiped at you?"

"Only after Roy gave me a nudge and Rudy swatted through my front half. Doctor up in Helena said I was lucky that my innards didn't slide free."

"Jesus, your brother must've felt awful."

"He didn't come back from Korea, so he don't have opinions on it."

The man's eyebrows go up, and he looks over Harry's

shoulder. A dull tubular bell rings, and then the man waves to somebody pulling in. Harry turns to see a sheriff's Blazer ease into the near drive, this side of the gas pump. Terror spills through him. The cop in the passenger seat looks in at the station owner and Harry.

Harry isn't sure whether to go back out yet or stall at the counter.

"Where you headed?"

"South," Harry says.

"You got a fly rod out in that truck?"

Harry says he does. His heart is trying to leave his throat.

"You'll wanna head over to Tin Cup Creek, off the Bitterroot. Make a left on Miles Avenue. Then hang a right onto Water Street and follow it out till you pretty much smack into the crick."

Harry makes a show of using a scrap of paper off the counter to write this all down. The station owner watches him, repeating the directions, adding details. Harry shakes it wildly but the pen's dead. He takes up another from the counter, starts jotting down things the owner's saying. A reservoir on somebody's property he'll need permission to fish. Further out on the river, but it's stinking full of trout: browns and cutthroats and rainbows. Harry writes down "stinking rainbows." The man tells Harry to ring the buzzer on the porch and let the old guy know that Bill sent him.

"He's got a red hound dog like your Grendel," Bill says.

Harry glances back over his shoulder. The cops are chatting and the taller one is peering through his aviators into the truck's open window where Greta's set up.

Harry starts collecting a few things to stall.

He pays in cash for a big cup of coffee and a gallon jug of water, a bag of corn nuts, and even tongs a hotdog off the rotisserie.

Harry comes out with an armload and he watches the skinny cop's hand reach through the truck's window where the top of Greta's head presses up at it for a scratch.

"You got a fine birddog here," he says.

"Oh, yeah. She's—*big time.*" And with that, Harry stuffs half of the hotdog into his mouth, bites down, chews.

The cop takes Harry in through his dark glasses.

"You hunt pheasants with her?"

Harry shakes his head, gets the door open. But the cop follows him around to the driver's side.

"Grouse or what?"

Harry's scalp and face flush with heat.

He swallows. "Wild, uh, turkey hawks."

He reaches over the side mirror for the coffee he'd set on the hood, but halfway into sitting back down the Styrofoam cup splits inward and pushes out steaming coffee, pouring it onto Harry's lap. He cries out, scalded in his crotch.

"You okay, bud?"

"*Ow*, shit—"

The stockier officer is at the window patting Greta now and when he sees what Harry's done, he comes around the front with a big flag of blue paper towels in his hand.

Harry takes the bunched wad from him and presses it all down into the hot stain on his jeans and starts to dab at the zipper area. He has to sit up when a pool of coffee puddles under him, and Harry wipes at that like he's soiled himself.

The cops watch him. "Thanks a lot," Harry says.

He starts the engine, smiles at them both with hotdog bun gunked in his teeth, and trains his head forward like he's all set to pull out.

The taller cop nods, heads inside, his tight slacks up over his ankles.

"You like this thing?" Handlebar says. "My brother-in-law's got an older model and says it's always double-clutching on him. Course, he's a moron so there's that."

The cop laughs a dry sort of vacuum-packed *hee-hee-hee*. How many unlucky assholes had heard that getting shoved into his Blazer?

"Yeah," Harry says. "I like it alright."

He isn't sure that his plumbing's not burnt off, and this cop is smiling at him with the sun glinting off his long mustache whiskers.

"Before you go, we're canvassing the county. You seen any suspicious characters?"

Harry gives him an empty look, but his eyes bounce all over the cop's face, which is inches from Harry's. The cop's breath is weak garlic and he rests his elbow on Harry's side mirror, reaches into his back pocket and pulls out a sheet of paper. Begins unfolding it.

Harry glances over to the station's office, where Tight Pants is now chatting up Bill inside.

Harry squints thoughtfully and squeezes his mouth shut. It's a black and white photograph of a younger Tommy, but it's him alright.

"Oh *yeah*…" Harry says, adding a little too much gee-wiz

to it. "I think I saw this guy on the news the other day."

The policeman tucks the Xerox back into his pocket before Harry can glean any stats below the photo.

"What'd he do exactly?"

"Shot a girl at a party. Outside Missoula."

"A girl?"

"Yeah, well, just barely eighteen. So, technically a woman. But she wasn't even out of high school. Indian girl. He's wanted in connection with a number of other violent crimes. Highly dangerous individual."

He tells Harry to call in if he spots the assailant and Harry promises he will.

"We're off to the races," the cop says, giving Harry a nod and starts away.

"Hope you catch that stubby-ass motherfucker."

"What's that?" he says, coming back around.

"Sorry, I just meant shooting a girl and everything."

"Mind if I take a peek at your ID?"

"I'm not really from here," Harry says.

"We saw your plates."

"Cool."

The officer leans into the cab and looks over the back seat. Harry pulls the wallet out of his jeans pocket. He's burned on his thigh and the moist denim chafes where the coffee's scalded him.

"What happened to Bowser here?"

"Porcupine," Harry says and they both look at Greta, her tiny black scabs visible in the red fur of her nose and neck.

There's that folded scrap in his wallet: *GET THE FUCK*

OUT OF MONTANA.

"I, uh, lost it," Harry says.

"Well that's no good now, is it? Wait right here."

Greta's breathing happily. There's white spittle on her tongue as it falls out of the side of her open mouth. She's made so many new friends this morning!

Handlebar gets back behind the wheel of the Blazer, and Harry watches as the officer's hand takes the CB receiver up to his mouth just like that cop on the precinct steps had done.

Harry's head is screaming at him to pull out of here. He looks out on the road and hears faint sirens. Harry's sure he's delusional or just paranoid, but he puts the truck in gear and then back into park and tries to keep breathing.

His heart is whapping the bottom of his throat like a clubbed fish. He hears it again. A far-off siren. It grows louder in his brain, and then he sees Greta's ears perk up too.

The sheriff's engine turns over and the skinny cop inside the store dashes back out in long strides. Harry puts his truck in gear once more and waits. Two cop cars speed by going north out on the highway, back up toward Missoula, and the sheriff's Blazer tears out of the lot and veers back onto the road following them. An ambulance trails them all and Greta then joins the piercing sirens, howling out through the open window and Harry pulls his pickup out of the station and heads the opposite direction, toward Idaho.

Harry doesn't stop again for another hundred miles.

By that time he's well into a wide, empty valley, flanked

on either side by mountains smoothed to round scoops of ice cream that have gone dark brown in the withering heat.

As far as he can tell, Idaho is comprised of scorched hay-fields and spooky hawks haunting the power lines like a videogame background going past him in nauseating redundancy. Now and then a jackrabbit zips across the road, but there are more of those than vehicles out here, which is fine with him.

Harry stops at a tiny post office/filling station in Tendoy, called Peter's Pump & Postal. His cell has battery, but no reception out here, so he's about as cut off from the world as he can be, and relieved when no attendant emerges from the little shop that looks to be the local restaurant, mail center, and sporting goods store all in one. There are rifles on the wall, and for a half a second Harry thinks he might go in and buy one. The idiocy of this thought manages to put a smile on his face.

Two old white men, identical twins in blue and red ball caps, are drinking coffee at a table inside. They gaze out at Harry, filling up his tank, and then he takes Greta out to stretch along the road and gets her nestled back into her bed before settling up inside for the fuel. A heavy-set woman wearing an American flag sweater and matching earrings makes change for a dollar.

"What kind of name is Tendoy?"

"This is Tendoy."

"The name, I mean—"

She shrugs and shakes her head.

"I'm from Bonners Ferry. I only moved down here six years ago."

Harry thanks her, nods at the oldsters, and goes outside to

the payphone, leaning on the ice chest to favor his foot.

It's time to call her now. The black payphone's receiver feels good and heavy in his hand and he chews his thumbnail as it rings through.

He's sure he'll get her voicemail and realizes as it begins to ring in his ear that even a recording of Leah's voice will fill him with heartache.

"Hello?"

"Hey, it's Harry."

"Where are you?" she says.

Harry tells her that he's in Idaho. That he's in some trouble but that he hasn't done anything wrong. He pauses to look at Greta who's staring at him from thc truck's open window.

"You just took off, Harry. I was worried. I called your sister."

"Yeah, I'm really sorry about that. And I'm sorry for what I said."

"You mean you're sorry that you *proposed*?" Leah says, laughing without humor in her voice.

"That was stupid. It was a complete mistake."

"It's alright," Leah says. "You just caught me off guard. Is Greta alright?"

"She had a little party in the woods with a porcupine but she's fine. We should be back home in a few days. I'm gonna head to L.A. first to see Adrienne, I think."

"Well, it's good to hear your voice. I'm glad you two are okay."

There is a long silence. Harry isn't sure if he should tell her about his mother, or save it for when he gets back to Tucson.

"You didn't read the email I sent, did you?"

"No," he says. "I've been a little tied up, why?"

"Never mind. I should probably go, Harry. But thanks for calling."

He looks down at his bandaged foot in its muddy grocery bag, next to a yellow M&M wrapper in the dirt, sighs, and thanks Leah for inspiring him to figure out what happened to his mother. He tells her that he's found out only this morning that she died in a car accident. Then Harry tells her that he loves her and he misses her, and that he understands if she never wants to see him again.

"Oh, Harry. You sound like you're in pretty bad shape. Look, we'll talk when you get home, okay?"

"Okay."

"Just take care of yourself and drive safe. And please give Greta a kiss for me."

He says he will and they hang up.

When he turns, he sees that Greta's still watching him through the open window. Harry wipes his eyes and nose on his sleeve and glances at the two men at the table inside in the store. The one wearing the red hat raises his arm and offers a thumbs up. Harry returns the gesture and climbs back into his truck.

HUNTER

By the looks of it, somebody's gutted a deer on the pumpkin orange carpet of Harry's room at the Traveler's Inn between Orem and Provo, Utah.

The motel's flickering sign shows a pig with a bindle and handkerchief, advertising rooms for $49.95 a night, which is the cheapest Harry's seen without an accompanying rate by the hour.

After driving south till dusk from Tendoy, Harry finds himself in a distracted, ugly mood. He'd only stopped to refuel at busier stations and pulled the bill of his baseball hat low over his eyes and let the nozzle flow as he took Greta to pee out by the dumpsters or in the nearby patches of burnt grass. Radiohead's *Amnesiac* repeated itself and helped pass the day at a low volume. Harry could only hum along intermittently as his mind was unable to sponge in more than a phrase or two from random songs. One track in particular sounded not unlike a siren, and Harry had to skip to the next one each time it came on.

The cars and semis in his rearview mirror morphed into every variety of police vehicle: sheriff's rover, bulbous 90s squad car, paddy wagons of ridiculous proportion—Harry even flinched at the navy-blue fender of a tractor carrying bales of hay on the highway shoulder somewhere between Salmon and Elk Bend. But he drove exactly the speed limit on cruise control as Greta gave off periodic sleep whimpers from her bed next to him.

Whenever Harry spotted an actual highway patrol vehicle tucked in under an overpass or poking its nose out from median foliage, he hovered his right hand over Greta's soft belly as she dreamt.

Thus, Harry's panic has receded into a low-grade headache, and his nerves are so frazzled that he's basically forgotten what it feels like not to be the conduit for a hormonal dribble of paranoid doom scenarios. He'd busted a taillight on his pickup when he bashed into the squad car at the precinct, so he isn't about to chance it by driving after dark—and anyway he's shattered.

The Traveler's Inn is an astonishing place. The young clerk's face is ravaged with acne, and he appears to be talking to himself when Harry comes in.

He looks up and gives Harry a dentist's empty smile.

"Have you got any rooms?"

"Let me see here…"

After a moment, he offers Harry his pick between one with a "problem bed," a room recently fumigated, and one he simply calls the "Hunter's Den." The clerk doesn't mind that Harry has no driver's license, so long as he has a credit card. Though he does study it, front and back, like he's never seen one before.

"Whichever's the cleanest."

"They're all pretty clean, but some people like a choice in accommodation. And every one of them's the same rate."

Harry turns up his palms as if to say, *Help me out, kid.*

The clerk nods and holds out the golden key to whatever lays behind door number 206.

Then he adds, "Go ahead and let the water run to get the rusty stuff out of the taps."

"Rusty stuff?"

"Yeah, it's fine to drink though. If you give it a minute."

The clerk sets the tasseled bookmark against his forearm and starts using it to lightly scrape upwards, in a careful combing maneuver. Then he hands Harry a long remote control.

"Can I do anything else for you?" he asks, his eyes searching Harry's face.

The clerk's half-smile, this lingering question, it hangs there. He asks the clerk if he wouldn't mind if Harry checked his email on his computer, and as he comes around the desk and takes a seat to get logged in, the kid hovers over him, his hand on the back of the seat, just touching the edge of Harry's shoulder, breathing. He notices a magazine concealed under papers called *Bad Daddy Party*. Harry hums a tune, the slow computer laboring to bring the site up, pretending not to see the clerk's reading material next to a stained paper cup he's evidently been using for a spittoon.

Harry's email inbox is days of junk, save one message from Leah. It had arrived while Harry was still out at the cabin—which already seems like a month ago. Its subject line says "Harry" but nothing is in the body of the email's message box, and he sees that there's an attachment.

Harry asks the clerk if he'd mind printing out a document.

"I can try," the clerk says. "But the printer can be a little feisty."

"No problem."

Of course, Harry knows this kid will read Leah's note, whatever it is, but that's a small price. And it isn't like he's going to sit here and pore over it in this chair, with the clerk leering over his shoulder, breathing onto Harry's head.

The two of them switch places, and Harry glances out onto the dark highway wondering what the hell he's doing, leaving passwords and computer files and fingerprints all over this place.

Greta lets out a solitary bark from the front seat when she sees that Harry's reappeared. He tells the kid to ring him in his room if he manages to get the printer to work. The kid's clicking furiously on the printer icon's status window when Harry goes out.

He opens the door for Greta, and she leaps down from her seat in the truck to stretch. Somehow, just seeing Leah's email there, he feels sure that he's gotten free. He might well be home to Tucson with his dog beside him in twenty-four hours—maybe less if he gets up early enough and risks getting back on the interstate. He could visit Adrienne another time.

Harry would get off Interstate 15, and follow the long, slow route through Moab and the outskirts of the Grand Canyon. Then cruise around the decrepitude of greater Phoenix, well after rush hour, into the hot darkness of the Sonoran Desert.

He lets himself imagine walking up to Leah's apartment, ringing the doorbell, waiting. Greta bounding through the door. Leah sitting barefoot on the floor, reading with a cup of tea. The life he'd fled is coming back into view now, and it's been transformed by the passage of time and wild adventure.

That, or the cops will kick in the door of the Hunter's Den in the middle of the night and Harry will be arrested for murder.

He and Greta locate the room in question, among every other, in a milky-smelling corridor. The thought of surprising Leah puts him in mind of a long, hot shower. The smell off of him is nothing short of poisonous. But when he pulls back the curtain on the tub, which hangs out of joint with the wall where black mold has formed a gleaming colony, he decides he doesn't need to bathe quite yet. Sugar ants march in a long line up the seam of the grayed caulking, and they pour industriously—as if in liquid formation—out from behind the vanity.

Harry appears to bother them about as much as the room's previous occupant, who, despite his wish not to conjure him, Harry nonetheless pictures as Calvin Hogan in his coverall snowsuit onesie with a fresh kill of game to butcher here in the soft glow of the television set. Flipping through the channels, smudging the remote's array of buttons with elk blood.

Harry sits down on the bed's comforter and reaches over to turn on the TV. Its audio comes first, and the drab picture of a hairy Italian-looking guy follows. The man is fucking a blond woman half his age, wearing only cream-colored riding boots. He's going hard, saying, "Take the salami. *Take eet.*" Harry changes the channel, but that's all there is, this one stomach-churning scene, repeating. He shuts it off and exhales deeply through his mouth, as though to expel the man's voice from his head. But it's still in his ears, echoing faintly.

When Harry unlatches the chain and peeks out into the hallway, he can hear the hairy guy moaning and grunting down the narrow corridor, emanating through the thin walls from the television sets of other rooms. Harry pictures half a dozen TVs showing the same scene—a young couple transfixed, or a gaggle of bible boys pretending not to hump their pillows once they'd agreed it would be sinful to leave it on.

The smell in the hallway stops him. He stands there for a moment with Greta looking up at him, wondering about her dinner. But Harry's trying to place the odor—there's cigarette smoke marbled into the walls. There's grime wiped down with citrusy disinfectant. But there's something else here—an undersmell that wafts in through his nostrils into the back of his skull—the weird, unlidded lubricants of the doctor's office in childhood. It smells faintly of his home in Denver, after Sally started filling the rooms with dolls.

A thin thread of sadness enters him, and he wonders how his dad is. He can't go back to Denver now. Even Tucson—what's there for him, if not Leah?

He shuts the door and sits down on the bed, and lets himself run through what Leah's letter might say: *Come home soon, Harry. I don't want to be with you. I'm so glad you went to find your mother. How could you just take off like that in the middle of the night? I need you. Don't bother calling me when the cops break down your door. I'm still in love with Ryan. I miss you. You make me sick.*

After the kid at the desk points out a local department store called Quincy's, Harry picks up a bag of dog chow and a new black collar for Greta.

He buys a pair of work pants and a shirt, a three-pack of boxer shorts, a six-pack of white tube socks, a blue tarp, duct tape, a packet of gauze, a new duffel bag, and a pair of child's scissors for 99 cents.

Harry needs a Laundromat more than new clothes, but he doesn't want to spend the evening sitting in public someplace, even this far down into Utah. Under the bright lights of the gas station's store, Harry stuffs himself with a personal pepperoni pizza out of its thin grease-stained box in the cab of the truck—perhaps the single best/worst meal he's ever had in his life—and heads back to the Traveler's Inn.

He doesn't know if the police are after him in hot pursuit or if that's a fun joke his mind has been playing on him all day.

Harry considers calling Kristin to tell her what happened at the cabin, but figures he'll wait until he gets home. And hopefully they will have picked up Tommy and Frank, and they're ratting each other out by now. Then Harry remembers what happened to Frank, and his stomach works itself into a complicated knot around the mini-mart pizza wedged in there.

He considers making an anonymous call to the police, but he's afraid he'll get tripped up by a detective like Calvin had warned, or have the call traced to Utah and somehow they'll know it's the driver of the getaway vehicle on the line.

Harry gives himself a quick rinse in the squalid tub and the hot water creates a great quantity of soapy steam. He keeps a plastic bag from Quincy's rubber-banded around the wrapping of his injured leg, fearing mold and ants and god knows what else worming inside his bite holes, delivering him back to square one. And once he dries himself off, and redresses the wound with fresh gauze, he lifts Greta into the tub too and scrubs all the dust and blood and shit out of her fur. She's as happy as before, her tongue lapping and biting at the water as it comes from the nozzle he's hosing her off with. She even lets him rinse her porcupine quill scabs and they look a little better.

He pulls the comforter off the sunken queen bed, which is adorned in great cancerous-looking gardenias. Tossed to the floor in a ball, its under-fabric shows such a vibrant yellow he first takes it for the actual color of the material and not the massive remnant of dried fluid he realizes it is.

Though it's his first shower in days, Harry's skin crawls with scratchy, insectoid awareness. He'd brushed his teeth with the water from the gallon bottle out at the open door of the truck, and then spent the better part of a half hour duct-taping a rectangle of blue tarp to the open passenger-side window. It was a ragged, ugly job. He'd broken a sweat ripping the plastic with his teeth after snapping the scissors in two just getting them out of their package. If his truck isn't exactly roadworthy, it's serviceable enough for the home stretch.

After a final stroll with Greta along the dandelions at the highway's edge, Harry remembers the spattered duffel bag, and transfers everything into his new one, tossing the bloody one into the dumpster behind the steakhouse next to the motel. Then he feeds Greta and they repair to their hideout for the evening.

"Mr. Gopher rings in the dead of night."

"I'm on the road, Calvin. I didn't make it to the police."

"Well do *not* divulge your coordinates with me then. I don't want to have to falsify anything to the sheriff's minions. If I don't know, I don't know. So, enjoy Acapulco. Meantime, I got intel."

Harry leans back on the bed and stretches out. He hasn't removed anything but his boots and hat and does not feel especially compelled—in his fresh duds, newly bathed—to disrobe further, let alone slip between the linens.

"Fire away."

"I went to see Paul Tillett's folks, night before last, Greg and Tonya. I meant to tell you at Flo-Ann's, but we got interrupted by the goon squad."

"Yeah, I remember. She was in the ER with Paul."

"I heard."

"What do you mean?"

"Evidently you were correct, Harrison. Paul skipped out into that moonlit meadow to try and extract the rifle from Tommy. And he got a hold of it alright, but Frank Keene and Tommy outmatched him, tugged it back, and then one or the other struck Paul in the solar plexus with the butt-end."

"You had that figured out at the cabin."

"Not the critical part, however, because Paul said that's when the shot was fired and hit the girl. At which point, everybody went ahead and dispersed. I guess that's about when you were playing Twister with Kujo."

"So, why didn't Paul say that in the ER? He told me that he hid all night in the garage."

"Greg verified that part also. Paul got home the next morning, but his mother was terrified. She thought he'd been killed, since Paul's buddies were in hysterics, phoning for him at home. They went ahead and told Tonya all the fun parts. So, when the sun came up—and still no Paul—Tonya assumed the worst.

"Knowing that he'd had his mitts all over the gun—and the less-than-friendly character of the boys he was dealing with—Paul guessed that they'd lay the killing on him. So, he hid out. Evidently, they'd cracked a rib and bruised his lung, and he couldn't run for it anyhow. Still couldn't take air too good when he got home in the morning.

"His mother, as you know, drove him into the doctor's. Logic being, she'd already lost him once, and wasn't going to watch him cough up enough blood to drown on the couch like a consumptive after he'd just emerged from the dead."

"Yeah, I remember. She was pretty jumpy—split the moment I got in there."

"Tonya thought they were gonna put Paul away for good—one way or another—since by morning word was out that the girl was in bad shape, and that they'd flown her to Billings. Besides, Paul's older brother Walter didn't come home from his tour in Fallujah—so she was past her limit in the dead kid department.

"Evidently, when you popped into the exam room—nice going, by the way—it startled her. Tonya slid out and called Greg on her cellular to tell him somebody named *Larry* sneaked in to chat with Paul. Greg went ahead and dialed the police himself, on his own kid. He figured that was preferable to finding the cops in his driveway, with their Glocks drawn. Take the bull by the ring, and so forth."

"And then Greg followed me…"

"And then Greg Tillett followed you out for a little Coors in the sun, with yours truly none the wiser."

"But why did Paul lie to me in the ER then?"

"Didn't wanna leave any breadcrumbs putting him at the crime scene, is my guess. Same reason you lied to me at Flo-Ann's that morning—no?"

"Okay…So, Paul comes home to a houseful of cops. They bring him to the station, he lays out the whole thing for the detectives, and they believe his story and let him go. And then what?"

"Greg heard him in the shower early, said Paul stunk like an outhouse when he'd gotten home from jail. I guess he wanted fresh air, and stepped out around dawn to go get some Copenhagen. Then *whammo*. Knocked down and left for buzzards. Greg was standing in the front room with his morning coffee when they clipped Paul and peeled off. Saw that black Mazda, just couldn't make out the driver."

"And the prosecution's key witness is dead."

"Exactly. And that's that, Harrison. All sewn up. Put a fork in it."

"But why the hell were Tommy and Frank after me?"

"Must've thought you knew the whole ball of yarn."

"But I wasn't even out in the field when the shit started."

"We know they were tailing Paul, so they probably spotted you traipsing into the germ farm after him and figured he'd spilled the story to you in there."

"Maybe so, but they figured out where I was out on Rock Creek, so why not just shoot me through the window, or run me over in the road?"

"Good question. Those are fine ideas, all of them."

"Why ransack the cabin and put a note in my wallet and try to scare me out of Montana?"

"I guess they wanted to keep you from discussing anything with Boss Hogg."

"Killing me would've solved that. That's how they took care of Paul."

"You raise some puzzling elements, Harrison. In point of fact, when I hadn't heard from you this evening, I figured those two had you roped to a chair, and commenced taking turns poking you with something hot and sharp."

"For what purpose exactly?"

"I saw that in a movie."

"Thanks, Calvin."

"You're absolutely correct though, Harrison. It's not over. Those boys haven't emerged since they came to chat with us at Flo-Ann's. I tried to tell them you were long gone, but they'd seen your truck and the red Vizsla in the lot. You must've appeared over my shoulder like a little bluebird. They spotted you and you know the rest."

"What were you yelling at me when you came out of the back of Flo-Ann's?"

"I was hollering, '*Flee, little gopher, flee!*'"

Harry pauses here, he wants to tell Calvin that Greg Tillett came by the cabin and blew Frank's head off. But he doesn't want to put Calvin in a spot where he might have to betray his friend. Harry knows he'll find out soon enough, if Calvin's not also bluffing to shield Paul's old man.

"You heard any more from Greg Tillett today?" Harry says.

"Not a word. But I went to see Tonya after you skipped out on breakfast. She said Greg was going hunting for the night. Get his mind right before the service for Paul on Sunday. How come?"

"Was Greg in the war with you and Dad?"

"Nah, high school, though. He and Pat went to the same junior high, too, I think."

"They were friends?"

"What's with the pop quiz about Greg Tillett all of sudden?"

"Never mind. Calvin, one more thing."

"Name it."

"It's about my mom."

"Oh, boy. What now?"

"Why did he tell people that she had cancer and leukemia and all that stuff?"

"Ahh, Harry...you're *killing* me here. You know Pat'll have to take that one."

"Just tell me, okay?"

"I don't know, bud. Cut Cal some slack. If I had to speculate—and that's all I'm doing—I'd say Pat probably felt responsible, and he didn't want anybody to think he had a hand in it...It wasn't anybody's fault. But I'd guess that—"

"Don't guess. Just tell me."

"Harrison, you're missing the point. We never talked about it. None of us did. Not then and not the day before yesterday when we chatted on the phone just like you and I are doing right now. Not ever.

"Even when Ginny and I were with him in the hospital, he wouldn't say anything. We just sat there in that hellhole.

Snotty nurses with their chins in the air going this way and that. I mean, it wrecked him. I'm sorry, kid. That's just how it is with him."

"Hospital, huh?"

"Exactly," Calvin says. "Been trying to tell you. That place sucked the life out of him. Your old man hasn't been the same since."

LETTER

Harry lay awake most of the night with Greta on the motel bed beside him.

His mind is still in the cabin: Frank's corpse slumped in the corner, the odor of gunpowder, that sewer smell coming off Tommy.

Every time he thinks of Leah, he cringes. He was stupid to propose, of all idiotic things he could've said. It was a hideously desperate move. He's lucky Leah had the sense to say *That's not a good idea*. But it still stung him.

When he looks over his actions, each one seems to have been carried out by a different Harry. One humiliated and exposed. One spurned and afraid. One belligerent and irate. And one longing to connect, desperate to be known. But all childish in their way—each one oblivious and grasping.

Harry must have fallen asleep at some point because many men were climbing through his dream—blond automatons in military fatigues—scaling walls and skillfully repelling down. Harry jolts awake when Greta starts barking from the bed.

She leaps off and goes at the light coming from the crack beneath the door. Laughter in the hall. A woman's voice, then wilder, chesty cackles. Greta scratches at the wood surface like a cat, and Harry pulls his boots on and stands next to her to listen, his ear on the door. He tries to muzzle her with one hand, the other poised on the knob, slick to the touch.

He hears the shuffle of steps in the hallway and somebody's loud whispering and then a man's low moan. It's amorous and drunken.

A woman's voice says, "Is this it?"

The brass doorknob of Harry's room wiggles in his hand, and Greta snarls at the door. The woman screams out on the other side.

"Two-o-six. Shit. We need two-o-*nine*, girl."

"I hate dogs!"

"He won't get you," the man's voice says. "I'll shoot that motherfucker down if it flexes."

Harry stands there, holding Greta's collar as she pants and whimpers and sniffs at the door. A thin string of slobber falls to the orange carpeting, and the voices recede behind the door of a room nearby. A bolt is drawn shut. A chain rattles and slides home.

It's 4:44 a.m.

Too early to be up. Too late to fall back asleep. Harry opens the door and goes down the corridor, out the back exit to let Greta pee. The sky's starting to get blue over the buzzing pre-dawn blackness in the parking lot. There's a chill in the air. It all smells ripe and buggy out at the truck under hundreds of moths and smaller insects assaulting the lights over the vehicles. A possum emerges from the dumpster, scales down to the asphalt, and disappears into the unmown grass beyond, escaping Greta's notice.

The same night clerk is asleep at the front desk.

His computer monitor now displays a quadrant dividing four smaller screens, each showing the static angle of a closed-circuit television camera: the vending machine alcove; the parking area where the truck is; the hallway Harry's just walked through; and the front desk where he's standing, from which he can now eerily see his own face from above.

He feels fairly certain that with a single keystroke the clerk can toggle to four other clandestine and downward-peering shots of the bed areas inside any room along that rank hallway.

He quickly replays the night he's had and feels relieved he hasn't gotten up to anything incriminating himself. But as he looks at the young clerk, Harry feels a surge of something sad go through him. The kid is wearing the same short-sleeve polo. There are crumbs of bread or chocolate in the lap of his khakis, some of this is around his mouth too. And he dozes with his head back and mouth agape like a man who's been shot, repositioned into a "sleeping posture," and left for dead. Except that his fists are tucked into his pants pockets.

Harry figures the jangle of Greta's collar will rouse him, but the kid—his name plate on the desk reads, "Hello, I'm *Mitchell*"—is conked out. Harry doesn't want to embarrass or startle him, but he's impatient and clears his throat.

Mitchell simply opens his eyes a few millimeters and perceives Harry, without moving any other part of his body, like a statue coming to life.

"Don't wanna bother you there. I just wondered if you had any luck printing out that document."

Mitchell sucks in some drool from the side of his lip and brings his head into an upright position. He blinks and asks

Harry to repeat himself. Mitchell's tongue appears to be jousting around the inside of his mouth—for food or something—and Harry actually has to turn and look slightly over his shoulder as Mitchell begins making mouth noises, opening and closing, and tonguing-around sounds.

"I was in 206. Hunter's Den. I had something you were going to—"

"Morning prayers," Mitchell says quickly. "I wasn't asleep."

"Sorry about that."

"It's right there, Mr. Harrison."

On the counter beside the bell is an envelope emblazoned with the Traveler's Inn logo. Across the front, a neat cursive hand has written: *Stables 206*.

Harry takes it, thanks him, and sets the room key on the counter.

"Did you enjoy your stay?"

"Sure."

Harry turns to go and Mitchell then asks rather plainly, "Were you able to make any friends?"

Harry looks back at him.

"No, actually, we did not…make any friends."

"I'm sorry to hear that because Orem's a pretty friendly place."

By now Mitchell is working something free from the back of his molars with a finger, and Harry thanks him again and pushes open the door.

He stands with Greta for a moment outside the motel as the trucks shake by on the highway beyond the cars parked in the front lot.

There's something in the road—a tire fragment, a deer carcass, some big piece of debris the size of a coffee table—that every southbound vehicle has to slow down and swerve around to miss.

Blackish sky going blue and cool wind and the smell of summer plants and exhaust all mingle together out here. A pigeon squeaks as it flaps onto the roof over the pull-through at the entrance and startles Harry. Greta wanders over to urinate near some trash.

The snow's starting to get shiny on the range of eastern mountaintops as the sun rises behind them. Harry sits down on a bench outside and looks at the envelope as Greta noses an empty Arby's bag that's fallen out of the overfilled garbage can.

Dear Harry,

I'm not upset with you anymore. I'm just numb. The story you sent the other day made me angry—and then it just made me feel bad for you, because I realized a few things.

It's been a confusing couple of weeks. Honestly, I've been torn. You proposed to me out of the blue and I'm sorry I didn't respond more gently. But you didn't exactly leave me much choice. We could've talked about it, and taken our time. And now I'm embarrassed to admit that I actually considered it after you left. I really did. I thought maybe you'd show back up with a ring and get down on your knee. Then I found your note.

Harry: you just took off. And I was worried about you and Greta. When your sister told me you went to Montana, I was furious. But I realized that whatever you're going through doesn't have anything to do with me. Because if it did, you wouldn't have left like that in the middle of the night. I told Ryan I knew nothing about what you did to his car, but God, Harry. I don't know if you thought that would scare him or impress me somehow, but when he told me what you wrote on his door I felt mortified.

I really did love to be with you, which is what makes this such a hard letter to write.

I know this isn't what you want to hear, but I still have feelings for him, and Ryan and I have decided to get back together. I think it's better if you and I don't see each other when you get back. Please take good care of Greta in Montana. Don't let the bears get her. Or you either.

Leah

PROPOSITION

There's a thick-sounding thud on the roadway when a black van strikes the large item, and it lifts up a bit and remains in traffic, in an upright position now, though it's still too dim to make out what it is: a mangled box or half an elk, maybe.

Harry folds Leah's letter up and slides it into the motel envelope and tucks it into the back pocket of his new pants. He and Greta jog across the highway toward the silhouettes of a playground slide and swing set, where a couple of kids are smoking. The two of them are perched on the edge of a red merry-go-round.

Greta trots over to the kids, and Harry lets her drag the leash behind her, as he stands staring at the mountains, struck dumb by the frankness of Leah's letter.

Harry's cell phone rings in his pocket.

This early, it's got to be Calvin calling, or Adrienne. But when he looks at the screen of his phone, his heart starts to pound.

The number on the screen belongs to the cabin's landline—that old black rotary-dial phone—out on Rock Creek.

For a moment Harry pictures Frank Keene's headless corpse dialing his cell from inside there. Harry lets it ring, and Greta greets the two boys in hoodies on the merry-go-round, muttering to each other, passing a cigarette back and forth.

It stops ringing. Harry waits and stares at the tiny green screen of his phone, but whoever it was leaves no message.

He opens the missed calls and checks the number again. It's the cabin's.

Was it the police? But why would they call from the cabin's phone? Had Kristin gone back out there to find Harry for some reason? She had the number, but she didn't know where it was, unless Tommy had told her. Maybe it was one of the neighbors wondering what had happened or wanting to know if Harry had managed to find Greta—but with the corpse of Frank slumped in the corner? None of these scenarios made any sense.

Harry slides the phone back into his pocket and feels something turn inside his stomach. He chides himself for not having answered it. And then the phone rings again. It's the cabin's number.

Harry clicks *send*, brings it to his ear, and waits.

"Harry?"

That voice. Harry says nothing, just holds his breath.

"It's Tommy. Do not hang up."

Harry lets out of a huge sigh. "Turn yourself in, Tommy. There's nothing I can do for you."

One of the kids sitting on the merry-go-round is scratching his leg with a stick as the other one pets Greta, and they both look out at the big carcassy thing on the highway. A yellow corvette swerves to miss it and revs off into the distance. Fat blue bands of light are coming up from behind the mountain ridges, and the darkness is turning grayish and grainy as the stars are dimming now. Harry notices a deer in a nearby yard, nibbling in somebody's garden next to a sprinkler.

"If I go to the cops, I'm gonna have to tell them you did it, Harry."

"Go fuck yourself."

The two boys perk up at this and look over at Harry. He gives them the oldster's thumbs-up and turns around to see the doe, now tentatively crossing the street, her head dipping down in rhythm with each step.

"Tommy, I'm calling the police right now to tell them exactly where you are," Harry says. "You'll have a few things to explain out in the cabin, I guess."

"The only part of that story they'll be excited about is that you're missing from your little hideout on the creek. But go ahead and give 'em a ring."

"Maybe you're forgetting the guy with his brains all over the fucking wall. And nobody in their right mind is gonna wonder why I didn't sleep in that bed last night. Anyhow, all I have to say is that you and Frank trashed the place, and I thought you were gonna kill me so that's why I took off. You think I was dumb enough to throw away the note Frank put in my wallet?"

"Goddamn it!" Tommy's breathing hard, then he lowers his voice again and slows down. "Okay, Harry, listen to me. Don Hunt and I were messing around, but *Don* accidentally shot Lucy. And the rifle belongs to Don's old man. So now they got him in custody and that piece of shit is blaming the whole thing on me. But it's his word against mine, which is what I need you for. To just call them up and back my story.

"Now, I'm sorry I said that stuff to scare you—but you and me are both on the run. And we can help each other out of this thing. So, work with me, Harry. Please."

"No thanks, Tommy. Not interested."

"A girl got killed at a party and one of the suspects flees *the state of Montana.* They're gonna snatch your ass up and bring you home—I don't care if you get to Alaska. I happen to know that they got pictures of you in your truck. License plate, everything. And I got your ID right here in my hand. But if you and I *both go in together* and tell them Donny did it, then the two of us walk."

"I'm not running anywhere, Tommy. I'm—"

"Ian told me they spotted you down by Idaho, yesterday, which means you're probably to Salt Lake by now. So, don't lie to me, Flowerboy. I got eyes on you."

"I know you killed Paul Tillett. I know he tried to get the rifle from you. I don't know which of you shot Lucy, but I'm just gonna let the Sheriff figure that out."

"Wait—please don't ruin my life over this, Harry. I'm sorry I threatened you, but Kris and I are having a baby, okay? And you need me just as bad as I need you. Plus, Don has to pay for what he did, doesn't he?"

Harry's standing under the overhang of the playground's public restrooms by the water fountain. Greta's digging at something beneath the shiny metal slide with a single front paw. Her ears are flapping back and forth.

Tommy's desperation and lies are lucid now as Harry feels something slow and wonderful take hold of him, like he's finally lowering himself into a warm bath.

"I didn't kill anybody, Harry. *Don* did it. That's why I left Don's ass on the road. Frank ran over Paul, okay? I didn't mean for that to happen. I told Frank not to."

The playground's radiant now as the sun's come over

the mountains, and the sky's a perfect swimming pool blue. Harry can see that the two high school boys are not boys, they're girls—both with short hair under the hoods of their sweatshirts. One of them's talking to Greta who's biting at the twig she's tossed into the sand.

"Bye-bye, Tommy."

"Turn on any channel. You're all over the news, Harry. They got video of you in your truck, pulling out of the precinct and smashing that cop car. There's a police van outside your fucking apartment in Tucson. If you call now, then you can end it—for me and for you—but we need to say that Donald Hunt did it. That Don shot Lucy."

Harry hears the cabin door open and the old rotary phone's muffled against Tommy's vest. Harry can't pick out the voices, but it's quiet for a moment, and Harry puts his hand over his other ear and shuts his eyes to listen. There are more stifled swishes and scratches before voices are arguing over each other, and then he hears Tommy yelling. And the line's dead.

APPLE PIE & COFFEE

Harry walks over and picks up Greta's leash, and they make their way back across the highway—past what he now sees is an animal mangled so badly Harry can't tell what it had been—to where the truck's parked in back of the Traveler's Inn.

Harry's tarp job on the busted window had blown halfway off in the night—it's making a crinkly snapping sound in the breeze.

He's shaking and yells at Greta to get up onto her seat, which she doesn't want to do. The truck's cold and it smells of mildew and last night's pizza. The fuel tank's nearly empty, and Harry needs coffee. And a toilet. Something to eat.

First thing in the morning and his nerves are already fried from Leah's letter and Tommy's call. He leans over the nozzle to breathe in its fumes as he fuels up down the road at a Texaco already teeming with morning commuters.

He has a bad feeling, but he's almost certain that there can't really be a dragnet for him. *Almost* being the operative word here. Calvin would've said so on the phone last night if there'd been a search underway, and if Harry's picture had been on the news that would've been the first thing out of Calvin's mouth. But doubt lingers in his empty stomach like a lit match, dropped and smoldering there.

Harry tears the flap of tarp and duct tape off the window and stuffs it into the garbage between the pumps, knowing his shoddy work won't last a mile on the interstate. Greta pokes her head out of the window, like he's playing peek-a-boo with her. Harry reaches in to pet her and he looks her tiny black scabs over.

"You ready to go home?"

He swipes his card three times, but the pay-at-the-pump reader keeps saying "***See Attendant***"

He looks into the storefront, where a short bald man is arguing with the clerk and there are three or four others in line behind that guy, all distressed-looking.

Harry gets back into his truck, sees that the fuel gauge reads full, and pulls out to go find some breakfast.

It's barely 6 a.m., but Cole's Diner is somehow already bustling with big Mormon families, featuring well-brushed blond children of every stage of pre- and full-blown puberty.

Young mothers with sad smiles rocking infants, getting tugged at and slapped by toddlers. Loads of happy dads. Harry waits for a few families to get seated and has a look around the place like he's stumbled into a restaurant on Neptune.

The men in here dawdle over to the spreads of one another's tables, hands in their pockets, to loom behind the children, smiling painfully over each other's broods in silent surveillance. These men—how else to say it?—they look insane to Harry. Clean-shaven, each and every one dressed the same as Mitchell over at the Traveler's Inn: baggy khakis and short-sleeve Polo shirts and white sneakers double-knotted with pristine white laces.

The teen host greets Harry at the register. His black Dockers are pulled high above his waist. He puts Harry at the counter and fills up his water glass.

Harry orders coffee and a slice of apple pie with ice cream for breakfast. He places the Traveler's Inn envelope, with Leah's letter inside it, face-up on the counter beside his napkin.

Leah.

Harry doesn't know whether to be livid or relieved. Mostly he just feels humiliated.

All his life Adrienne had told him to get off the fucking fence already. *Stop dithering, Harry. Go after something. Women like it when you assert yourself. You don't have to be a brute. Just tell her how you feel.* But Harry hadn't told her how he felt. He hadn't bothered to ask her what she wanted either.

I thought maybe you'd show back up with a ring and get down on your knee.

It meant he'd actually had a chance with her.

Harry pours copious amounts of cream and sugar into his coffee and is still stirring it when the pie comes out on a small blue plate with a melty glump of vanilla ice cream. The big slice has teardrop holes in its crust, and gooey apple hunks fall out of either side, letting off steam. There are fat crystals of sugar on the pinched parts of the crust edges, and it's glorious.

Tommy's story—pinning it on Harry or Donald Hunt—the whole thing reeked of desperation. And Harry starts to revel in the sloppiness of Tommy's scheme.

He loads up a forkful of steaming pie, dabs it into the white glop, and takes an exquisite bite—simultaneously burning and freezing the roof of his mouth.

Tommy's threat of a dragnet was just a Hail Mary tossed as the clock ran out on him. The fact that he was still out at the cabin with Frank Keene's slumped-over corpse was enough to confirm as much.

Tommy seems pitiful now to Harry, almost trivial. A little boy hiding under the bed from his father dangling a bike chain. He almost feels bad for him.

Then he remembers Kristin's cousin Lucy, running out to the field after Kristin had warned her, only to be shot down behind a trailer because a couple of drunk rednecks wanted to screw around.

The moment Harry finishes off the last of his pie and a second cup of coffee, it's as though he's being lifted up in a hot-air balloon, high above the doublewide and cars out front, the bonfire's lapping flames.

Then the party, everybody clustered out in the field, Kristin and Paul Tillett, the white dog bucking around in the grass, Frank Keene in his Stetson, the sisters passing in front of the truck, and that pizza box folding in on itself in the fire—every shred of it seems a long, long ways away from the counter of Cole's Diner in Orem, Utah.

Harry floats higher and higher, as Tommy, in his yellow hunting vest, covered in dust and blood, holding a splintered mop handle, becomes even smaller, before he finally disappears.

Harry's cell buzzes in the pocket of his jeans and he fishes it out at the counter, sipping his coffee as he looks at the screen.

It's a 406 number. Missoula area code, but not the cabin's

landline this time.

"Hello?"

"Harry, this is John Dowd calling from the Missoula Public Library."

Relief floods into him and he sets down his coffee cup.

"Hey, John. I'm sorry I haven't gotten back to you, I've been on the road."

He remembers John coming over that morning to the computer terminals, before Harry hobbled out of there and made his way to the Emergency Room.

"I left you a message at your cabin, but realized you might not have gotten it if you're no longer in town."

"I had to hit the trail a little early, actually. Something came up."

"My friend over at Providence found the records of your mother's hospital visits."

"It's okay, John. I found out about the accident from my dad's friend. So, I know all about the car crash. Sorry I didn't tell you earlier."

"Well, that's a relief," John says. "I'm very sorry about your mother, Harry. And I hope it provides you some closure to know what happened."

"Thanks. Seriously, I appreciate all your help. Please do thank your friend for me. I hope I didn't put her to too much trouble, digging through old records in some warehouse."

Harry stands up and motions to his waitress for the check.

"I will tell her, of course," John says. "So, you *do* know about the hospital visits before her accident then?"

"What do you mean?"

"There were three others."

The waitress slips the bill across the counter to Harry and smiles at him. He turns from the counter, slides a hand over his ear.

"Three other hospital visits?"

"July, August, and one in early October of '79."

Harry remembers Calvin saying the crash had been Halloween night. Ice on the road. A fox crossing the highway. Swerving to miss it.

"Does it say anything about what she'd gone in for?"

"Looks like routine check-ups on the baby."

"What?"

"I'm sorry, I thought you knew, Harry. Your mother was pregnant."

—

As he settles up with the host at the register, Harry notices the cursive scrawl below the sign for Cole's Diner: *Family-Friendly Fun for Fun, Friendly Families.*

Harry has to call his sister right now. He decides then, fishing a toothpick out of the holder on the counter, to veer off and head to Los Angeles, and crash with Adrienne and Ronnie for a few days. They can take Greta to the beach and he and his sister can make a plan to head back to Missoula. Calvin can take them to the spot of the crash. Finally, some clarity about what Pat had been avoiding all these years. He hadn't killed his wife. But Calvin must've been right, and Pat had to have felt responsible for all of it—the baby, too.

The young man at the register is shaking his head,

muttering something.

“What’s that?” Harry says.

“I already ran it twice,” he whispers. “Do you have another card I could try?”

Harry glances out to Greta in the truck and sees two plain-clothes cops getting out of a blue patrol car.

He ducks quickly around some children fussing at a candy machine—the cashier calling out “Mister?”—and Harry gets into the bathroom, where he locks himself in an empty stall and waits for a moment, trying to catch his breath.

This is nothing. Those two cops are simply coming in like everybody else for the early bird special.

The toilet next to Harry flushes, and he peeks out through a crack at somebody who’s now at the sink. But this person’s wearing a long floral-print dress and white Keds with frilly pink socks. Harry glances down and notices a metal receptacle for feminine products mounted next to the toilet roll dispenser. He nearly chuckles, realizing what he’s done the same moment he understands that even on the slim chance that the “dragnet” has located him, they certainly aren’t coming into the ladies’ room to arrest him.

He’ll give it a couple minutes, and then slip through the doors, and hop in the truck—he’s got a full tank of gas, and he’ll be back on the road with Greta in no time.

Finally, Harry gets it.

It’s not about lunging forward or sitting on the fence. It’s about seizing the right moment. Calm deliberation. To strike with absolute perfect timing.

Hadn’t there been some lesson in Calvin’s story of that

defanged, unfrozen snake and the shocked dog?

The hand dryer comes on and then the ladies' room door squeaks open. Harry hears low voices asking the woman if anybody else is in there. He's breathing a little too hard to make out her reply. Harry steps up onto the plastic toilet seat and crouches down into a squat, his feet straddling the bowl, leaning awkwardly on the toilet paper dispenser to keep the weight off his bad leg.

"Harold Stables?"

This isn't possible, is it? Technically his name is Harri*son* Stables, so Harry just squeezes his fist into his mouth and shuts his eyes. Deep breaths.

"Come out of the stall, Stables."

"I'm…occupied at the moment. What's this about exactly?"

"Stables. Out of the stall. *Right. Now.*"

When Harry unlatches the door and pulls it inward, the two tall cops are standing there in stonewashed jeans and sneakers and black shirts tucked into their waistbands. They each take hold of Harry's arms and frogmarch him out of the women's restroom, through a gaggle of children in the restaurant's foyer, and out to their patrol car. In front of the eighty windows of the fun family diner, they arrest him for driving off without paying for sixteen gallons of unleaded gasoline at the Texaco across the highway.

They ease Harry into the back of their car, parked next to the truck where Greta now pops up her head to check out the action. She's panting, looking nice and happy. And when he leans forward to ask the cops if he can please get his dog, they say *no* in unison.

SALLY

After booking Harry in, certain calls are made, and he's led to a room where another prisoner is seated, his back against the wall.

A business guy, in a charcoal suit. Slicked back strawberry blond hair, and his skin is blotchy.

He comes over and asks Harry if he'd been picked up in the solicitation sting last night, too. Harry tells him that he'd forgotten to pay for a tank of gas over at Texaco, and the guy laughs so hard a fleck of saliva flies out and lands on the tip of Harry's nose.

"My wife's gonna file for a divorce, and you're in here for two squirts of flippin' *gas*? You pocket some Tic Tacs on your way out, too?"

The man keeps undoing the knot of his tie and pushing his chin out this way and that, like a boxer. When they hear footfall in the corridor, the guy stands up from the metal chair and re-cinches his tie knot, fluidly lifting his head off his neck like a swimmer trying to see over waves. He undoes and re-ties the knot again and again, mumbling to himself, arguing, disgusted.

"What *that* was? That was coercive entrapment," he says. "That was illegal, what those turkeys did to me last night."

"I was gonna go back over and pay," Harry says. "It was a long line. I really had to use the bathroom."

"Zip it, Tic Tac man. They're gonna throw me out of my congregation."

"Are you a minister or something?"

"No," he says gravely, like Harry's insulted him. Then he whispers, "I'm the second counselor and brother in the Sunday School ascendancy of the Church of Latter Day Saints."

The guy sits back down in the corner with his arms folded.

An officer calls Harry's name and he's escorted to a phone, where he has exactly one call, lasting no more than two and a half minutes. He tells Harry the line's being monitored and will cut off after the allotted time. He stands a few feet behind Harry with his arms folded.

Harry dials Adrienne's cell and waits an eternity. He never hears it ring, finally she's just there.

"Harry?"

"Hiya."

"*Hiya*?! The recorded message thing asked if I'd accept a call from an inmate in a corrections facility in *Utah*. Please tell me this is a joke."

"Hilarious, I know. Look, *allegedly* I took some gas. Borrowed, really. I was gonna pay for it, but I had to pee really bad. I think the credit card swipe-thing must've malfunctioned or something. The cops came and got me in a restaurant across the street. It sounds worse than it is."

"Leah told me you were in Idaho."

"What the fuck? Are you two like best friends now, or what?"

Adrienne wants to know everything he found out about their mom. But Harry tells her he only has two minutes.

"I'm coming to L.A. for a couple of days, and I'll tell you

the whole thing. Will you please look on the internet and see about getting me a lawyer in Orem. I know I already owe you the $1600. I'm really sorry."

"Oh, you owe me alright. What about Greta?"

Harry starts to tell her that Greta's—

The line's dead.

"Fuck."

He turns to the guard. "That was not two and half minutes."

The guard shrugs. "Including the outgoing message to the recipient it is. Guess I forgot to mention that." He yawns and leads Harry back to the cell.

Harry turns to the officer. "Do they press charges? What happens now?"

"Depends. We can hold you for up to thirty-six hours. But it usually doesn't take that long. They said something popped up in your file. So, you're gonna have to hang tight."

Three or four hours have passed when a different officer arrives, and Harry's brought back into the front room where some microwaved chicken nuggets and a warm, unopened can of generic cola await him on a metal table. Harry sits down and starts putting them into his mouth though he has no appetite.

An older black cop taps him on the shoulder, and tells him to hurry up, that he's being transferred. Harry asks him why, but he shakes his head and says his shift's just started. Harry asks about Greta, and he says to check in at an animal shelter called Fuzzy Buddies in Orem once he posts bail. His pickup will be towed over to the police impound yard behind Orem High on Ellis Drive. Harry tries to sear these details into his memory as he stuffs the last two nuggets into his mouth, one on top of the other.

Four male police officers escort Harry out into the afternoon breeze—and they stand around him forming a kind of wall as he scoots into the back caged area of a white police van with black vinyl interior. They idle there in the lot for a long time as the men speak to one another and respond to garbled voices from their radios.

The older cop returns, finally, and hands over the bag of Harry's personal effects to the driver.

"Alright, Stables. You're set to jet."

He pats the van a couple of times.

"Did you find out where they're taking me?"

The cop shakes his head.

"Missoula, Montana. That's all they said."

Harry's mother died when he was not quite two years old, but he has one memory of her.

Whether it's a real memory or an invention he's collaged together from something Adrienne said and fused to his old photograph, he doesn't know.

But it goes like this: It's summer and he's splashing around in a wading pool on their front lawn in Missoula. Their father's set up a makeshift slide for Harry, and from the photograph he carries around in his wallet, he can see that the "slide" is a kitchen stepstool jury-rigged to the bright pink door of his sister's play castle.

Harry's stark naked, shin-deep in the water, facing the

camera. He has on swimming goggles, pushed up over his forehead into his hair. And Adrienne is a happy blur, dancing in the lawn sprinkler behind him. She's got on her Minnie Mouse bathing suit.

Their mother is on the porch, sitting next to her friend and they're chatting as the two women keep their eyes on Harry and Adrienne.

Elizabeth's mouth is open as though she's in the middle of saying something like *Please don't take my picture*. Her dark hair is tucked behind her ears, and her knees are up. She's wearing blue shorts and a white tank top, like a man's, and her bare feet are just *young*-looking. There's a cigarette between her fingers. She would have been twenty-eight that summer, not much older than Harry is now.

Each time Harry goes down the slide, he knocks the contraption over, and then he shouts for help getting it put back together. His mom tells Adrienne to fix it for him. After helping her brother a few times, Adrienne loses interest and then Harry's crying and Elizabeth puts down her cigarette and comes out herself, barefoot in the grass, and fixes the slide for him. Harry stops crying for a minute and does it all over again.

By the time Harry was seven, Pat had married their Aunt Sally, and their mother's sister became their step-mom. Sally and Pat simply avoided the topic of Elizabeth altogether, so Harry and Adrienne were left to animate the few photos they had of her themselves.

If they asked Pat at the dinner table, he would say, "When you're old enough, I'll tell you about your mother." Then he'd glance over at Aunt Sally and she'd look down at her plate, or pretend she'd forgotten something in the other room and not come back, even to finish her meal.

When Harry was ten, he and Adrienne found the last photo album Elizabeth had made—color photographs of the four of them, of Harry and his sister as babies, six or seven of Adrienne staggering around in yellow footie pajamas before Harry was born. Whenever Adrienne asked their dad about this or that photo, Aunt Sally would start to cry and Pat would shake his head at his daughter and then go work on something outside or smoke in the garage.

By Adrienne's fifteenth birthday, she'd openly scoff and glare at Pat, and Harry would sit there at the dinner table and watch them carefully, hoping it wouldn't spill into a fight, but not wanting to get up and leave in case Adrienne managed to pry something out of their father.

She was sick, he'd say. *She was in the hospital.*

Once Harry heard Adrienne and Pat fighting. Harry came out of his bedroom and crept half-way down the stairs and listened to them in the kitchen.

"It was complicated," Pat said. "The doctors had competing diagnoses."

"You just don't want us to know."

"Oh, would you stop already," he said. "It's not like that."

Harry could hear how upset his dad was and wished Adrienne would leave him alone. But he could feel how furious Adrienne was and Harry wanted almost as badly to know what really had happened. It wasn't just how she died—it was her whole life that he and his sister were forbidden from mentioning.

Harry was a freshman in high school with lackluster

grades and his sister was a gifted senior heading to art school, when they overheard Pat on the phone one afternoon. They looked at each other after Pat took the call into his study, the long cord trailing after him.

"That's correct," they heard him say through the closed door. "She passed away. Yes. That would've been November 1, 1979. Um, leukemia, we think. But it was—thank you. It was a long time ago. You bet. Will do. Okay, goodbye."

Adrienne was right. Their father had lied. They didn't even know who he was talking to. Someone from the bank? An insurance agent? One of their mother's childhood friends from Helena who'd never heard?

As Pat opened the door, Adrienne grabbed ahold of the phone cord and whipped it like a jump rope.

Pat pulled the cord from her. "Adrienne, stop it."

"Why did you tell that person it was leukemia, *we think*?"

Pat put his hand up, as if to halt traffic. "I don't want to get into this with you."

"You lied. We both heard you. Harry, you heard him, right?"

Harry was watching and waiting, but he was frozen.

"*Harry*," Adrienne said. "You heard Pat say it was leukemia, didn't you?"

They'd been calling Sally by her first name for as long as Harry remembered, but it was the first time Adrienne had called their dad by his given name.

Harry nodded, looking between them, avoiding everyone's eyes, trying not to lose it.

Pat lit a cigarette, blew out a big plume of smoke, and shook his head.

"You know this upsets your Aunt Sally, and yet you push and push and keep pushing."

"You're a liar," she said. "We both heard you."

"That's enough! She's *gone*. Let it go," Pat was red in the face, tears welled up in his eyes. "Why can't you let her rest in peace?"

"Easy for you to say," Adrienne said. "You knew her. We have nothing."

Aunt Sally was sobbing and pleaded with them to quit, shouting from the couch in front of the television. Harry wanted to know as much as his sister, but more than that he wanted the fighting to stop—so he stood there, mute, trying not to take sides and make everything worse.

Adrienne was gone a few months later. She moved to California, where she came out to Harry after meeting her girlfriend Ronnie. And if it wasn't any easier with Pat and his Aunt Sally then, it was much quieter with Adrienne gone.

Harry moved up to Boulder for college, and every time he returned to the house in Denver for dinner or to do his laundry on the weekend, there was more and more of Aunt Sally's stuff heaped up. Adrienne's old bedroom was soon filled with dolls and plastic babies and stuffed animals. Before long, the collections became stacks and the stacks grew into massive piles all over the house.

When Harry was shoving off to start grad school in Tucson, Pat was already in and out of the hospital. There were better days and bad ones, but he didn't like to be visited after bouts of chemo.

When Harry's friend Jake came with him to pick up his

dad's Toyota and help Harry move a few things, Harry hadn't been to the house for months. He had planned take Adrienne's old bed with him, which she said he could have, since he'd been living on a ratty mattress in Boulder for so long.

Actually, Adrienne said, "Take whatever the fuck you want, Harry. I'm not ever going back there."

When he and Jake got to the house, Sally wasn't home, and Harry found the hidden key in the watering can near the shed out back. By then, there was just a slender path through the house, dividing all the sacks and piles of debris. Harry picked his way through the mounds of clutter and went upstairs to look into his sister's old bedroom. The door could barely open before hitting more bags of junk.

Everything smelled of cigarette smoke and mothballs. It would take Harry at least an hour to uncover the bed from all the Cabbage Patch Dolls and stuffed animals and Beanie Babies, let alone carry the frame and mattress down the stairs, which were piled high with stacks of magazines, jackets and snow equipment, cardboard boxes and dolls—many still in their packaging, or sprouting price tags from their heads.

"Whoa," Jake whispered. "This is pretty intense, man. Is all this your sister's crap?"

"It's my Aunt Sally's," Harry said. "I didn't realize it had gotten this bad."

"I'll give you a hand. But this is gonna take a while, so you're buying the beers tonight. Breakfast alone isn't—"

"Never mind," Harry said. "We need to get out of here."

They stepped over piles of toys and old coats and more boxes and plastic bags of garbage and newspapers and what looked like a kid's dollhouse that had been out in the rain. Jake found his way to the front door, Harry scribbled a quick note to Sally in the kitchen, and they made it outside.

The fresh air and sunlight were a godsend. Jake laughed nervously, but Harry said nothing. He was dumbstruck. Then he was angry, then just horrified, but when he got into his truck and started the engine, he felt a lump of inarticulable sadness take hold of his chest. Whatever this hoarding had become had to do with Harry's mom, and Harry felt sure then that he and Adrienne would never find out what had happened. He needed to move on. Cut ties. Take his dad's Toyota and start his life over in Arizona, and suddenly he felt so relieved that he'd gotten into the grad program in Tucson. Like he was escaping something in the nick of time.

He and Jake took Pat's pickup, and the two of them made their way down to Breakfast King. Harry drove in silence for a while, heading out on Colfax, and taking Broadway south.

"No offense," Jake said. "But that was pretty fucked up in there. You said it was sort of cluttered, but I've never seen anything like that."

"Me neither," Harry said, slowing down to stop at a light on Alameda, not looking over at his friend. He hadn't realized the depth of dysfunction he'd grown up in until he'd gotten a sliver of distance. It's when you come back that it hits you like a fist. All these years, Adrienne had been right about the evasion, secrets, or dissembling—whatever it was. It had materialized and piled all the way up the stairs, and taken over every room of the house. It made Harry dizzy to let his mind wander from one overflowing room into the next.

And for some reason, Adrienne's room was the source of it, as if those dolls and toy animals had been reproducing on their own in there.

A woman in a yellow coat was leading a troop of toddlers through the crosswalk, and she lifted her arm and waved to Harry in the truck as the children waddled by.

Jake said, "So many scary-ass dolls. I thought that clown from *Poltergeist* was gonna reach out and grab my ankle and pull me under the bed."

"Yeah," Harry said. "It's gonna swallow them."

BOG SPRINGS

Harry wakes up just as they're passing the old service station in Darby, where he'd spilled coffee on his lap talking to those two state troopers.

They're about a hundred miles from Missoula now. And Harry tries to think of what he'll say when he calls Calvin out on Old Pond Road from jail, but for some reason he's distracted by the memory of having sex with Leah for the first time.

Harry and Leah took an excursion into Madera Canyon, in the Santa Rita Mountains, bordering Mexico. Leah was hiking fluidly up the rocky incline on the trail up to Bog Springs.

She was wearing wool socks and her mother's old school leather boots that looked like they'd carry her up the side of a Norwegian fjord. Leah was tuned into the surroundings, and staring at her long, graceful strides was the only thing Harry had to keep him plodding that hard up the path. She'd never hiked as quickly before, but Harry was too embarrassed to ask her to slow down.

When Leah stopped to take in a view or kneel down to study a lizard sunning itself on a rock, it wasn't ever long enough for Harry to catch his breath. And after two hours of ragged, sweaty huffing, he'd fallen well behind her and Greta, who was trotting up the trail at Leah's side.

When they finally took a real break, Leah leaned back on a red boulder overlooking the canyon. It might have been

Guatemala, it was so dense with lush foliage after the summer monsoons had started in southern Arizona. A wisp of gray mist threaded itself into the greenery.

There was a hot breeze, but it had been utterly quiet. No birdsong. Just the sound of Greta lapping water out of the portable dish Harry had set down for her in the dirt by a scaly juniper.

Harry wiped the sweat off his forehead and his eyes met Leah's. She was wearing a funny expression, as if she was unsure if she should share a dirty joke.

"What's gotten into you?" Harry said. "You're hiking like a crazy person. I was dying back there."

"Can I show you something?"

Harry took a long drink from his water bottle and braced himself.

"How much further is it?"

"Follow me."

They hiked another grueling ten minutes, Greta back in stride with Leah, who was practically jogging and both of them were gliding easily over roots and jagged stones on the trail. Leah stopped once more and turned around to wait for Harry to catch up. He cleared sweat from his face and neck with the sleeve of his t-shirt.

Leah pointed at something.

"What is that?"

"That," she said, "is the cairn."

All Harry saw was a stack of reddish rocks on the trail edge. He shook his head, not following.

"Okay…" he said. "But what's it doing there?"

"It leads to a surprise."

Leah hiked up another twenty feet to the cairn, reached down for a small stone, and placed it on top of the pile. When Harry got there, he saw bootprints leading to an offshoot like a herd path through a thicket of shrubs.

Leah diverted off the trail onto the side route through the spiny foliage and Harry followed, but she was moving even faster now, and Greta was loping to keep up with her.

The secret pathway curved down into a valley full of leafy shade trees. Harry started tromping to keep pace, but Leah and Greta were moving still faster, Leah's pack bouncing up and down on her back, fifty feet ahead of Harry, then farther.

"Why are you running?" Harry called.

"Just hurry up. You'll see."

But Leah had flown ahead and Greta was racing, bounding like a greyhound. Leah's laughter echoed through the valley as she raced in an all-out sprint behind Harry's dog now, who seemed to sense where the trail was leading.

Harry's lungs were about to burst. He stopped and turned around to get his bearings. Behind him he could barely make out the ledge of the main trail they'd come down from into this valley. All that was there were thick shrubs and a big thatch of prickly pear. When he turned back, Leah was maneuvering around a far outcrop of red boulders.

Harry got to the enormous rocks a few minutes later, only to spot Leah at the edge of a meadow. She was removing her clothes in the shade under two big oaks quavering in the heat.

Naked, Leah scaled another smaller cluster of rocks surrounded by blue agaves.

By the time Harry had finally gotten to Leah's backpack

and discarded clothes, his chest was soaked in sweat and he was panting like a whipped animal. Perspiration was streaming down his temples, behind his ears. His back, his feet, his ass—everything was sweaty. Greta reappeared from some nearby bushes, stopped, and then darted past Harry with a huge stick in her mouth and veered off to find a good spot to gnaw on it.

Harry let his pack fall to the ground and went for his water, sucking in air between gulps off the bottle.

He took his shirt off and monkey-crawled on all fours over the boulders he'd seen Leah scale, bare naked, like a wood-nymph. On the other side of the rocks, there were three pools of clear water: Leah was already submerged in the biggest one, the other two were shaped like oval hot tubs between enormous red boulders. Each pool was being fed by the trickle of a translucent stream. There was nobody here but Leah. Her hair was soaking wet and pulled back on her head. She was beaming.

"Don't just stand there, Harry."

"You didn't tell me to bring my swimsuit."

"It's unbelievable," she said, dunking her head.

"Is it warm enough?"

Leah spit water his way. "Come on. Jump in."

Harry pulled off the rest of his wet clothes. He crept onto the near boulder, then tiptoed out to the edge.

"Just close your eyes and do it, it'll feel amazing."

Harry leapt in. The water was arctic. He sprang out, gasping, and shrieked like a burned chicken. Leah was floating away from him on her back, giggling. Greta poked her head through the vegetation to have a look at whatever had been disemboweled.

"I take it you've been here before," Harry said, trying not to let his voice break with cold.

"The trick is to run down the trail and race through the meadow and get as hot as you can and then pull off all your clothes and jump in."

Even with the hot sun on his shoulders, Harry's teeth were chattering, less from cold than nerves. He sat up on the slippery stone edge to get some warmth onto his face and chest. Leah edged over to him. Her eyes were big and brown, her mouth open slightly. Her breasts out of the water, the sunlight all over her face and shoulders.

"Don't you love it?"

Harry nodded, clenching his jaw to keep her from hearing his teeth clatter.

"Are you *shivering*? You're from Denver!"

"So?" he said.

"I thought Colorado was all snow-skiing and Rocky Mountains—that winter wonderland beer commercial crap. It's eighty-something degrees up here, Harry. Tell me this isn't incredible."

Leah was right. It felt good now in the sun, as she slid closer and put her hands on both of Harry's thighs under the water and held them there, looking into his eyes. Suddenly Harry was neither hot nor cold.

"I bring you all the way here for a surprise, and you're not even going to kiss me?"

"I was just waiting," Harry said, "for the right moment."

She slipped beneath the surface, swam off and emerged on the other side, pulling her hair back into a long strip down the nape of her neck.

"Well, don't wait too long. You might miss your chance."

Harry climbed out of the pool and followed Leah into the shade behind some rocks under a tree. Leah turned and kissed him, and their mouths opened, and she pressed herself into him—and Harry went from shivering cold to a flush of heat out in the hot air.

They had sex in the grass, on top of all their sweaty clothes. Harry shut his eyes, and after he was inside her, Leah said, "Look at me. I want you to look at me."

Harry opened his eyes, but he couldn't keep staring at her or he'd come.

He shook his head and squeezed his eyes shut and she said it again, "Look at me."

And she was breathing deeply, these long exhalations with this throaty sound at the end of each one. Harry wanted to stop up his ears, distract himself, vanish. Feel it and not feel it somehow at the same time. Her nails were in his back. She was making that sound at the end of each breath. Like she was trying to push the air out of her body all the way—and it was that sound, not a moan or a word, just an *uhn* that squeezed the last of it out—as she sunk her nails deeper into the skin between his shoulder blades. But he couldn't keep going like that, Leah's sound in his ear. He slowed down.

"Don't stop, do *not* stop."

"I can't—"

"Keep fucking me," she said, and she made the sound

again, and it was as if that sound she made was coming from inside him now, and he started again and he was sweating on her and she said, "Look at me."

Harry said something roughly approximating, "No, no, fuck, oh god."

And Leah made that sound at the end of her breath again and again and again.

And that was it.

ISLAND

The jail corridor smells of wet clay, something primordial and mossy.

A single bumblebee cavorts upside down on the flat panels of fluorescent lighting overhead. The concrete floor is clean and swept, but the odors from deeper inside are sending out foul wafts.

When the guards completed his intake, they told him that Detective Ridge was gone for the evening. That she'd be in early to speak with him. Then they advised Harry to use the restroom before proceeding. He told them he didn't have to go, that they'd stopped at a rest area just outside of town. They looked at each other and the female guard shrugged and said, "Okeydokey, let's do this."

Harry tries not to breathe in through his nose, but he can soon taste the smell of dank animal. He'd smelled it in the cabin after that black bear had come in and devoured his strainer full of blueberries. There's an effulgence of something fecal in here and Harry's nauseous.

The male guard's aftershave was applied in what would've been an offending quantity, but having his own cloud of cologne is probably the only thing that keeps him from vomiting. The guards walk on either side of him but do not touch Harry's arms or back or head. Neither of them looks at him or at one another—he feels their steady gaze aimed straight ahead in the deadening light of the hallway. And he hobbles fairly well between them.

They turn the corner of another long corridor, and now Harry can see many men in one enormous holding cell. There's urine and shit and the scent of burnt paper emanating from within. The prisoners wear vacant expressions, but a few look up at Harry with something shy of curiosity when the guards get the cell door open and let him inside.

Several prisoners are speaking in low voices without facing one another. One man is stretched out on his side in a long *S*-shape, like he'd fallen through the roof and gone to sleep where he'd landed.

In the absolute center of the holding cell there are human feces floating in what has become a sort of wading pool. The solitary toilet—brushed steel and seatless—stands agape beside a single metal sink. No one stands near either amenity. The latrine appears to be done overflowing shit and toilet paper. For now, it's topped-off at a quiet standstill. Many blue bottle and black flies busy themselves in the mire. And Harry realizes that occasionally these men will simply have to go ahead and add to it.

The putrid outflow of sewage has formed a kind of reverse island—the dry land making a ragged skirt on which the prisoners are clustered, their backs to the gray cinderblock walls or bars where the urine and filth have not quite reached their feet.

As the female guard draws the sliding cell door shut behind him, Harry turns to look at her but she avoids his eyes. He can see that she's trying not to take air. Her face a frozen wince, her eyes nearly shut.

Someone yells out, "You have to fix this fucking toilet in here—now!"

The lanky guard, without turning, says, "You're hired. When can you start?"

Harry pinches up the collar of his uniform to cover his nose under the tent of his shirtfront, and three men begin to jab elbows into each other's ribs and chuckle at this. One says, "Hey, check out Smelly over there," and a cackling comes from those three and a few others.

Not lingering on anyone in particular, Harry looks from one man's face to the next, going around the room—trying not to inhale at all and their faces become a blur of emptied-out eyes as he gets lightheaded. He lets fall his shirt collar and places a single hand over his mouth and nose, but there's nothing to prevent the odor from seeping in—and he gives up, just focusing on not tasting the smells entering his mouth.

An older pinkish man is slumped over. He's crying softly into his white sailor's beard. Snot comes into his mustache, and he weeps with a strange sound like a cat laughing.

One dark-haired kid, alone in the corner, is definitely too young to be in this holding cell with the rest of them. Harry thinks he can't be sixteen, and he recognizes him from the library the day of the party. The kid had been sitting at the computer terminal next to Harry, talking to himself, seeming to look through the screen into the blackness beyond.

In here, he's the only prisoner younger than Harry, and he mutters in the exact same way he had at the library. Gesticulating, pushing out his elbows. Many expressions—delight then rage then despair—pass over his face, one after another, as he stands alone with some invisible conversant. Harry watches him for a moment, relieved at even this distant familiarity.

When Harry looks down, his new white socks accidentally touch the edge of the great puddle, and he limps back to the bars and leans against them, facing the throng of prisoners around the island of water.

The men, clustered together in groups of three here and five or six there, speak in low voices that form a not unpleasant wall of murmuring: Spanish and English and indigenous dialects fusing together.

Cameras point down at them from each corner. Their lenses secured behind their own individual cages, almost like canine muzzles. And for a moment Harry thinks of where Greta must be, and a terrific sadness washes through him.

Everybody's feet, including Harry's, are clad in socks. Everybody's but one: the tormented young guy is barefoot, which Harry feels sick about given the creep of the wastewater. The goal now is to breathe in the putrid air as little as possible, and Harry negotiates his urge to throw up with quick mouth breaths, his eyes half shut to aid in conducting only the shortest inhales he can manage. Sneezing is a delicious relief. Yawning a kind of physiological nightmare triggering his gag reflex.

When it's phone call time, Harry now knows not to waste even the shortest moment. And, with Adrienne still in LA and probably assuming her brother's still in Utah, there's only one person who can help bail him out, Pat having bailed *him* out of whatever squabbles Calvin had found himself in over the years.

Harry dreams of what exactly he'll say to him when Calvin picks up, and labors to mentally rehearse a twenty-second description of the circumstances and ends by begging him to bring money down and extricate him from this pit. Harry almost smiles, remembering Calvin doling out a pocketful of coins and rumpled dollar bills to pay for their breakfast the morning they'd met at Flo-Ann's.

It seems like a year has passed between then and now. When Harry counts the days, somehow a single week has yet to elapse.

A voice comes from a group of men congregated closest to the flowing-over toilet.

"Hey you."

It's the ghost from the road. The big guy Harry had ditched with Tommy the night of the party. Donald Hunt from Coeur d'Alene, Idaho. Long white shirt. Red basketball shorts. Harry had only seen him once since then—and that was his mug shot on the TV above Silas's bar after his day on the river with Calvin. And now Donald Hunt is looking straight at Harry, calling out to him.

Hunt is wearing that same long white shirt, and it hangs over his gut almost to his knees. On its front, a big splotch of mud or shit, maybe. The perspiration rings of his underarms are two brown moons. Don's hair is tousled and flattened like he's slept in here.

It's been several days since the party. This guy obviously hadn't posted bail, or maybe it hasn't been set. But from across the septic pond, Don stares at Harry, nodding like he can't believe his luck. The man's eyes belong to a beaten doll—they are wild and alive and seem to have been pushed back deep into his head by somebody else.

Harry tries to say something, but when he takes a breath he gags and falls into a coughing fit. Don waddles his way over to him, avoiding having to put pressure on his bad side, a gimpy maneuver Harry knows well by now.

Two other men had been standing with Don, and they're now staring at Harry and back at Don again. He doesn't recognize them from the party, but Harry doesn't want to hold eye contact and make any unwitting invitations to join him.

One of those near him is a Native guy with black hair half way down his back. The other man is much shorter and white—his pallor is that dead gray of bad hamburger. And he looks like a skeleton, with the protruded jawline of a Halloween skull in a shop window. Harry can see from here that some or all of his top teeth are gone. His cheeks are dents. His skull face appears frozen in an expression of sucking at wind.

Don holds his eyes on Harry and comes slowly around the watery outflow, pushing past the other men, calling out "Hey!" again and again, and Harry would really prefer if he stopped that. The other prisoners are turning to discover who Harry is, what misery or fortune he might have brought in with him. And Harry can't tell if Don's coming over for a bear hug or to bash his face in.

Don sticks out his big moist hand and the two of them shake then, like any couple of chums in a jailhouse.

"I'm so glad it's you, man," he says.

"Why's that?"

"It means you didn't run. Tommy was gonna try to scare

you and get you out of town. It means Tommy's fucking scheme fell apart."

"Oh yeah?" That's all Harry has.

Don just shines his wild-looking eyes on him.

"What did Tommy tell you?"

Don glances over at the young kid jabbering in the corner, still fidgeting and carrying on with his invisible cellmate.

"He and Frank were gonna say it was this guy Paul Tillett, and then he talked to Ian, and Ian told him that Paul already ratted him out to the cops. So, Tommy had to come up with another story and that's when—"

"Tommy was in here with you?"

"Yeah," Don says, his eyes back on Harry. "But he called Ian and Ian got him out and Tommy said he was gonna go scare the hell out of you. Since it was his word against Paul's. But Tommy was worried, because he'd already changed his story with the detectives at least twice. Then he said he and Ian got in a fight over it."

Tommy had smelled like an open sewer at the cabin when he showed up with Frank that morning and it was now pretty apparent why.

"Tommy said he was gonna put it on you," Don says. "But he had to get you to run first, to make it look like you'd fled town."

"Well, Tommy got me to run alright."

Don chuckles, like Harry's kidding. Harry just stares at him. The capillaries under Don's eyes and across the bridge of his nose are broken, enflamed. The whites of Don's eyes are bloodshot with thick striations of pink and red.

"Where'd the cops pick you up, anyway?"

"Utah."

"Ho shit! You *were* on the run. You steal a car or something?"

"Something," Harry says.

He thinks of Greta sitting in the truck, her porcupine cuts visible from the back of that patrol car.

"Don't worry though, man. Paul Tillett knows everything. He's already told the detectives it was Tommy and Frank who shot Lucy. Paul's gonna—"

"Paul's dead," Harry says.

He doesn't want to tell Don, it just falls out of Harry's mouth like so much drool.

"No he's not…" Don says, and then to the young kid mumbling in the corner, Don yells, "Shut the fuck up over there!"

But the kid's in pain, grimacing and gesticulating with his palms up, arguing or pleading, maybe.

"Paul told the cops," Don says. "Tommy said Paul told them what happened and—"

"Don, they ran him over in the street in front of his house, while his dad stood watching from the window. Paul Tillett's dead."

Don shuts his eyes for a moment, like he's suddenly realized that what he's staked everything on is a mirage. Harry doesn't want to tell him what Tommy had told him on the phone when Harry was at the playground in Orem. He doesn't want Don to lose it in here. Who knows if he'll attack Harry or keel over into the filth or what.

"Shut up!" Don yells at the kid, who is chattering louder now. Then to Harry, in a stage whisper, "I didn't kill her. But it was *my* gun, so they won't fucking let me out of here."

Don's eyes seem to siphon light out of Harry's, and Harry has to look away. He's darkened Don's world, and Harry knows things that will make it worse.

"What are they charging you with?" Harry says.

"First, they said maybe manslaughter, but later they said minimum is accessory or something. They wanted me to say Tommy did it, but I told them I didn't know. Plus, I don't have a lawyer. And they have the Ruger. It's my dad's rifle. It's registered in his name."

"Everybody shot that rifle though, right?" Harry says, trying to throw him a bone.

"But the cops found me on the road. They made me take them to where it was in the weeds and if Tommy—Shut the fuck up!" Don says to the kid again.

A couple of the men speak to Don now, words of warning to leave the young guy alone.

"Don, he's not well," Harry says. "Just let him be."

Don doesn't hear this. He's someplace else now, far back in his brain, someplace where the story is closing in around him.

"What happened out there?" Harry says.

"Tommy ditched me. I twisted my ankle *bad*."

"No, I mean, out in the field at the party."

But Don keeps going, "Tommy just left me out there in the fucking dark, so the cops found me on the road before the sun even came up. I didn't try to hide, because my leg was so fucked."

Don's bloodshot eyes are glassy with tears that won't fall. He'd seen Tommy fire over his friends' shoulders. He'd seen Tommy hatch plans to put it on whoever popped into his little brain next. Don knew without having to know, because he knew Tommy.

He comes in as if to tell Harry a secret. "You left us out there, man. And you didn't have to do that."

Harry leans back from his pungent breath. "I panicked, Don. I'm sorry, but I—"

"I didn't shoot Lucy," he says. "Is that what Tommy told you?"

Harry doesn't want to say it, so he stalls. "Don't they have to appoint you a public defender or something?"

"Yeah but they said it could take *days.*"

"Jesus."

The other men are watching them, listening now.

Don doesn't seem to notice them. He's glaring instead at the young kid in the corner, like all his problems would vanish if this poor guy would stop babbling. Don barks at the kid, an animal sound. The kid flinches and it makes his chatter wilder, louder. The very tall man with long black hair and the shorter, gray-faced one both step forward.

Harry doesn't want to deceive Don. He doesn't want to crush him with word of Tommy's scheme. For all Harry knows Don had fired the shot himself. Plus, Don's a big guy and Harry's not sure what he's capable of.

With the men watching them, he can't tell if some of them are protecting Don, or what, but Harry doesn't want to get stomped to death in a jail cell. Yet everything inside him is saying don't lie to this guy.

"Don," Harry says, "who shot Lucy?"

"Honestly, it could've been either of them. Paul was talking to Tommy, saying all this shit to distract him, or to get him to quit shooting over everybody, and Tommy hit Paul with the rifle and Frank jumped on him when Paul got his hands on it—and it went off and got Lucy in the chest."

"What was Paul saying to Tommy?"

"It didn't make any sense."

"What was it? Do you remember?"

"Paul kept saying, 'It's mine, you piece shit. Not yours, it's *mine.*' He was saying it in this weird way, over and over, but the rifle wasn't Paul's, it was my dad's so I didn't know what the fuck he meant. Maybe Paul was just wasted, but it made Tommy furious, and that's when Tommy fucking jabbed him with the Ruger. When Tommy and Frank pulled it back from Paul it went off."

Kristin's baby. It was Paul's.

Don speaks without looking away from the kid now, who's getting louder and louder. The kid looks like an actor on a stage, rehearsing the climactic scene of a play, going over each gesture and nuance, getting all tangled up inside it. And he's holding his right wrist with his left hand, kneading the muscle there compulsively, massaging a wound or getting at a mosquito bite.

"Tommy and Frank came out to my dad's cabin on Rock Creek yesterday morning. To scare me off or kill me, or to try to get me to lie to the cops. I don't know. Before Tommy even got around to it, somebody came into the cabin and shot Frank."

"Is Frank okay?"

"Frank," Harry says, "is not okay." He lets out a sigh. "Frank's dead too. But listen to me."

"Tommy killed Frank?"

"No," Harry says. "A man came in and blew his head off." Which was true, but Harry's stomach is twisting now, like he'd eaten something he shouldn't have, just stuffed it in and swallowed without chewing.

Don's gone red and sweaty. Tears are pooling over his bloodshot eyes. He's putting it all together, but he keeps staring at the poor kid in the corner, who's wrestling with something terrible—bickering and imploring. Losing to whatever it is.

"Tommy called me yesterday," Harry says. "He wanted me to say that you'd done it, Don. He wanted me to go to the police and say it was you, or else he'd put the whole thing on me."

Silence. Don can't seem to take his eyes off of the kid.

"Don, did you kill Lucy?"

Tears fall from Don's eyes, and streak down his dirty cheeks. He won't look at Harry. He watches the kid, who's still rubbing his wrist, twisting with hurt and stammering convulsively.

Finally, Don says, "Tommy shot Lucy."

"You're sure?"

"Frank was on the ground after they tried to pull the rifle back from Paul. Tommy got it from him, I think."

"You *think*?"

"Paul was yelling. And Tommy got the gun away from him and Frank, and it went off and hit Lucy and everybody fucking ran. You have to tell the police, man. You have to tell them."

Then the kid in the corner meets Don's eyes, still working at something on the inside of his wrist. He tugs down his shirt sleeve and goes at it, scratching. Harry doesn't want to remind Don that he can't corroborate Don's story, even if it's true.

Harry hadn't been out there, but Don's coming apart now, his chin quivering, crying.

"I'm going to kill him," Don says. "I'm going to beat his head in if he doesn't shut up and stop staring at me."

"Don—" Harry touches his elbow. "He's not right. Just—"

Don's arms go up in the air, and he tells the kid to stop looking at him and shut the fuck up. And then Don says it again much louder and goes over to him around the water on the floor and swats the air in front of the kid, though the young guy's ten feet off, still in his corner. And the kid sees that Don's coming toward him and begins screaming louder now. Not words, just brain-emptying cries.

Don limps up to the kid and shoves him against the wall. There's a muffled slap of the kid's back making contact with the cinderblock. But the kid is curled over, working something out of his sleeve with both hands now. He hadn't been itching his wrist. Harry can see what looks like white wire from a straightened coat hanger. The kid slashes Don across the mouth with it, almost like he's scribbling on Don's face with a pen.

Don screams and this brings over the tall man and the gray-faced man from near the flooded latrine and they walk right through the water and shit in their socks.

Don swings at the tall one with long black hair. And that man turns his face, grimacing, and takes Don's fist on his ear. The skeletal one comes up behind Don in the shit. The short gray man is biting his own tongue, watching Don as his eyes seem to come forward in their sockets, and then he jabs Don very hard somewhere low in his back, locating a kidney maybe. And Don doubles over, gasping, and Harry takes three steps backwards into the cell's cold bars.

The skeleton draws Don back up and holds him now. And then the tall one takes up a fistful of Don's hair to steady his head on his neck and begins to punch at Don's mouth. He punches at his teeth and at his lips. He lands one on Don's eye and Don cries out like a wounded dog. And the skeleton lets him fall, and Don goes down to the water on the floor.

And the two men, who become four then, are upon him. And they kick at Don with their feet, in white and black and brown socks—at first in his ribs and stomach. Then at his legs and back and face.

Harry's sure that they can't kill a man kicking away at him in their socks. But the tall man with black hair goes to work at kicking Don's nose in, and that man looks like a puppet tugged by a possessed master. Soon there's blood from Don's mouth on the man's white sock, which becomes longer like a child's when his socks slip partly off and are dragging behind his feet.

Now Don is bleeding in the filth and water on the floor of the holding cell. And Harry begins to yell. And the young kid in the corner comes out from behind the shield of his own arms and begins to scream and yell with Harry. And Don is moaning now too. And Harry screams for them to stop. And the men in their socks, still kicking and kicking, must've collapsed Don's lung, because Don is gasping like a netted fish and one of his eyes has become unsocketed. Harry turns to face the corridor, as if in a Saturday afternoon movie, and he grips the bars with both of his hands, and screams for the guards.

When the two guards arrive, they beat back everybody

near Don's fallen body. They strike the skeleton and the tall man with long black hair. And they strike at some of the men who had tried to pull the assailants from Don when the shouting had begun. And Don's still on the ground, prone, in the shit and water of the cell floor trying to figure out how to breathe without lungs now. He's drawn a hand up to cover his loosened eye. The other hand is palm-down, flat in the sewage, readying for a push-up that won't come.

The men who'd been at Don with their fists and feet have either fled to the corners or received a club to an ear or shoulder. One of the men, a stubby blond-haired white man, like a much older Tommy, slides in the mess as he scurries off, and he goes up into the air like a circus clown slipping on a roller skate. The stubby man's legs come out from under him—pedaling the air—and he hits the floor hard with a watery smack. Some of the other men jeer with laughter at this. And the blond man who looks like old Tommy gets up on his knees and he holds up his hands, which are covered in excrement. The man cackles. Harry turns and throws up in his corner of the cell.

And then it's over.

Don is alive, but he's a fish on the wet floor of a boat and looks to have been beaten like one. The guards remove him by dragging him out by his trousers, as his shirt is badly torn.

Harry gets a solitary whiff of the guard's magnificent cologne, and then it's gone. There's a slender red scratch from Don's ear across his face from the kid's wire hanger. Don's white gut hangs over the waistband of his red shorts, and there's purple and black bruising now. And Harry sees what looks like a blue spotted leopard tattooed onto Don's belly and ribs, and it looks right at home there.

Harry stands in the corner next to the kid too young to be in here with any of them.

And the kid continues to chatter and murmur and shout intermittently. His wire hanger must be tucked back under his sleeve now. When they patted him down, they probably hadn't felt a thing. It looked to have been thin enough that the kid could have used sleight of hand and simply distracted the guards with his stream of chatter. Or perhaps it was made of plastic, and the wand had missed it entirely.

Harry stands close to him. He doesn't know if it's to protect this young guy from the others or to keep himself safe in the shadow of his anguish, but Harry stands with him and weeps without sound, his chin on his chest, one hand a spider over his face.

Had Harry helped to spawn such violence? Could he have prevented Lucy's killing? Maybe, maybe not. But Paul's death might have been avoided if Harry had confessed what he'd seen to the police. Behind his eyes in swift succession: Frank's slumped-over corpse, the unbroken mop handle across his quivering leg, then the long strand of tobacco saliva over Greg's arm in the doorway of the cabin, then Don's kicked-in face. And for some reason the two smacks of the thrown newspapers hitting the glass door of the Sapphire that last night with Kristin.

Harry squats down into the corner in a ball and stays like that through the night. Each time he nods off, he flinches awake to make sure his socks and pant legs aren't touching the water. The young guy whispers and talks on beside him, and Harry lives in the sounds of his muttering, in a sort of waking dream.

Finally, Harry's got time to ponder this nightmare and reckon with what's happened, with what he's seen and done, but he's obliterated. Emptied of anything like perspective.

The countless domino-like effects of his own zig-zagging maneuvers fade into the kid's murmuring, as with scraps of ash a roaring fire offers the breeze.

Harry threads together a child's verse to keep from losing his mind:

Kristin's awake and Lucy's asleep
As Paul is gone and Tonya weeps
Greta's in Orem at Fuzzy Buddies
and Leah's with Annie at home.
Betsy was killed when she saw a fox
and it's time for Harry to go.
Frank is dead and Tommy has fled
and Don was kicked to his bones
If Harry gets out he'll ring up the guide
who lives on Old Pond Road.

Harry chants this half-rhyme of doggerel in his head until he dozes off to the sounds of the kid whispering beside him, and the buzzing of the flies working over the water.

Around dawn, a few of the men begin to stir and moan and grumble to each other. Harry watches as three and then four and then five of them urinate directly onto the pool in the holding cell, and eventually he stands up and gives in to doing so himself.

A new guard with his hair in a loose ponytail appears at the cell not long after the sun's risen. He calls out something through the bars.

"Stabble?"

Harry looks around. No one replies.

Then Harry says, "I'm Stabble."

"You're out, Stabble. Let's giddy-up."

The prison guard slathered in aftershave from yesterday is waiting for him at the intake desk. He hands back Harry's possessions in a Ziploc baggie, and says there'll be no charges filed against him in Missoula County. That he's free to go.

"I was in there for almost twenty-four hours," Harry says. "They drove me—"

"Usually folks aren't trying to pick *up* charges," Cologne says, pausing to look over at the other man with the ponytail. "I bet Russ here can work up some other ones. What do you think, Russ? You wanna call Detective Ridge back and tell her this kid wants to be a suspect after all?"

Russ chuckles and shakes his head.

"Can you tell me what happened to Donald Hunt?"

They look at each other, then at Harry. "Don't know, but he must've had it coming for something." One of them laughs. The other scratches his ear.

"Is he dead?"

Russ narrows his eyes and shrugs.

Cologne sighs, and slides a single sheet of paper across the table to Harry: a memorandum detailing a $517.47 fine for the misdemeanor larceny of removing sixteen gallons of unleaded gasoline without purchase from Texaco, in addition to time served. Payable to the City of Orem Justice Court, Orem, Utah. The invoice for which will arrive in the mail in seven to ten business days. Failure to pay the balance will prompt a police warrant, up to six months in prison, additional fines.

"That's it?"

Cologne looks at Harry, his forehead wrinkling. "Stables, this is the part where you turn around and push open that door right there behind you."

I'll tell you what else. I think that my desire to remain totally fucking ignorant about shit that will only get me in trouble is both deep and abiding. I'm going to say that it is just damn near a religion.

— Cormac McCarthy

PART 4
HOMECOMING

OLD POND ROAD

Harry walks two blocks over to the Grizzly Grocery in the street clothes he'd purchased at Quincy's in Orem and buys a bottle of orange Gatorade.

He comes out on the curb and looks at his phone. It's dead.

There's an elderly woman in a pristine chocolate-colored Jaguar in the lot, and she's smoking behind the wheel and reading *People* magazine. On the cover, Harry can see a celebrity couple getting married. It's a close up shot of them kissing. Harry smiles at the woman, and she returns a half-smile and cocks her head as if to see whether she recognizes him before returning to her magazine.

When Harry notices the payphone, he goes back inside to ask the cashier if he can get some quarters. He has one dollar in his wallet. The cashier says he can only make change if Harry purchases something, so he buys a single ten-cent mint to get the register open. Harry smells wretched enough that the cashier puts the coins on the counter and takes two steps back and watches with a look of revulsion as Harry goes out.

He glances over at a newspaper vending box with a copy of the *Missoulian* face out. The headline reads: *CABIN KILLER CAPTURED*, below which is a picture of Greg Tillett. Under the subheading follows: *Greg's Foreign Auto Shop Owner Charged in Rock Creek Revenge Slaying.*

Beside the payphone is an ice chest adorned with a goofy

cartoon penguin. The penguin has on a red stocking cap with a fuzzy white ball on its peak, its black flippers akimbo, as he's doing a slippery dance. Harry puts in one quarter and dials the number zero.

When he gets the operator, he asks for Calvin Hogan's number. On Old Pond Road. The voice thanks him mechanically and he hears a click. The line seems to go dead, but Harry holds the receiver to his ear, and he looks at the dancing penguin, and then it begins to ring through to the phone at Calvin's. The plastic receiver feels good against Harry's jaw, and hovering there near his mouth. He could almost break down and sob, but he's done with that for now.

Harry touches the slender accordion coil of its silver cord and draws the tip of his finger along its serrated length where it disappears into the plastic siding of the phone box. Somebody has carved the words FUCK YOUU, like that, into the shiny metal plating where the coin slot is, under the lever to pull down and surrender your change.

It rings a third time, a fourth, yet somehow Harry knows he'll answer it. He can almost see Calvin watching two guys yapping at each other in an aluminum boat, trying to net a big marlin on the fishing channel. He'll set down his bottle of beer, shush Herkimer on the way over, and pick up the phone.

Harry shuts his eyes and he pictures it all.

"Yell-o?"

Harry opens his mouth to speak, but it feels like there's cotton in his throat, over his tongue. He coughs a few times.

"Amanda?"

"It's Harry."

"Oh hey, Harrison. You make it home yet or what?"

"Not quite. But I'm on my way."

"So, what do you make of my proposal?"

"I have no clue what you're talking about, Calvin."

"Didn't you get my message?"

"Phone's dead. Honestly, I'm not sure I can handle any proposals right now."

"Sure you can. I need an aide-de-camp, Harrison. Somebody to tie up flies. Shuttle stockbrokers from the Radisson out to the crick. You know, assist old Cal in hauling the big game kills down the mountain."

"I don't think so."

"Don't be so hasty, Harrison. You ain't even heard what I pay."

"What do you pay?"

"Cold beer and puma stories, to start."

"No," Harry says.

"Just joshin' ya, kid. I'll throw in bologna sandwiches for lunch. Don't it sound like a boatload of thrills n' spills?"

"Calvin," Harry says, smiling now, "have you lost your fucking mind?"

"Probably," Calvin laughs. "But what's that got to do with anything? You think it over. It'd be a hoot: we join forces, fight crime, solve little murder mysteries out on the rivers and streams, all while reeling in the fishies, drinking ice cold cans of—"

"Sounds like you need a gopher."

"If you wanna be fancy about it, then yeah. I need a gopher."

"Thank you, but there's not one chance in hell."

"Harrison, you're already as good a gumshoe as what's her face. Old Jessica Fletcher on *Murder She Wrote*." Calvin's snickering. "We'll find you all kinds of captivating yarns up here to scribble onto your notepad."

"I'm literally never coming back to the state of Montana, ever in my life, Calvin."

"Alright then, Mr. Snooty Britches, you better stop at the Grand Canyon on your way down. That thing's supposed to be huge."

"I think maybe I will do that."

"You hear what happened, Harrison?"

"You mean about Greg?"

"I meant about your valentine. Old Cal was a step ahead of you. Your playmate Kristin…"

Calvin pauses a moment and Harry turns around. The woman in the Jaguar is gone. In her place, a guy is unloading crates of beer from a truck emblazoned with a gargantuan bottle of Budweiser exploding out of a lot of wet ice. Harry's going to need one that size.

"Harrison?"

"Yeah, what happened?"

"Oh, man." Calvin says. "They're gonna lock her ass up, you can bet on that. Haven't you seen no news?"

"I've been on the road," Harry says. "What the fuck is going on?"

"Well, Kristin went ahead and shot the little guy. Six times. Put him down over at Child's last night. About ten people sat perched there on their barstools and watched her stroll into the saloon and sprinkle him with lead like it was the Wild West. I'm still waiting for the coppers to get it cleaned up. I mean, that's my watering hole for Pete's sake. Anyhow, I talked to Rod behind the bar and he said he saw the whole thing like it was in slow-mo.

"Tommy comes in and says he's buying everybody in the place a round of Jäger shots. Rod says, 'If you're gonna do that you gotta pay the tab up front.' I guess the twerp tried that once before and slipped out the back after everybody drank up and patted him on his head."

The operator interrupts and says to put in another twenty-five cents. Harry's hand is shaking and he loses the first quarter, as it rolls under the cooler. He kicks it hard and cries out. He takes a deep breath, and then gets the next quarter out of his pocket and eases it into the coin slot.

"Calvin?"

"Aren't you listening to this, Harry? *Sheesh.* So, short stuff pulls out a C-note splattered with blood and whangs it down on the bar, and Rod says he was still holding it up to the light behind the register, turning it this way and that, when your gal slips in through the door, pistol in hand. Kid hadn't even washed his whiskey down before she fired at him."

"Jesus."

"Rod said the first bullet went into Tommy's open mouth—he must've been hollering or something—and it came out the back of his head and landed in the dart board. I guess the second one missed him and went into the jukebox, so Rod's gonna have to get that repaired again.

"But your pal Kris, she walked right over to the little guy, gurgling and flopping on the floor like a baby squirming in a crib, and emptied numbers three, four, five, and six into his ribs. Then she turns and struts out. Never said a word to nobody about nothing. Like Merry Goddamn Christmas. Now Child's is all webbed off with yellow crime tape, if you can picture that."

The delivery guy rolls another stack of beer cases down the truck ramp on his handcart. He's sweating and gives Harry a nod as he wipes his forehead with his arm and pushes his load through the doors.

"Did they arrest her yet?"

"Not yet, evidently," Calvin says. "She done bolted, solo. I talked to Rod last night so they probably have bracelets on her by now. Unless of course she's peeking over the edge of the Grand Canyon with you, Mr. Tiptoe-Out-Of-Dodge-City-After-Breakfast...."

"Very funny. How'd they know it was her?"

"Everybody knows her, man," Calvin says. "You crazy? She's in there all the time. She didn't have on any *costume*. Just waltzed in wearing her blue jeans and—bang-bang—got the job done."

"Is that it?"

"Not hardly. Old Frank Keene got his pumpkin shot off out at Pat's cabin, but I guess you probably knew that, huh?"

"I didn't want to get you in trouble."

"Yeah," Calvin says, chuckling, "that's quite a mess out there now. You see that thing transpire?"

"I might've, yeah."

"Greg's got his mug slapped all over the news."

Harry wants to tell him that Greg and Tonya are going to be grandparents, but he doesn't know that for sure—and who knows what's going to happen to Kristin or to her baby now.

"Hey, Calvin, do you think you could come downtown and pick me up?"

"What do you mean? I thought you said you was on the road?"

"I'm in town. Over on Ryman."

"Look, I got a date with Amanda, Harrison. Where'd you put your truck at?"

"Orem," Harry says.

"*What*-um?"

"Orem," Harry says. "Utah."

"Shoot, bud. I don't have time to pick you up on Ryman *and* make my date. Can't you get somebody else to fetch you?"

"Calvin, Jesus Christ, man. I'm standing outside the fucking Grizzly Grocery, and I'm just out of jail and my cell phone's dead, and I'm down to my last quarter, okay?"

"Jail, huh? Ain't you full of surprises." Calvin lets out a big sigh, like Harry's swung a wrecking ball through his weekend. Finally, he says, "Yes…Harrison…I'll cancel on Amanda for you, but you're gonna owe me for this one. This gal's got a full dance card and it wasn't easy to—"

"Thanks, Calvin."

PATRICK

Sally called Harry several times on his long bus ride back to Utah, but his phone was dead until he found another charger for it at a Radio Shack when he had to switch buses in Pocatello, Idaho.

By the time he finally plugs it into an outlet on the wood-paneled wall at the Sizzler, across the road from the bus station, there are six messages from his aunt. Harry makes the mistake of listening to them all at once in a corner booth of the empty restaurant.

The first ones are short. Six seconds: "Hi, Harrison, it's Sally. Give me a call when you can." Ten seconds: "Not sure where you are, but please call me back. Your father'd like to hear from you."

But then they grew longer: twenty-eight seconds and more frantic. The last one's nearly two minutes long: Pat's been moved to hospice. The cancer's spread to his lungs. It's time to buy a plane ticket and come say goodbye. Sally ended by saying, "Call me back as soon as you get this, Harrison." By that time, the last message is already two days old.

Harry walks out to the parking lot of the Sizzler and stands in the late afternoon shadows, debating. But there's nothing to debate. If Harry doesn't call right now, that'll be it. He won't ever call. And it'll be too late.

Harry scrolls through his contacts, finds his dad's cell

number, dials, and Sally answers.

"Harrison? Thank goodness."

"Hey there."

"Hang on a second, I'll put Pat on."

Sally muffles the phone. Harry hears his dad's voice. Sounds tired but he's alive.

"Hey, kiddo. You back in Tucson?"

"Not quite," Harry says, letting out a breath he didn't realize he'd been holding. "How are you feeling?"

"I might ask you the same thing. Cal said you got into some debacle up in Rock Creek."

"Something like that. But I'm fine. Anyway, what are the doctors telling you?"

"Oh, a variety of things. Depends on which one I care to listen to."

Harry can hear his Aunt Sally tell Pat to ask when he's coming to Denver, but his dad ignores her. He pictures Adrienne's room erupting with his aunt's dolls and shudders.

"That Missoula sheriff's detective called me."

"No kidding."

"You don't sound too surprised, Harry. Why's that?"

"What'd he say?"

"Matter of fact it was a lady sheriff," Pat says. "Detective Ridge. You get tangled up with that Francis King somebody-or-other?"

"Frank Keene," Harry says. "What'd she tell you?"

"Well, they found him dead as a rat out in the cabin. Miss Ridge wanted to know what the deceased was doing on my property. I said, 'Deceased how?' and she says, 'Set down with a twelve-gauge scattershot at close range,' and that it was something colorful in there. I says, 'That's news to me.' And I asked her for a description of the body since I figured it was probably you. But she said the cadaver had long dark hair. Although that was about all she could offer on account of the man's face being blown half off."

"Sounds about right."

"Then she asked me when I'd last seen my son."

"What'd you tell her?"

"I told her it'd had been a while, but that you'd moved to Tucson about a year ago. That you'd left for school down there."

"I didn't kill him if that's what you're thinking," Harry says.

"You sound like a regular outlaw to me, kiddo."

Harry hears Pat smile on the other end, ice clinking inside a glass.

"You're getting to be like that little boy in the storybook with the purple crayon who scribbles himself into all kinds of trouble." Then Pat starts coughing, which sounds dry and painful.

"Anyhow, I had Cal head out to Rock Creek to poke his nose in there. He confirmed that it's a macabre scene: cabin door flung wide open, animal tracks through the gore—"

"Calvin told me what happened to mom."

There's a pause before Pat says, "No kidding."

"You don't sound surprised. Why's that?"

"Well, I figured you'd find out before much longer, Harry."

"Why'd you lie to us?"

Pat lets out a big sigh. "I never once lied to you."

Harry thinks he can hear his dad light up a cigarette, but his mind must be been filling in the silence on Pat's end.

"She died in a car wreck."

"Wrong, Harrison. She died in the hospital from any number of things. I was laid up at the time myself, so don't—"

"But why wouldn't you ever tell us what really happened? Why'd you make up those stories?"

"I didn't think you were up to hearing about it, Harry."

"What do you mean, *up to it*?"

"Maybe I just didn't think you could stomach it."

"*Stomach* it?"

"What's with the echo?" Pat says, louder now. "We in a cave here?"

"So, it's our fault you lied to us? Is that what you're saying?"

"Cripes, Harry. You never wanted to know anyhow. I've had about enough of this for the day. It was hard on us. Even harder on Sally, and your mother—"

"I know she was pregnant. Adrienne and I had a right to know that."

"Listen to you, whimpering about your rights." Pat says. "Your sister's a *pest*. And you know what else? I got tubes sticking up my nose and a needle in my arm with Bob Barker dancing around in a yellow suit on the boob tube in here. And your Aunt Sally's in pieces now. I give you my pickup truck, you leave a dead body to rot in my cabin, and now you're flinging this old nonsense at me?

"Your mother's gone. We moved *on* from it. I don't know why you two couldn't do the same, but that's your problem—not mine."

Harry wants to scream *fuck you*, to throw his phone at the asphalt and shatter it, but he's squatted down, his free hand over his ear, hot with rage. He can hear Sally muttering to Pat and Pat tells her to hush, but she keeps on chattering in the background.

"Enough," Pat says to her. "Harrison, Sally wants to me ask you when you're getting to Denver."

"I'm not," Harry says, standing up and walking through the parking lot to a patch of grass in the sunlight. "Adrienne and I are heading back up to Missoula to say goodbye to her."

"Goodbye to who?"

"To Betsy," Harry says. "To our mother. Calvin's gonna take us out to the spot on the Clark Fork."

"I hope you kids have a ball," Pat says. And he lets out a long, wearied exhalation.

"Aren't you at least sorry?" Harry says, his throat constricting around the words. He's too mad to cry. But Pat says nothing and Harry says it once more: "Aren't you sorry about what happened? That she lost the baby?"

"Is *that* what you finally called to hear me say? You're not really giving me the sense that I'd misjudged your abilities to act like a grownup. Have to admit I liked you better when you minded your own damn business."

"You know what? You're right," Harry says. "I'm an idiot for defending you to Adrienne. Avoiding bringing up mom to protect you. I might be a dumbass, but you're a coward and a liar."

"Defending *me*?" Pat says, amused now. "Protecting *me*?"

"I gotta catch my bus."

"Go run and catch your little school bus, Harry. I warned you about going up to Missoula."

"Yeah. You warned me all right, *Pat*."

Harry hangs up and starts jogging as quickly as he can with his leg giving off dull throbs of heat up his spine to the back of his brain. He's still two blocks away when he has to slow down. He's screaming, waving his hands, out of breath—and the Greyhound to Salt Lake City pulls away.

Outside Pocatello the next morning, Harry has little to no service so he shuts his phone off to conserve battery.

He's not in the mood to hear any more from his dad or Aunt Sally anyway. He had a long conversation from the motel with Adrienne about his talk with Pat, and she stayed remarkably calm throughout. In fact, she was unfazed by Pat's lack of apology or contrition. Then Harry finally told her about their mother's baby and Adrienne lost it.

Before they'd hung up, Harry thanked her for sending him bus fare to Western Union in Missoula. When he showed up at the office, there was money waiting for him. He slid his passport into the compartment and the clerk opened it and held it up against the transparent partition, eyeing Harry. She slid an envelope full of fifties and twenties back out with it, along with a page-long, yellow receipt—its paper as thin as an onion skin. He flipped through the bills with his thumb. Nearly five hundred dollars. On the line where it said *Message to be sent*, Adrienne had scribbled a three-word note: "Go home, dummy." Harry couldn't help grinning at that.

On the phone later, she said, "Just promise me it's not for drugs."

"I probably *should* be on drugs by now, but do I really

sound that fucked up?"

"Meth would make quite a bit more sense at this point."

"Maybe I'll try to find some."

"Don't even joke. By the way, I spoke to Calvin Hogan. I want to go Missoula right away."

"No fucking chance," Harry said. "I literally just got out of that place for the second time. We'll go for Thanksgiving. I can get Mrs. O'Brien across the street to look after Greta. I already missed my fucking bus to Salt Lake yesterday, and I'm gonna need a month to sleep and eat Little Debbie snack cakes while I watch Sesame Street."

Adrienne wanted to know where Greta was and why Harry hadn't called to check on her. In fact, he had and she was fine. He called the shelter earlier that day, stuck with nothing to do but watch Cinemax at the Tomahawk Motel out on Pocatello's scenic Bench Road for the evening.

"She's at Fuzzy Buddies in Orem."

Adrienne laughed at this.

"I'm so glad you think that's funny," Harry said, electing not to mention that it wasn't the first time he'd lost Greta this week. "I'm lucky somebody didn't try and adopt her. Or trade her in for some meth."

"Get some sleep," Adrienne said. "I'm glad you're out of Alcatraz."

"Not as glad as I am. Thanks for everything, Adrienne. I promise I'll pay you back. I love you."

"Yeah, yeah," she said. "Okay, Harry."

Harry drifts in and out of sleep in his seat on the back of the bus most of the way down from Idaho into Utah, passing through Ogden and Salt Lake back into Orem.

The animal shelter closes at 5 p.m. and it's already 4:15 by the time he hoofs it from the bus station over to the tow lot after a chatty police dispatcher tells him where to find his truck.

Harry hands over $156 and a bald man with milky eyes and an extremely long beard slides over his keys. After Harry climbs into the truck, he takes a deep breath and the engine turns over. He lets it run for a minute and wonders why nobody's called him all day. Then he remembers his phone's been off since early that morning, when the bus left Pocatello.

The truck's clock reads 4:38 p.m.

The moment he gets his cell back on, Adrienne's calling him and he doesn't answer it. He just needs to get Greta from the shelter and then they can chat all she wants.

Harry pulls into a gas station to get directions to Fuzzy Buddies, and when he gets back into the truck he notices that there are three messages from earlier in the morning, several missed calls from his sister. A message from Sally, one from an unknown number in Denver, and another from Adrienne. But nothing from Calvin or Kristin, and no calls from Missoula or Rock Creek.

Harry gets that tobacco acid-feeling in his stomach again. Not now. He just has to get Greta and it's 4:48 p.m.

He'll deal with everybody once he gets to his dog.

Orem's street names are all dizzying numbers, and he has to do a U-turn on 800 North to head right onto 100 West, and drives over the center median to pull into the lot of Fuzzy

Buddies. The faded sign on top of the strip mall roof features a large, badly-painted cat and dog, surrounded by faded pink hearts. Just two other cars out front. It's 4:56 p.m.

Harry hops out of the truck, and sees Greta right there in the entry through the glass doors sitting by the front desk. She barks twice when she spots him and leaps up onto the door to get out.

Harry squats down on his knees on the curb, looking in, to rile her up. Somebody was nice enough to let her out for him, or maybe she's just come in from a stroll before they closed up for the day. Either way, he's made it in time.

Greta's going nuts now, bounding around in circles and barking at Harry. He pulls open the door and Greta lunges, slapping her front paws on Harry's chest.

"Surprise!"

Adrienne's got a hold of her leash, and Harry goes to the floor so Greta can maul him.

"What the hell are you doing here?"

"I've been calling you and calling you," she says.

Greta's all over him, licking his face, bouncing around, spinning in circles, barking, her tail going like mad.

"I'm so sorry, Greta. Do you hate me so much now? I'm a bad Harry, I know. I keep losing you."

Harry gets himself up, wipes Greta's slobber off his neck and mouth, and thanks the woman behind the desk for looking after his dog. He hugs Adrienne as she's wiping tears out of her eyes, but Harry's so happy to be back with Greta—and so stunned to see his sister in person—he's beaming.

There are only a couple of spots on Greta's snout where

you can see the tiniest black scabs, otherwise she's all healed up from her escapade in the woods.

"Very sneaky," Harry says. "*Now* I get why you were asking all about where Greta was last night. I had no idea."

As they come out into the parking lot, Harry turns to his sister.

"Where's Ronnie?"

Adrienne takes ahold of his arm.

"Dad died this morning in hospice."

GILPIN

"Hey, Sally, it's Adrienne again and we're about forty-five minutes from Denver…Not sure if you're still at the hospital, or what, but we'll just head to…the house."

Adrienne hangs up and looks out the window, her hood drawn up over her head, the drawstrings pulled tight.

They've been on the road from Orem since early that morning, Greta poking her head into the front between the seats, getting scratches from Harry and his sister, who's riding shotgun with the wide-open window blowing air in her face.

"We gotta fix this," she said, before getting in. "Or I'll drive and you can see how you like it with 70 mile-an-hour wind going up your nose."

"That's Greta's seat," Harry said. "She loves it like that, so finally I just went ahead and shot it out for her."

They spent nine hours trading the wheel, driving back to the house in Denver they'd both grown up in, just north of Cheesman Park, at 13th and Gilpin.

"If it's snowing in the mountains, we're stopping for the night and getting drunk."

"Too early for snow," Harry said. "But your backup plan sounds better than what we have to deal with. Sally's gonna be in rough shape."

Their aunt had left Adrienne a message when they'd been out of range, and Adrienne listened to it when they stopped for gas in Grand Junction. Harry took Greta to pee and gave her some water. Adrienne looked flustered when she put her phone back in her pocket.

"She sounded weird."

"Makes sense," Harry said.

"Yeah, I don't know though."

"Her husband of—what?—twenty-plus years died yesterday. I mean, it'd be weird if she *didn't* sound a little unusual. What'd she say?"

"I couldn't make it all out. It's too windy out here. Let's get going. I'll put it on speaker in the truck."

Adrienne is right.

Sally sounds weird in the message:

"Hey you two, looking forward to seeing you both. Just come on in when you get here. Sorry about the mess in this place. I've been at St. Joe's so much that it's been a little hectic with your dad and everything." Then there's a nervous, almost girlish laugh. And she says, "Okay, drive safe. Bye-bye!"

"Whoa," Harry says. "She sounds kind of—"

"Chipper?"

"Yeah, kind of chipper. You're right."

"I told you," Adrienne says.

"Well, the woman's in shock."

"I guess, but it's not like this hasn't been coming for months though, right?"

"Yeah," Harry says. "I don't know. Weird."

Then he proceeds to tell Adrienne what the house looked like the day he and Jake tried to haul out her old bed before Harry moved to Tucson.

"It was a full-on hoarding situation," Harry says.

"You're exaggerating."

"The thing is—I'm not. There were dolls and newspapers and winter jackets and just piles of god-knows-what everywhere."

"So, like really messy?"

"Adrienne, you couldn't *walk* through the house, except along this narrow sort of trail through the heaps of garbage. It would've taken an eternity to even find your bed. But trying to haul that thing down those stairs? We just said fuck it. Went and got shitfaced after breakfast."

"You never told me any of this."

"I must've blocked it out. It was a bad scene."

"Why do all her creepy dolls have to be in *my* room?" Adrienne says. "Not like I thought they'd keep it how I left it, but still. It makes my skin crawl."

"I don't know. But you have been replaced, that's for sure. Jake thought the clown from *Poltergeist* was gonna pop out and drag him under the bed."

Adrienne laughs.

"You'll see," Harry's laughing now, too. "It's not funny, though."

But they're both laughing.

After a while Adrienne tries calling Sally again. Again, no answer, as they pull off the interstate into the city.

Harry turns up the radio. It's Bob Seger's "Night Moves."

"No more Budweiser rock, please. What's that smell?"

"That's Denver," he says, cranking the music up. "Autumn breeze…with a touch of dogfood in the air."

"I hate this redneck town."

After nine hours on the road through Utah into Colorado, they're both listless.

And both Harry and Adrienne have an aroma. Greta's antsy to get out of the truck, perking up every time whoever's driving taps on the brake. They've said little about Pat, except to mull over why he would've kept their mother's accident shrouded in fog all these years. And after hearing her message, neither Harry or Adrienne is particularly eager to see their Aunt Sally or help out with preparations for what needs to happen next.

Sally had called at 4:30 a.m. the day before. Adrienne happened to glance at her phone on her way back to bed from the bathroom an hour later, and by seven Ronnie was dropping her off at LAX to catch the first flight to Salt Lake. Then Adrienne had taken a shuttle down to Orem to find her little brother at the animal shelter.

They passed the first half of the day with Harry catching Adrienne up on his exploits between Rock Creek and Missoula, and after that Adrienne took over driving and Harry slept with this mouth open, even with the wind flooding through the missing window. All he needed was Greta's head stretched onto his lap and he was out for hours.

"I just realized something," Adrienne says, breaking a

long silence.

"What's that?"

"This is going to be an awkward time to come out to Sally."

"You know, I doubt that's really gonna be a thing."

"Fuck you."

"Sorry, I just mean that Pat's gone. And that's probably gonna pull Aunt Sally's focus off of us slightly, don't you think?"

There's another long silence before Adrienne says, "I wish I could've told that asshole what he robbed us of."

"I'm pretty sure your feelings on the subject of mom weren't exactly a mystery to him."

"Not for Pat's sake, Harry. For mine."

When they pull up to the house on Gilpin, it's dusk, and they're exhausted.

"I didn't think I'd ever be back here."

"You know what?" Harry says, getting out and stretching. "Me neither."

"But I'm glad to be out of this disgusting truck."

Greta leaps out behind Adrienne, trots into the next-door neighbors' yard, and promptly shits in their rose bushes. The Barlows? Who knows if they even still live there.

Adrienne laughs. "Good girl, Greta."

"It'll fertilize their flowerbed."

The door's locked. Neither of them still has a key, so they ring the bell—but there's no answer.

"She must still be at the hospital."

"Or making funeral arrangements?"

"I know where they hide the spare," Harry says.

Adrienne and Greta follow him around back. He finds the watering can next to the shed, and the key is right there, waiting beneath it.

"*Voilà*," Harry says, and he opens up the back door and calls out for Sally.

No answer.

"Well," he says, "are you ready to see this place?"

"I'm really not," Adrienne says. "I need a gin and tonic first."

Greta barks, paws the door, and the three of them walk into the kitchen.

"Aunt Sally?" he calls again. "It's Harry and Adrienne…"

Nothing.

"She'll be back soon, I bet."

"Wow," Adrienne whispers. "This is *bad*, Harry."

There are flies at the sink, swarming in a lazy circle around plates and pots and bowls piled high on the counter, and deeply encrusted food in pans of every size on the stovetop.

Harry puts his hand on his forehead. "I didn't think it could be worse."

"How is this *worse* than when you last saw it? This is a total nightmare."

Many Lean Cuisine boxes and Swanson aluminum TV dinner trays, half-eaten, are stacked into each other. There appears to be a chicken or game hen in the microwave, the door of which is ajar. And that's just the kitchen.

It no longer smells of dust and cigarettes. The more prominent odors are straight-up rot and mildew, a kind of richer mold aroma that Harry recognizes from his evening in the "Hunter's Den" back in Orem.

"This place," Adrienne says, pulling her shirt up over her nose, "is fucked."

"We're not staying here."

"No shit we're not staying here. Are you crazy? Where would we even *sleep*? There's food on the sofa. Old food. There must be mice and—god-knows-what in here."

"Shall we have a look-see at Valley of the Dolls upstairs?"

"I don't think I can do it."

"Hold on," Harry says. Greta's snorting around in the kitchen, and Harry takes her back outside and ties her leash up to the picnic table in the overgrown yard. He doesn't want her chowing down on a rotten carcass scrap the very first night he's managed to get ahold of her.

When he comes back inside, the smell hits him again, this time he gets a whiff of that musty sort of burrowing rodent odor he recognizes from the cabin in Rock Creek.

It's not Alcatraz in here yet, but it's not far off.

"We take a *peek* upstairs," Adrienne says, "then we get the hell out of here."

"Deal," Harry says.

They pick their way up the carpeted stairs, over ripped-open bags of old toys and stuffed jungle animals and much-used barbies all tangled together, and they get to Adrienne's bedroom door. It just smells mousey up here now, so at least the fetid food decay is somewhat contained to the main floor. Adrienne lets her shirt go from her nose and shakes her head at Harry.

"You know what? I don't need to see this," she says. "I'm done.

This has already been enough to permanently ruin my dreams."

"If I had to see it with Jake as my witness," Harry says, trying to push open the door with his shoulder, "I assure you, you are not leaving the premises without having the full experience."

There's something blocking the door and Harry shoves it out of the way. They hear a tower of magazines spill over and Harry reaches in and flips on the light. He can see through the half-open door: dolls galore and hundreds of plush toys and mounds of rumpled clothes covering every surface.

"After you, m' lady."

Adrienne gasps.

"I told you," Harry says, allowing her to step through first.

"No," Adrienne says. "Sally."

He pushes open the door the rest of the way—as a second stack of magazines cascades over—and Harry sees a knocked-over chair, and his aunt in her long nightgown, hanging from the ceiling fan.

Strange how the night moves with autumn closing in.

— Bob Seger

PART 5

AUTUMN CLOSING IN

ALPHA PHI

Six weeks later, Harry and Adrienne check into their hotel room in downtown Missoula.

Adrienne says she needs something to eat. Maybe a cocktail before they reach out to Calvin. She wants to take it slow. Harry's looking out the window of their room at passersby on the street below, and tells her that he needs to grab a gift for someone. He'll meet her in the lobby in fifteen minutes. He heads down, purchases a bottle of Four Roses in the liquor store across the block, and meets Adrienne as she's coming out of the elevator, with a fresh shirt and jeans on.

"Come on. I gotta make a quick stop before we find food. It won't take five minutes."

He and Adrienne head down Main Street, cross Washington in the sun.

"I forgot to tell you: Leah called me over the weekend. She broke up with that Brian guy."

"You mean Ryan?" Harry says. "Why are you talking to Leah?"

"I asked her to look at something I wrote for Ronnie's birthday. I'm visual, you know that."

Adrienne follows Harry up the steps of the Missoula Public Library.

"Why didn't you ask me?" Harry feels himself blush.

"Don't be insulted. You lack a woman's touch. Anyway,

you're not exactly knocking it out of the park on the lady front."

Harry stops at the library door and faces Adrienne.

"I guess he was hooking up with some girl from his yoga class."

"What are you telling me this for, Adrienne?"

"Don't try to play it cool, Mr. Propose-and-Run. Wait, what are we doing here?"

"I have to drop this off for John, the librarian who helped us out. We'll discuss this other matter over lunch."

"Okay. Two minutes though. I'm starving."

They pull open the doors, and the library is bustling. A couple of people are standing in line waiting for computers, all the terminals full as usual. And a pretty woman in jeans with blond-grayish hair is reading a storybook to a group of itty-bitty kids in the children's area.

Harry walks up to the circulation desk and asks the young librarian if he can leave the bottle for John Dowd.

"Hang on," she says. "I'll go get him. He's in his office."

A moment later John comes out, wearing a green sweater and brown cords. He smiles when he sees Harry.

"Hey, John." They clasp hands. "This is my sister Adrienne."

"Nice to meet you, Adrienne. I've heard a lot about you. So, you're back in town, huh?"

Harry doesn't remember telling John anything about Adrienne—did he even mention her to him?

"We're just back for a couple of nights," Harry says. "I brought this for you. To say thank you for helping us out."

But John is distracted. His expression has changed and he's looking over at the kids' area. Harry holds out the bottle and John takes it, absently.

"Excuse me for a moment. I'll be right back." John walks past the bay of computer terminals, over to where the children are sitting.

"What's up with this guy?" Adrienne whispers, leaning on the desk.

"I don't know," Harry says. "Usually he's all fired up to see me. Maybe he's getting senile?"

John is interrupting the woman reading *The Hungry Caterpillar* to the preschoolers in a semi-circle on the rainbow carpet.

"You're busted, Harry," Adrienne says. "Probably forgot to pay your late fee."

Harry watches John put his hand on the woman's shoulder, as he leans in close to tell her something. All the little kids are watching them.

"I can't believe you're friends with Leah now."

"She said to say hi. But I told her you were in the pokey."

Harry looks at his sister. He almost hears Leah's *hi* in his head, and it's like a switch has been thrown.

"So he fucked some girl from his yoga class," he says. "How enlightened of him."

Adrienne touches Harry's shoulder and he turns back to see the woman in the children's area stand, nod a couple of times at John, and then she says something to the kids and hands the book to John, who sits down in her seat and resumes reading the story to them.

Adrienne says, "Do know this person?"

He shakes his head. The woman is now walking over to Harry and Adrienne, an expectant look on her face. She's in jeans, a University of Montana sweatshirt. Curly, shoulder-length hair.

As she comes up to them, the woman's eyes are wide and she reaches out and squeezes Adrienne's arm. "You're Adrienne."

"I'm sorry, have we met?" Adrienne says, glancing down at the woman's hand.

"Well, yes and no. You probably don't remember. I'm Carol Leeds. I recognized you from all the way over there."

Carol has this beautiful sad smile, and Harry can't breathe. Everything tilts on its side. The air in the library is hot then cold—then it's gone.

"I'm sorry. I'm not following," Adrienne says. She turns to her brother.

Harry takes a step back, dazed.

"You look just like your mother," Carol says.

Adrienne shakes her head.

"I used to look after you and your brother. I guess it's been almost twenty-five years. Your mom was my closest friend."

Adrienne looks at Harry and neither of them can find words to fit any of this. It's almost as though their mother herself has appeared.

"Oh my goodness, you're *Harry*," Carol says, covering her mouth with both hands. "I'm sorry I didn't recognize you and you're standing right in front of me. You were quite a bit smaller the last time I saw you."

Then Harry realizes this must be the woman who John's been in touch with at the hospital.

"You work at Providence," Harry says. "You found the files for us."

"Yes," she says. "Sort of."

And she's hugging Harry before he knows what's happening. She lets go, then reaches back up and takes him with both of her hands by his shoulders.

"Look at you," she says, like Harry's nine years old.

Harry's okay until he looks at Adrienne and Adrienne's crying and Harry loses it. He's wiping his eyes with the back of his hand. Smearing his nose on his shirt sleeve and then he turns and heads to the men's room, where he locks himself in the stall and breaks down, heaving sobs. He's gotta stop doing this in public bathroom stalls, but hey. At least it's the right one this time and there aren't any cops kicking down the door.

Harry collects himself after a few minutes and splashes some water on his face. There's one of those old hand dryers in here, so he puts his face under it as an old man wearing big hearing aids and a cardigan comes in. Harry stops at the door and pulls the picture out of his wallet: Adrienne in her swimsuit, dancing in the sprinkler. Little naked Harry with his tiny swim goggles pushed up on his forehead. His mother smoking a cigarette next to her friend.

When he comes out of the bathroom his eyes are still red and he's got a wad of toilet paper in his hand. John's back from story time, standing beside Carol, the bottle of bourbon in his hand.

"Thanks for the booze, pal. Sorry I got diverted there. I wasn't sure if Carol would want to meet you, but I figured this might be the chance for it to happen. I had to check with her. Anyways,"—and John raises the bottle, admiring it from afar—"Four Roses. I hope it was on sale."

"Don't worry about it, seriously," Harry says. "Thanks for everything."

"Harry, we're going to get lunch," Adrienne says. "Across the street. Carol's gonna tell us about mom."

"My treat," Carol says.

"You knew all along?" Harry says to John.

"I did and I didn't," John says, his hand raised up, scout's honor-style. "Carol's my wife, Harry. When you said your mom was an Alpha Phi sister in the early seventies, I had a hunch they'd crossed paths."

"But there weren't any files," Carol says. "I knew the dates because I went to the hospital with your mother. I checked my old diary, which *was* in storage, but that was up in our attic. I feel bad about the fib, Harrison. But when I found the diary, sure enough, it was all there—and a lot of memories came back.

"I asked John a few questions about you, and when he told me your name was Harry, that you were about twenty-five, and that Betsy was your mom, I was so flabbergasted that I needed to buy myself a little time. So, I told John to make up a story. Then I felt terrible and didn't want to turn you away, especially after you'd come all the way to Missoula to track your mother down. Finally, I told him to call you until he got ahold of you, to make sure that you knew about the accident. And the baby."

"This is insane," Adrienne says.

"It's not quite as crazy as it sounds," Carol says. "Missoula's a small town. Back in the 70s it was even smaller, and your mom and I were in the same class at U of M.

"It had occurred to me every so often that I should look you two up, but I didn't know what your father had told you—if anything—about what actually happened. I was a little worried that you both had grown up thinking Sally was your mother, to be honest. Which is why I didn't try to get in touch. I didn't know what I'd be stirring up."

"Pat told us less than nothing, Carol," Adrienne says. "He made up a lot of vague stories that referenced her being sick with different things, *blah-blah-blah*. Anyways, I don't even know what to say. Mostly I'm just stunned that Harry pulled this off."

"Very funny," Harry says, reaching for his wallet. "I have something."

He pulls out the picture, and sets it on the desk and everybody crowds around, leaning over it.

"You keep this in your wallet?" Adrienne says.

"Oh my gosh," Carol says, picking it up.

"That's you with mom, isn't it?" Harry says.

Carol's got her hand over mouth again. "Yes. That's me. This was your house over on Hastings. Look at you, Adrienne. God it was hot that summer."

"You remember this?" Harry says.

"Not the exact day," Carol says. "But of course I remember. It would've been June or July '79. That was the summer before the accident."

John says, "Is that you guys? Look how cute you were."

Adrienne asks John to join them for lunch across the street, but he declines. He has to stay at the library and work. John holds the bourbon up.

"But this'll make the day go quicker. Tipsy librarians and *The Hungry Caterpillar.* What could go wrong?"

Harry feels his phone buzz in his pocket, thanks John once more, and says he'll meet Adrienne and Carol across the street in a few minutes.

Harry steps outside into the sunshine and answers his phone on the front steps of the library.

"What's the word, Harrison?"

"Hey, Calvin. We ran into mom's friend, Carol Leeds."

"*Leeds*," Calvin says. "Haven't seen that gal for years. She was an exquisite beauty, Harrison. Matter of fact, she was runner-up in the Miss Montana Pageant, which was rigged that year by the Mayor of Butte. Put the sash on his step-daughter, homely as a moose calf, and Carol was plain robbed. Didn't I tell you to track her down?"

"You did," Harry says. "But I believe I was still in the custody of Missoula County at the time."

"Oh, yeah, your big stint doing hard time in Folsom," Calvin laughs. "I nearly forgot, since it lasted about as long as a turtle fart takes to break the surface."

"Wow," Harry says. "I'm gonna miss the way you violate the English language."

"Yeah, yeah. You missed all the giggles up here so bad you clambered back for more action. I knew that offer of mine's been burning a hole in your brain."

"Sorry, Calvin. This is the end of the trail for me. We're headed back the day after tomorrow."

"You say that now, but once you get a look at that pretty river they call the Clark Fork down there, you'll be begging me to take you under my wing."

"I doubt it. Though I have to admit I'm vaguely flattered. Calvin, we need an hour to catch up with Carol."

"Okey-doke, kid. Ring me when you're ready to ride."

When they hang up, Harry sits down on the steps. He can almost see the corner where the Sapphire Mountain Bed & Breakfast is and realizes he forgot to ask Calvin if he'd heard any more about Kristin. He decides to walk down the street and peek in the Sapphire's window.

There's a woman at the counter—red hair, tied up with a white frilly thing—who greets him as he comes in. The bell on the door jingles, giving Harry a shiver of memory from the night those newspapers smacked the glass. He looks around. Except for one cat, the front room's empty. The woman closes her *Glamour*, and asks Harry if he's checking in.

"No, I just stopped by to see a friend. Do you know if Kristin still works here?"

"I don't think so," she says. "But I only started a few weeks ago."

"You ever hear anything about her?"

"No, I'm sorry I haven't."

Harry thanks her and goes out. The thought of Kristin sitting in jail washes through Harry's chest, and he tries to let it go.

He'll ask Calvin when they meet up at the river.

Harry finds Carol and Adrienne at the coffee shop down the

block.

He slides into the booth next to his sister. Carol's already got a cup of tea in front of her, and Adrienne's sipping the foam off a latte. The server—a freckle-faced high schooler, wearing a dopey soda jerk costume with a bowtie and paper hat—comes over to see if Harry wants something.

"You do milkshakes?"

The kid nods, smacks his gum. "Lots of flavors. You can check the board. I like the banana nut."

"Let me get a chocolate shake," Harry says, "a club sandwich, fries, and a cup of coffee, cream and sugar."

"Jesus. You want apple pie with that?" Adrienne says.

"Usually, I take my dessert *after* my meal. I'm not a barbarian, Carol."

"Will you bring us an extra order of fries?" Adrienne says. "Carol, fries?"

"No, but thank you." She smiles, shakes her head. "I already ate, but you two help yourselves."

"I'll share mine," Harry says. "Adrienne's a hog. And we're buying, by the way."

"We'll see," Carol says. "I should've said earlier that I'm very sorry to hear about your father and Sally."

"Thank you," Adrienne says.

Harry's looking for the right words, but after a silence he says only, "We'll spare you the gory parts, Carol. It wasn't a pretty scene when we got to the house in Denver."

"Total fucking nightmare," Adrienne says. "Excuse my language. Just beyond description."

The two of them fill Carol in on Adrienne surprising her

brother at the animal shelter on the occasion of Pat's death and relate a PG-13 version of discovering Sally. Adrienne calls Pat a son of a bitch more than once. Harry notes that this doesn't seem to register one way or the other with Carol.

Adrienne asks Harry to take out the picture again.

They're quiet for a moment as Adrienne studies the photograph. The kid in the paper hat brings Harry his coffee and he's relieved to have something to pour cream and sugar into, and he stirs it up a couple hundred times.

"I just realized that picture was taken before your mother knew she was pregnant."

"The cigarette?" Adrienne says.

"Exactly," Carol says. "She quit the day we went to the hospital."

"I really do look like her, don't I?" Adrienne says.

Carol nods and sips her tea.

"Well, I'm more than happy to tell you about your mom. And I promise I'll share everything I can remember—depending on how much you're ready to hear, of course. But will you two tell me what you have been up to first? I've missed out on quite a bit."

"It won't take long," Adrienne says, turning to Harry. "May I?"

"Be my guest."

"Harry graduated from CU-Boulder and moved to Arizona, where he got kicked out of grad school in Tucson for losing a fist fight. I got the hell out of Denver as fast as I could after I turned eighteen, racked up sixty-grand in debt at an art school, and now I work for a rich sculptor in LA." Adrienne turns to Harry. "That everything?"

"You should be in P.R.," Harry says. "Though you failed to mention my botched marriage proposal."

Adrienne laughs. "Harry's had a big year, Carol."

"I prefer the term *self-actualizing*," Harry says.

Carol's smile fades and she looks between them, seeming unsure of whether this is part of their sibling banter or not.

"Harry's been *self-actualizing* on our futon in Malibu for over a month, and he's heading home to Tucson very soon—aren't you, Harry?"

Harry nods, sips his coffee.

"You two seem to be such close friends," Carol says, lifting up her tea. "I can't tell you how pleased I am to see you both all grown up."

"Adrienne," Harry says, "aren't you forgetting somebody?"

She looks at Carol and seems to consider this.

"My partner and I just moved a few blocks from the beach. And we have a cat named Chico. Been together five years. That's pretty much it. And Harry here has a marvelous dog named Greta. What kind is she again?"

"Vizsla," Harry says. "In her free time, she enjoys long walks on the beach, chasing after porcupines in the forest, and, evidently, eating out of Chico's litterbox while on vacation in California right now. But Adrienne's right. She completes me."

Adrienne laughs, but Carol's eyes glaze over a bit. There's a long pause then, when it's Carol's turn. She's straightening the knife and spoon on her napkin.

Harry sets the photo down next to Carol's tea cup and she

studies the picture for a moment, and looks up at Harry and then at Adrienne.

"Well," Carol says. "Are you two up for this? The mood's so festive."

Harry sets his mug down. "Never mind us, Carol. We're just nervous as hell."

"Everything," Adrienne says. "Please."

"Pat and your Aunt Sally had been seeing each other for about a year before Betsy discovered them one day over at Sally's house.

"Your mom was just stopping by to borrow something and Pat was in the kitchen, having a cigarette. With his shirt off."

"Oof," Harry says.

"Motherfucker," Adrienne says. "I knew it."

Carol's studying the flatware, not looking up much between Harry and his sister. Carol takes a breath and goes on.

"Betsy confronted Pat when he got home that night, and they argued. Pat denied it. He had some excuse about needing to do laundry, but he wouldn't come clean. It was a real mess, since Sally was married to Greg."

"Not Greg Tillett?" Harry says.

"No, Greg Warren. Why?"

"Thank God," Harry says. "Just had to make sure."

"Would you let the woman speak?" Adrienne says.

Carol smiles her sad smile, then sips her tea.

"Your mother wasn't sure what to do. You have to remember that it was different then. She had her hands full with two small children and was trying to figure out if she could break up her marriage *and* possibly her sister's marriage, too. This was 1979 and in Montana divorce was not unheard of, but it was still a last resort. Even if you weren't a religious nut, it was a real no-no. Your mother had a teaching degree, but she wasn't working. She was at home looking after you two.

"Anyway, your mom called me, hysterical. She'd missed her period. So, I told her I'd go with her. There weren't any tests over the counter at that time. You had to make an appointment with a doctor, and it was the last bit of news she needed. She and Pat hadn't planned on having a baby after you were born, Harry. The two of you were plenty, I think."

"Harry was plenty," Adrienne says. "I was a princess."

Carol laughs at this.

"You were a handful, actually. But you were a lot of fun, Adrienne."

"Why am I not surprised to hear that?" Harry says.

"Betsy still hadn't decided whether or not to confront Sally about the affair with Pat. She was furious, of course. Because it would mean either living a lie with your dad. Or basically just ruining everything with her only sister. In those days, we all knew each other in town. Everybody was fairly tight-knit. So, it was a huge deal to even say something."

The kid in the paper hat sets down a basket of fries in front of Adrienne along with a cobb salad, and sets down Harry's sandwich, then follows with his shake.

"You sure you're alright with tea, ma'am?'

"I'm fine," Carol says. "Thank you, dear."

Adrienne takes the first big slurp on Harry's shake and calls the kid back. Orders her own—strawberry. They start in on their fries and Carol sips her tea and continues.

"I came by one afternoon and the four of us drove to the hospital to see the doctor. I remember, it was the hottest day of the year, and you two were miserable. You'd been out on the lawn playing in the sprinkler and now you had to get stuffed into the car. Adrienne you were mad as a hornet. I remember you insisted on knowing why we had to go to the hospital. Your favorite word was *why*. It was every other word out of your mouth."

"Still is," Harry says. Adrienne elbows Harry sharply in the ribs without glancing at him.

"Well, sure enough, Betsy was already a few months gone. Pregnant with number three."

"Knocked up at twenty-eight with her *third*?" Adrienne says. "I'm twenty-eight, Carol. And me and Ronnie can barely handle our cat."

"It was really a different time," Carol says. "In so many ways. And even for your mom it was too much. But she didn't believe in abortion. She loved her kids. And she felt it was her responsibility. So, she decided that afternoon she was going to take you two down to Helena. She made up her mind, because she'd need a lot of help with another baby on the way.

"She called me up later that night. I was sitting on the burnt-up lawn out front on a bath towel, since it was still so hot in my little apartment. I remember running back into the house when it rang, because the phone cord only stretched out to the porch—we didn't have cordless phones or cell phones or any of that.

"She said your father..." Carol pauses here, looks down, and takes a breath. "Pat didn't want her to keep the baby. They fought about it, but your mother was determined to have it. I don't know if she ever pressed him anymore about what she'd seen over at Sally's. But I know for a fact that she confronted Sally about it.

"Of course, Sally was a wreck. But she didn't deny it like Pat had—and that's how your mother found out it had been going on for so long. Your mom told her that if Sally wanted to be with Pat, then so be it. Then she told her that she was pregnant and that she was moving back to Helena. I guess Sally didn't take the news well, about the baby. I'm not sure if she and Greg couldn't have their own, but she was crushed."

Harry looks at Adrienne. Carol pauses to give them a moment.

"What?" Adrienne says.

"The dolls. Your bedroom," Harry says. "Adrienne, you look just like mom."

"Harry's right." Carol says. "You must've provided Pat and Sally with quite a reminder."

"At the dinner table every single night, no less," Harry says. "Between your resemblance to mom and knowing that the baby died in the accident."

"No wonder," Adrienne says. "Every time I mentioned mom, Sally would just get up and leave the room."

"It must've been why Aunt Sally used *your room*," Harry says, "for all those dolls and stuffed animals."

"And," Adrienne says, "for how she ended it."

"That summer and fall," Carol says, "I was over to help out with you two a lot.

"I'd get off my shifts from nursing school and come see you three. And your mother and I discussed it every other day, just about. Finally, she decided she would leave at Thanksgiving. They'd all go to Helena together. And your mother and you kids would stay with your grandparents and not come back to Missoula.

"That was Betsy's plan. She didn't know how Pat would react, but she just had to make it to Thanksgiving. She'd pack everything up like a normal family holiday trip. Her logic was that if she was surrounded by her family, she knew Pat would have to acquiesce and eventually he'd go home, I suppose. She invited me to come along, so I could be there to help with you two if it got messy. And I'd known Betsy's folks, of course, for many years.

"Keep in mind that your grandparents knew nothing of the affair between your father and your aunt Sally, of the new baby, or that she was planning on leaving Pat—none of it. But as you've probably gathered, your mother was a very determined woman. She'd made up her mind. She'd figure it out. She had you two to think about—and the little one on the way.

"Meanwhile, your dad had an old friend from the service, coming down to Missoula from Whitefish or Kalispell, I think."

"Calvin Hogan," Harry says.

"Exactly," Carol says. "You've really been scouring every corner of the state, haven't you, Harry?"

"More than I care to share, Carol."

"I can tell you that your mom was in no mood to entertain company. She had morning sickness all day long and wasn't in a hosting way, to say the least. But Calvin, your dad's old friend, had just tied the knot and they were down on a little honeymoon to see Pat. That was Halloween, it wasn't even a weekend. It must have been a Tuesday or Wednesday night.

"I remember that we talked that afternoon, before Pat got home from work. Your mom was going to try to get through Calvin's visit and then hang on another three weeks till Thanksgiving. She and Pat were barely talking by that point, and he was staying out later and later, coming home falling-down drunk from lord knows where. As you probably know, that was the night it happened."

"Who was with us that night?" Adrienne says.

"I was," Carol says. "You were both at my place, which you loved—my little efficiency over on 6th and Hazel, right across from the Greek Orthodox Church. I haven't thought about that place for a long time. Anyways, Harry you were fast asleep. Adrienne, you should've been too, but you'd woken up in the night upset about your tooth. I was reading you a story, trying to get you to doze off again. I remember you were working on getting one of your front teeth to come out. You were very excited about the tooth fairy, as I recall.

"At about 11 p.m., the phone rang. I don't even remember who called me, but it was probably Sally already at the hospital. I had finally gotten you to fall back asleep, Adrienne, and then had to wake you both up again and get you into my car—and it was cold already. I remember that. Harry you slept in the back of the VW. I bundled you up in my old quilt and buckled you in, but we didn't have kids' seats or anything. It probably seems crazy now, but you were fine back there.

"There wasn't much I could tell you. All I knew was that your mom and dad had been in a car wreck. That they'd both been hurt, but that everybody was alive.

"When we got to the hospital, I carried you in, Harry. And Adrienne, do you remember any of this? You marched right through the doors, holding my hand. And Calvin and his new wife—I'd never met her, she looked like she was about sixteen—met us there in the waiting area. They smelled like a roadhouse, both of them. They'd been in the back seat and were badly shaken up, but had only scratches, mostly from climbing out of the car. They told us that they'd slid on a patch of ice and went through the guardrail and smashed into a bunch of trees and nearly careened into the river. Calvin was worried sick. His new bride was white as a ghost, in complete shock.

"The doctor told us that your mother was with child, which, of course, I knew. And your Aunt Sally went to pieces. She was not in a good way. I'm sure the guilt was ripping her up, from the inside out. And your dad was in the other room, recovering. His eyes were black and blue, but he was conscious, and he was worried about your mom. Pat's leg had broken badly, but compared to Betsy, obviously he recovered.

"I remember very clearly that your dad didn't want either of you to see him all bruised up in the face. He didn't want to scare you. So, I just told you we had to wait and that everything would be alright. Harry, you were so disoriented, you cried and cried. But we bundled you back up, and I rocked you in my lap, and eventually you fell back to sleep. Adrienne, I didn't know what to tell you, but you were remarkably calm, serious even. And since the doctor had let the cat out of the bag, I sat with you and told you that you were going to have a new little baby brother or sister. And that your mom would be okay."

"I'm sorry I have to stop," Adrienne says. She's crying and Harry gets up to let her out of the booth, and he thinks his sister's going to hug him, but she pushes past Harry and heads to the restroom.

"Harry, I said too much," Carol says, dabbing her napkin at the corner of her eyes.

"No," Harry says, "this is what we need to know. We've been waiting our whole lives to hear it. Dad never told us any of this. And Sally was a ghost. She was good to us, you know, she made dinner every night, and took us to soccer practice, but she was gone. Every time we asked about mom, she got so distraught she'd lock herself in their bedroom and not come out. And Dad would be furious at us for upsetting her. Adrienne was right, it was just an awful scene, walking on eggshells all the time."

"I'm really sorry," Carol says, smiling. "I wish your mom could see you two."

Adrienne comes back after a long time. Harry slides into her spot and she sits back down.

"I thought I could keep going," Adrienne says, her eyes puffy. "But I had to call Ronnie and tell her. And then I was crying and I couldn't stop. I'm sorry about that."

"You don't need to apologize," Carol says. "I never dreamed of telling you two so much all at once. Why don't we just give it a rest and we can talk another time? I'll write down my number and you can call me and—"

Harry and Adrienne insist that she continue.

"I'm okay," Adrienne says. "Please."

"Well, that was pretty much it. Pat and Sally, were next of kin, and they had to make some decisions. There was hemorrhaging. I don't know if you know, but your mother severed her spine in the crash, and even in the best-case scenario, she'd have been paralyzed from the neck down. But her brain scans were showing no sign of activity. And after the longest night of our lives, the doctors advised us to say goodbye. And Sally and your father signed off on it, while I read to you two in the waiting area. We waited until about 8 a.m., after waking Betsy's parents up in Helena. Ray and Susan drove up, in the middle of the night, so they could see her. And it was the hardest thing I'd ever done. But we brought you two in, so that you could say goodbye to mommy."

"This is my first memory," Adrienne says. "It's like I woke up from the dream of childhood at that exact moment. I just remember she didn't look like herself, so I didn't really get it."

"Oh, she was so banged up. And bruised. Gauze wrapped around her head. It was scary for all of us. But you were a tough little kid. You wanted to hug her and say goodbye. Later you asked me when she'd be home and that's when *I* lost it. And then Harry was crying because we were all so upset."

Carol blows her nose. "Harry, I think I might need some of that bourbon you bought for John."

"Seriously," Harry says. He pushes his plate aside, sips his coffee.

"At some point, Sally took you both home with her. Your

dad got out of the hospital the next day. But he was in a wheelchair and then on crutches for weeks. It was a bad break. I still had some of your things, which I brought over. But you were both having a nap since you'd been up half the night at the hospital with us, and I didn't get to say goodbye to you two, which was very hard. I saw you at the funeral, but that was mid-November already."

"Jesus," Adrienne said. "I wish you could've taken us."

Carol laughs at that, but then it becomes more crying, and Harry says he has to get up and go outside and get some air.

"Hang on, Harry," Adrienne says, not moving out of the booth. "Is this the end?"

Carol looks at Harry and he nods at her, wiping his eyes on his sleeve.

"By then Pat and Sally and Sally's husband Greg had you both to look after, and they had to plan the funeral for your mother. It was the last time I saw you two, at the service. Your dad left you both with Sally for a few days, to go hole up by himself in that ratty little cabin of his out on Rock Creek, which must've collapsed years ago."

"I've been staying out there, actually," Harry says. "It's even worse now. Like, way worse."

"Oh my gosh, well you two did love it out there, playing down at the river. But it was pretty much in shambles back then. I can't imagine what it looks like now."

"We didn't live in that cabin, did we?" Adrienne says.

"Oh, god no," Carol says, laughing a high-pitched thing that puts a smile on Harry's face. "Pat went out there alone, probably to try and figure out what to do."

Adrienne looks at her brother. "We would've grown up in Helena."

"We would've had a little brother or sister," Harry says.

"We would've had *mom*," Adrienne says.

The kid in the paper hat brings over the bill, which Adrienne takes without a word. Carol looks at Harry, then at Adrienne.

"Obviously, Pat moved you to Denver where his sister's family was. And later Sally followed him out to Colorado just to 'help out' with you two—which nobody thought anything of at the time, since you were her sister's children, after all. But I knew, of course. And I suspect Pat and Sally had a hunch that Betsy had discussed their affair with me. But your dad and your aunt and I never spoke about it.

"In fact, after the service, I called a few times, but I never heard from them again."

RIVER

Out on Main Street, it's a beautiful, sunny early autumn afternoon in Missoula.

And Harry takes a moment alone to catch his breath before ringing Calvin. He watches the cars roll by and a FedEx truck whines to a stop and a delivery woman in a black and purple uniform hops out and starts unloading white boxes.

"Well, well, well, the prodigal gopher returns. Thought you might chicken out on our mission this afternoon."

"Calvin, we're gonna need a drink."

"That's the spirit, Harrison. But, FYI, Child's ain't what it was after the jukebox took a dose of hot lead. So why don't we go out and see Silas at the Trapper for old time's sake and he'll freshen you up a bit. It'll be nice to show your sis an authenticated hunk of Montana culture. I can even point out the spot where you lost your cookies over by the payphone."

"Thrilling," Harry says. "Before I forget, did you ever hear if the police found Kristin?"

"Funny you should mention that."

"Oh boy," Harry says. "What happened?"

"I talked to her step-dad Lionel not yesterday. Let's just say the piglets in blue haven't exactly pinpointed her whereabouts yet. Lionel thinks she should lawyer up because the police are nattering in his ear about getting her to come on home, to take advantage of a reduced-plea-bargain thingamabob since

Tiny Tommy the Terrible used to knock Kris around now and again.

"They're saying a self-defense story is better than the alternative. But like I told Lionel, with the crooked lawmen in this town—to say nothing of Tommy's kinfolk on the squad—Kris would be better off growing a pair of wings and flappin' her tailfeathers over the border on down to Cancún. Lionel said he ain't heard a peep from her since she shot that mouse turd in the skull. But then something strange happened."

"What's that?"

"Well, day before yesterday was Kris's birthday, evidently. After they had their bacon and eggs, Lionel says the phone in the house rang. Kristin's mother, Wilma, picked it up and there was nobody there, though she heard somebody breathing. The caller ID said the number was restricted. And then she hung up."

"But that could've been any old wrong number."

"Except the call came in at exactly 10:11am."

"Okay…"

"So, Wilma looks at Lionel and says that's the precise time Kristin was born on that day of the calendar."

"Weird."

"Coincidence?" Calvin says. "I doubt that very much. Anyhoo, we gonna yak on our tomato cans all day, or shall I just meet you two out at the Trapper?"

The memory of Kristin lying to Harry at the Sapphire, saying the party was for her birthday, sends a shiver down his spine. That bouquet of yellow irises sitting on the passenger seat.

"Actually, you gave me a better idea. How about if I pick

us up a half-rack at the Grizzly Grocery on our way out."

"Works for Cal. Just none of that apple-raspberry-flavored sewer swill you kids like to pour down your gizzards."

"I have no idea what you're talking about, but I think we'll find something in our price range to your taste. Calvin, last thing: what kind of landmark am I looking for?"

"You're gonna head east on I-90, Harrison, just past the turn-off for Bonner, probably one, not more than two mile markers after Marty's Mart, where it gets pretty steep right above the Clark Fork. You following this?"

Adrienne and Carol come out of the coffee shop and Harry turns and gives them a wave. Adrienne's smiling and Harry watches them hug. They look like they're emerging from a cave into the daylight. Yet they're both somehow radiant in the fall sun out here on the sidewalk.

"Yeah," Harry says. "I got it. A couple miles past Marty's Mart. I think I might've stopped out there for gas once or twice."

"Just pull over on the shoulder when you see my rig. I got Herkimer with me. He'll be hard to miss, since he's got one of them white cones wrapped around his head to keep him from chewing out the new stitches I had to put in."

"Rattler?"

"Nah. Bighorn out by Pat's cabin. This ram didn't like the idea of his little lamb frolicking in the meadow with my pooch for some reason, so he bopped Herky pretty good."

Carol comes over and squeezes Harry's arm. Sadness and warmth flow through him at the same time and he breaks eye contact with her to look across the street.

"Alright, Calvin. Carol's gonna take us over to our old house on Hastings to have a look around."

"River ain't going no place."

"Half-hour, forty-five minutes. We're on our way."

"I'll see you at the crossroads, Harrison."

ACKNOWLEDGMENTS

A hearty thanks to Jeff Alessandrelli, Adie B. Steckel, Joshua Stanek, Mike Corrao, and everybody at Fonograf Editions for believing this story was worth bringing into the world.

All gratitude to my friends who offered me invaluable feedback on the manuscript: Aurelie Sheehan, John Cleary, Abraham Smith, Kelly Andrews, Zachary Schomburg, Daniel Handler, Thomas Cobb, Terry Westby-Nunn, Farid Matuk, Tom Williams, Ingrid Wenzler, Mason Gates, Brandon Shimoda, Dot Devota, Nathan Lanman, Alexander Moysaenko, Andrew Crabtree, Zach Zulauf, Stacey Bennetts, and Jen Olson.

Kate Garrick at Salky Literary Management put a colossal amount of work into this story and I'm grateful for her wisdom.

Love and thanks to my friends: Ian Miller, Mathias Svalina, Fred Moten, Tim Rutili, Jaswinder Bolina, Jason Snyder, Kris Leja, Christopher Cokinos, Oliver Lockwood, Scott Lindsay, David Rubin, and Solan Jensen.

A fond thank you to Deputy James Allerton of the Pima County Sheriff's Department in Tucson, AZ, for helping me sort out the criminal particulars for Harry, and to Kim Vercande, DVM, at Best Friends Veterinary Care in Iowa City, IA, for her generous expertise about porcupine-related canine injuries. Nurses Yael Podebski and Jennifer McGeary Miller offered invaluable medical expertise for Harry-related injuries. Finally, my appreciation to the fine librarians at the Columbia, Beacon Hill, Lake City, and Broadview branches of the extraordinary Seattle Public Library.

And to my amazing students and colleagues at University of Arizona, Hugo House, Seattle University, Tradecraft, and Rhodes University in Makhanda, South Africa as well.

Infinite love to my family in Seattle for support and encouragement. Most of all, to my wife Lisa Wells, without whom this book would've languished, unfinished. And, of course, to my son Jude.

FONO
GRAF

1. **Eileen Myles**—*Aloha/irish trees* (LP)

2. **Rae Armantrout**—*Conflation* (LP)

3. **Alice Notley**—*Live in Seattle* (LP)

4. **Harmony Holiday**—*The Black Saint and the Sinnerman* (LP)

5. **Susan Howe & Nathaniel Mackey**—*STRAY: A Graphic Tone* (LP)

6. **Annelyse Gelman & Jason Grier**—*About Repulsion* (EP)

7. **Joshua Beckman**—*Some Mechanical Poems To Be Read Aloud* (print)

8. **Dao Strom**—*Instrument/ Traveler's Ode* (print; cassette tape)

9. **Douglas Kearney & Val Jeanty**—*Fodder* (LP)

10. **Mark Leidner**—*Returning the Sword to the Stone* (print)

11. **Charles Valle**—*Proof of Stake: An Elegy* (print)

12. **Emily Kendal Frey**—*LOVABILITY* (print)

13. **Brian Laidlaw and the Family Trade**—*THIS ASTER: adaptations of Emile Nelligan* (LP)

14. **Nathaniel Mackey and The Creaking Breeze Ensemble**—*Fugitive Equation* (compact disc)

15. **FE Magazine** (print)

16. **Brandi Katherine Herrera**—*MOTHER IS A BODY* (print)

17. **Jan Verberkmoes**—*Firewatch* (print)

18. **Krystal Languell**—*Systems Thinking with Flowers* (print)

19. **Matvei Yankelevich**—*Dead Winter* (print)

20. **Cody-Rose Clevidence**—*Dearth & God's Green Mirth* (print)

21. **Hilary Plum**—*Hole Studies* (print)

22. **John Ashbery**—*Live at Sanders Theatre, 1976* (LP)

23. **Alice Notley**—*The Speak Angel Series* (print)

24. **Alice Notley**—*Early Works* (print)

Fonograf Editions is a registered 501(c)(3) nonprofit organization. Find more information about the press at: fonografeditions.com.